OCEANBERRY BLUES
CHARMING MYSTERIES, BOOK ONE

JOANN KEDER

No part of this book may be reproduced in any form or by any electronic or mechanical means, including information storage and retrieval systems, without written permission from the author, except for the use of brief quotations in a book review.

Publisher: Purpleflower Press

ISBN: 978-1-953270-04-7

First Edition July, 2021

Edited by: Benedict Brown

Cover Design by: Molly Burton with Cozy Cover Designs

Copyright © 2021 by Joann Keder

All rights reserved.

ACKNOWLEDGMENTS

Thank you as always to my street team. That includes beta readers, Dayle and Barbara, editor Ben Brown, always quick-with-a-name, Andy Gold and the Keder Readers. Without you, this product wouldn't reflect my vision in a flattering way. Each successful writer needs not just one but many people in their corner, helping at all stages of development. I'm especially fond of the team of people I've assembled; each an expert in their own way. I'm fortunate that you are willing to share your personal areas of expertise with me. Doug, Mackensie, Meghan, Elise, Sarah and many others who answer endless seemingly nonsensical questions – you are appreciated!

"Without dreams, there can be no courage. And without courage, there can be no action."
Wim Wenders

For Sydney

ALSO BY JOANN KEDER

Piney Falls Mysteries

Welcome to Piney Falls

Saving Piper Moonlight

Tales of Naybor Manor

Lavender's Tangled Tree

Charming Mysteries

Oceanberry Blues

Tangerine Troubles

Emory Bing Mysteries

The Case of the Half-Baked Bing

The Case of the Rootbeer Bungle

The Case of the Fudged Features

The Case of the Chunky, Funky Monkey

The Case of the Clairvoyant Carrot

The Case of the Vegan Vixen

The Case of the Cream Cheese Caper

Pepperville Stories

The Story of Keilah

Secrets and Sunflowers

Franniebell and Purple Wonder

Be the first to hear about new releases! Sign up for my newsletter here:

http://www.joannkeder.com

CHAPTER 1

"What do you mean, he's missing?" Gemini Reed glanced worriedly at her husband, Leo, and then at the woman behind the imposing admissions desk of Charming General Hospital.

"Just what I said, ma'am. Unfortunately, he's out for now, but we've been told he'll return soon." She looked down at her paperwork, refusing to meet Gemini's harsh gaze.

"Let me get this straight." Gemini pushed her silver-gray hair behind one ear, signaling to Leo that she was struggling to maintain control. "We sold our home in Fassetville—the one we built together with our own two hands—"

"Four," Leo corrected her. "Your hands and mine."

She made a shushing gesture and frowned as she reached into her oversized turquoise bag, where she kept all of their paperwork. As she slammed the impressively thick pile of papers on the desk, they made a dramatic thwacking sound. Everyone in the busy lobby stopped what they were doing for a second, startled by the noise.

"We gave up our life to come here for this study," Gemini

continued, undeterred by the stares. "You owe me a better explanation."

A short, dark-haired man wearing a navy-blue jacket that barely met in the center of his body walked up to the desk. "Is there a problem here?" He scratched his chest, dragging his nails over a name tag that read, "Gary J., Maintenance."

"Yes, I'd say there is a problem," Gemini sputtered. "My husband and I are here so that he can take part in the drug trial for Atomycin. We've dropped everything to take part, and this woman tells me that Dr. Wilson thinks it's the time for a holiday? Cheese and biscuits! I'm flabbergasted." She placed one hand at her throat, still attempting to control her anger for Leo's sake.

Gary J. rocked back and forth, wrapping his arms tightly against his chest, causing his jacket to stretch to the point of distress. "I'll grant you, it's strange he would leave abruptly, but we can't really tell you anything further. They're investigatin'." He seemed oblivious to the receptionist, who was shaking her head back and forth violently.

"Investigating? Did something happen to him? Is he dead?" Gemini leaned over the desk. "I have experience in investigation. I could offer my services."

Leo pulled himself up shakily from his wheelchair to a standing position. "Gem, what you did for the law firm is hardly the same. I'm sure there is a logical reason for his absence."

"You shouldn't be standing, dear heart, "Gemini admonished. She moved quickly to assist him back to the sitting position. He was still just as handsome as the day they married—steely blue eyes and a movie star face that reminded her of 1960s actor, James Dean. Just a little thinner these past months.

When he was safely seated, she turned and glared at the receptionist. "We spoke with the man three days ago. He said this miracle drug—Atomycin—was going to cure Leo's cancer. He promised to meet us at check in; said that he was excited we were coming, Ms...." Gemini squinted to read the nametag. "Ms. B.?"

The petite brunette woman pushed her thick glasses up her nose. "It's a security thing the board president thought would be wise. None of us have our full names on our name tags." She hesitated. "But you can call me Beverly." She put one hand to the side of her mouth and whispered, "Beverly Buttons."

Gemini reached her hand across the desk. "Nice to meet you, Beverly." She grinned, her perfect white teeth gleaming. Her silver hair was still as thick as it was in her thirties and her bright blue eyes glistened. She always prided herself on being told she resembled actress, Rita Hayworth. If Rita and James Dean owned a hardware store, of course. Gemini and Leo always chuckled about that.

Gary J. cleared his throat. "Strangest thing. Yesterday, he didn't show up for work. They called all three of his phones, his golfing buddies and his next-door neighbor. Nobody'd seen him since the evening before. The police are trying to figure out exactly what happened. He never fed his dogs or opened his refrigerator. Got one of them fancy ones that's like a computer. I've been telling the wife we should invest–"

"Should we go back home and just continue as we have been?" Gemini asked Leo. "You haven't gotten worse this month." Despite his obvious decline, each day she told him how robust he appeared. She repeated it so often, she'd begun to believe it was true.

"We came this far. I don't want to turn around," Leo replied firmly. He glanced at the receptionist. "You said they are continuing the trial, even without Dr. Wilson?"

"Yes, sir. We're continuing everything with Dr. Natchez at the helm. He's well-regarded here at Charming General. This is Doctor Wilson's second drug trial, and he has everything set up to go smoothly. Doctor Natchez has been a part of every detail."

"Doctor Wilson likes his vacation time," Gary J.continued. "Always heading somewhere interesting. Wish I had that kind of money. You know the type—they don't have a clue how the rest of the world lives."

Gemini Reed put her hand on her forehead and looked around the spacious lobby of Charming General Hospital, where large plants filled every corner, complimenting the multi-colored floral-print carpet. Everyone was going about their business as if something terrible hadn't just happened in their midst.

"I'm ready to do this, Gem," Leo reiterated, smiling.

Gemini glanced at her husband and bit her lip. Their daughter had been resistant to the idea of her father leaving town to seek treatment. She could almost hear Sophia's all-too-familiar words. "I told you so, Mother." Seven long months he'd been fighting. When their doctor in Fassetville discovered this study, it felt like a sign.

"I'd feel much better if we could speak to this Dr. Natchez."

Beverly nodded. "I have sympathy for you. It's hard to try something untested. But I can assure you we've done drug trials before and everything has gone smoothly. Don't worry, your husband is in expert hands. Can I call an orderly and get him taken upstairs? So that he can be ready for his first treatment tomorrow?"

"I can take them up," Gary J. offered.

"We agreed to this adventure and the Reeds always follow through, Gem. I want to do this," Leo repeated as loud as he could muster.

"You're right, dear; this isn't about me or my concerns. I said I would support your decisions and I have your back, no matter what, my astrological mate." Gemini bent down and kissed the top of Leo's head.

He reached up with a thin hand and patted her arm. "We're always up for an adventure, aren't we?"

Gary J. pushed Leo's wheelchair while Gemini carried his bag to the elevator. The doors opened and Gary pushed the number four.

"You folks ever visited Charming before? We're mostly a medical community, but we get our fair share of tourists too, being five minutes from the Pacific Ocean and all. We're–"

"Why do you think Doctor Wilson would leave so abruptly?" Gemini interrupted, still irritated by this unexpected turn of events.

Gary J. shrugged. "I was about to say we're a friendly community. Doctor Wilson loves the water. That's why he moved here from Missouri. He's always snorkeling somewhere. He showed me pictures of where he's right next to a shark. Can you imagine?"

"In the middle of an important drug trial?"

The elevator doors opened, revealing a woman wearing bright pink scrubs. Shoulder-length brown hair framed her friendly face, and she smiled at the couple as though they were old friends.

"Welcome, Leo and Gemini! Beverly B. called ahead to let me know to expect you! I'm Denise and I'll be your nurse." She lowered herself so that she was at Leo's level. "Leo, shall we get you settled?"

Leo turned his head away and nodded. He was still shy around women, even at sixty-five. If she was being honest, Gemini always admired that about him.

Gary J. pushed Leo away from the elevator doors. "Looks like you're in expert hands. I'll be seein' you then!" He pivoted abruptly and re-entered the elevator before there was any opportunity for more questions.

Denise wheeled Leo into room 412 and set the brakes on his chair. "There's some of our attractive green wear for you on the bed. No fashion show tonight, unfortunately," she joked. "I'll let you change and then I'll come back to go over some paperwork."

When she'd gone, Gemini reached into Leo's bag and pulled out his fuzzy brown slippers, the ones Sophia had given him last Christmas. "Don't go getting funny ideas, Leo Reed," she chided him gently as she put them on his feet. "Nurse Denise's no match for my zodiac super powers." Gemini forced a smile as she helped him unbutton his shirt.

"No dating; got it," Leo replied. He used to be the first one to tell a joke. Now she wasn't sure when they even made sense to him. His brain was always fuzzy.

A sharp rap on the door startled them both.

"You're Mr. Reed? We've been expecting you." A tall man in an expensive, silvery-green suit moved to the end of Leo's bed.

Leo nodded. "You must be Doctor Natchez."

His dark brown hair was slicked back, and he had the scent of a lawyer trying to impress a new client. As a legal secretary, Gemini had learned all of their tricks. Not a single one had impressed her.

"Carson M.," he extended his hand to Leo. "I'm the president of the hospital board. We're delighted to have you in our study."

"Why do you hide your last names? It makes me feel like grade school, to be honest." She didn't dare look at her husband, who would say she was being too nosy.

"Purely for security reasons. We don't want an angry patient harassing a staff member at home." He smiled, displaying large, perfect teeth. "I can tell you're a man of honor, though, Mr. Reed. My last name is Moore. It's Carson Moore."

Gemini touched Leo's back and put her own hand forward. "I'm Gemini, the spouse. In all of our extended hospital visits, the board president has not greeted us once."

Carson took her hand, rubbing his thumb back and forth on her knuckles until she snatched it away. "Mrs. Reed, I take a personal interest in everyone involved in the drug trial. We're going to save lives." His eyes darted away from Gemini. "I'm assuming we arranged your housing? If not, I know of some spouses of patients in the program who found a housing together."

"My husband and I rented a place that's only a couple of blocks away. The management company says the owner plans on selling soon, but it should be fine for the six months that we're here. I suppose I'll adjust to the ugly shade of blue." Gemini winked at Leo and squeezed his shoulder. Leo winked back.

"Oceanberry," the spouses said in unison.

"My wife and I love to paint. A change in color is a change in attitude," Leo explained.

"Leo and I own a hardware store in Fassetville. Reed's Paint to Power Drills."

"Owned," Leo corrected her.

"We sold it last year. We were planning to travel around the world." Gemini sighed before realizing she'd done the very thing she promised herself she wouldn't do in front of Leo–complain. "Everything is an adventure, isn't it?"

"If this trial goes as I expect it will, the two of you will be eating pasta in Italy by this time next year." Carson rubbed his hands up and down the front of his silk shirt. "Last time I went, I think I put on twenty pounds."

Finding herself with waning energy and a bad feeling about Mr. Moore, Gemini pretended to yawn, putting her hand to her mouth. "I'm sorry. It's been a long day."

"I'll leave you two to get settled. If you need me, my office is on the second floor, right past the nurses' station."

As they listened to his expensive shoes clacking on down the hallway, Gemini remembered their most recent concern and scurried to the doorway.

"Wait!" she called after him. "Mr. Moore, what can you tell me about Dr. Wilson?" If he heard her, he made no attempt to answer.

"People make quick exits in this place," Gemini remarked, returning to the bed. "He was odd. I'll even go as far as to say, a bit creepy."

"You're always looking for trouble, my dear. It's not there."

She helped Leo change into his green hospital gown and sat beside him on the bed. "You know I'll be here so often you'll be begging me to leave. We've never had time to tire of each other's company. I should have quit working so much sooner. I wasn't appreciated anyway."

"The past is the past, Gem. We're not there anymore." Leo leaned back on his pillow. "Can you get me some water, please?"

Gemini turned to walk out the door and bumped into the pretty brunette nurse. "Oh, excuse me! I was just fetching my husband some water."

"I can do that for you, Mrs. Reed!" Denise offered cheerfully.

"Denise is such a lovely name. I knew someone back in Fassetville named Denise. She was a client at the law firm where I used to work." Gemini put her hand beside her mouth. "I can't tell you much, but let's just say she had a thing for slipping and falling at the most opportune moments."

"Gem!" Leo admonished, coughing as he grabbed his side.

"I'll run get your water and be right back, Mr. Reed." Denise disappeared, returning momentarily with a full pitcher and two yellow plastic cups. "Only the finest in dishware at Charming General," she quipped.

"Denise, how long have you worked here?"

Gemini had developed a curiosity of others during her years as a legal secretary for the Floris, Fealgood and Flem Law Firm that served her well. At least in her mind. Leo wasn't always so sure.

"I've been here ten years. I really love it. You meet so many interesting people. After I pay off my student loans, I'm going to find a nursing job in the tropics. I'm thinking of Jamaica. As long as my boyfriend can get his expensive suit addiction under control." Denise giggled. "It's terrible. We had to convert the pantry into another closet."

Gemini nodded. "And what about Doctor Wilson? Does he love his job too?"

The smile on Denise's face disappeared. "We're not supposed to talk about it. Hospital policy, I'm afraid. You're in excellent hands and I have confidence the rest of our team will take good care of your husband. I have some paperwork to go over with both of you, and then we'll get Leo all settled in. Does that sound okay?"

Another nurse knocked on the door, motioning for Denise.

When she returned, she explained, "just in case there is confusion with meals or mail, your room number changed at the last minute. Mrs. Ryan was in this room and is now in 419. I'll make sure I check on that every day, so there's no confusion."

Gemini crossed her arms. "I'm still uncomfortable with the state of affairs. Can you walk me through what happened with the doctor? We haven't really been told much of anything."

Denise's phone buzzed in her pocket and as she looked at the screen, she bit her lip. "I'm afraid your paperwork will have to wait. There is an emergency down the hall and I need to go check on the patient. I'll be back here soon and we'll go over everything, I promise."

Gemini watched her rush out of the room, all too familiar with hosptial emergencies after Leo's many stays."Leo, I'm getting a strange vibe from this place. Everybody acts like they're hiding something."

Leo laid back on the pillow, placing one hand under his head. "Gem, I know how your mind works. This is not one of your mysteries at the law firm. Hospitals are notoriously tight-lipped. Everything will be fine, I promise you." He reached over to the nightstand and picked up the television remote. "Why don't you find something good for us to watch on TV?"

"Mm hmm," she responded absently, as she took the remote and pointed it toward the television. A mystery series from the 1970s blared and Leo settled in to watch it.

Gemini fidgeted for a few minutes before standing. "I'm going to take a stroll and see what's down the hall."

"Gem! No!" Leo protested weakly.

She waved at him as she exited the room.

The floor was strangely silent. In Fassetville Regional Hospital, when there was an emergency on the floor, the place was abuzz for a good hour afterward. The nurses were always eager to share with Gemini afterward, even though it was a privacy violation. "You won't tell on us, right, Mrs. Reed?"

She was good at keeping secrets.

There was one nurse sitting at the main desk as she walked by, displaying the name tag, Esther C. "Excuse me?" She leaned on the desk. "I have questions about Doctor Wilson. We're supposed to have a meeting with him tonight, but no one has said where he is."

"Didn't they tell you?" she asked with surprise. "He's no longer in charge of the study."

"Oh?" Gemini asked innocently. "Did something happen?"

"You... who told you?"

"I'm not sure what you mean. We had a meeting scheduled with him this evening. He called us yesterday to make sure we'd be here in time." Gemini tapped her finger on the desk, glancing at two hospital employees who giggled about something as they walked by.

"He's not coming back," Esther C. replied solemnly.

"What would cause Doctor Wilson to leave with no word to his patients? It's terribly unprofessional."

Esther C. cocked her head to the side, appearing to size up Gemini's secret-keeping abilities.

"He was always secretive. But I never expected him to disappear like this."

She stood up and put her arms next to Gemini's on the desk. "You didn't hear this from me, but his maid showed up to clean and there was no sign of him. Hadn't slept there all night. His car was in the garage and none of his clothes were missing. Someone found his phone in a ditch outside of town. We're all very worried."

Gemini shook her head and clucked her tongue. "Such a shame. There's no reason he would leave abruptly?"

"I don't gossip, but between you and me, I think there's something funny going on. Someone knows more than they're saying."

Gemini leaned in even closer. "What exactly do you think happened to Doctor Wilson, Esther?"

Esther took a deep breath and looked around before whispering, "he was murdered."

CHAPTER 2

Feather Jones meandered slowly on the beach. Her combat boots kicked up sand as she moved, amplified by the energetic ocean breeze. She didn't mind the sand in her mouth. She came here to think some days after work when she couldn't find quiet anywhere else.

Two young adults flying a kite walked by her, staring at her beat-up leather jacket and multi-colored hair. She could hear them whispering and giggling.

"Hey! Lady! I think. I know you!" A boy of eighteen or so ran up beside her. "Hey! Didn't you hear me?" He poked her in the shoulder.

She stopped, turned around and grabbed him, pulling his arm behind his back and forcing him to the ground. The self-defense skills her boyfriend taught her often came in handy. "Don't you know how to speak to a lady?" She whispered in his ear.

His girlfriend ran up beside them, dragging her fingers through her long hair and dragging the black-and-white kite behind her. "He just wanted to say hello. You cut his next-door-neighbor, Olive's hair. He drops her off at the salon and she thinks you're wonderful."

Both idiots. He stole all the change out of the newspaper dispenser yesterday and she studies dialogue from reality shows to use on job interviews. Completely harmless, but idiots.

Feather let go of his arm and helped him up to standing position. "You know Olive? She's a regular."

He brushed the sand from his shorts and glared at her. "Do you treat everyone who asks you an innocent question like this?"

"I came out here to find peace, not to entertain. You need to take all the money back to the newspaper office that you stole from their machine. Every penny, or I'll tell Olive and she won't pay you to take her to her hair appointments anymore."

The two kite fliers looked at each other and then at Feather. "How did you know?"

She shook her head. "Doesn't matter. Just return what you stole and I won't share your secret."

The three strangers stood awkwardly for a moment. "Do it now!" Feather commanded.

They ran off, leaving her to her thoughts. Some days, she felt an overwhelming sadness. Whether it was because of her life circumstances or her "gift," she differed from everyone else she met. Up until this point in her life, she'd only truly connected with one other person. At least she had her impossibly perfect boyfriend, Tug.

She stopped, leaned her head back, and closed her eyes. She thrust her arms out straight, feeling the power of the ocean in her fingertips and a tingling sensation as it made its way to every corner of her body.

Opening her mouth, she tasted the salty air. "I'm not strong enough," she cried. "I can't do this anymore." Tears ran down her cheeks, making trails through the coating of sand.

CHAPTER 3

*C*harming was known for its medical community, the largest one on the Oregon Coast. In addition, it sported the dramatic tree-covered cliffs and an enviable front-door view of the ocean. Tourists often rented homes for the summer months, comforted by the fact that there was good medical care nearby if they were injured during a coastal adventure.

Gemini walked home from the hospital, appreciating her new surroundings. The cobblestoned major streets of Charming were a cacophony of sounds – cars driving by and kids yelling to each other as they raced their bikes over the uneven surface. In an empty lot, the community created a garden full of flowers and miniature, ornate statues. There were endless art galleries, and a Chinese restaurant next door to a Mexican restaurant next door to an all-you-can-eat spaghetti bar. It was a far cry from Fassetville.

The town where the Reeds owned a hardware store and raised their daughter was sixty miles inland. It had no distinctive features, other than an abundance of ragweed in the spring. It felt boring but familiar.

It wasn't as if she'd never left Leo in a hospital before. This just felt different, especially after the information the nurse gave her. One of Gemini Reed's many gifts was getting people to tell her their most private thoughts and feelings.

She'd discovered it when Sophia was in kindergarten. The teacher called to tell her Sophia had fought with another girl. "Your daughter is rude and doesn't follow directions well," the teacher began.

"We've taught her to think independently. That may not make her the most popular girl in the class, but she will be the most confident." Gemini replied; words that would come back to haunt her when Sophia turned thirteen. She was trying to think of what to say next, in the most firm but polite manner. Her head tilted to the side, and she stared at nothing in particular.

The teacher took the space as an invitation to share.

She burst into tears. "It's not really your daughter's fault. This class is just awful. The worst group of students I've ever had. I have at least one parent a day calling to complain about me. And my husband just moved out—"

That was the moment Gemini realized she had power. It wasn't something that took a lot of thought, just the ability to remain silent and allow people the space they needed to tell all. Whether it was her kind eyes or her open face, everyone felt they could confess to her. By the time she left the school that day, she knew enough about every other parent in the classroom to cover her back in case they made another complaint about her daughter.

"Mrs. Reed, I really shouldn't tell you this, but—" The more she tilted her head and closed her mouth, the more it happened. No one had ever discussed murder, though.

"You won't tell anyone?" Esther, the charge nurse on Leo's floor had asked, not waiting for her reply. "I don't normally gossip, but there's no reason for him to leave. He's treated like a god here. And Atomycin is having an astounding effect on people. One patient said it made him feel twenty again. Doctor Wilson mentioned that to everyone just last week. You know how doctors like to hear the sound of their own voice!" She rolled her eyes knowingly at Gemini.

Gemini rolled her eyes in response, mimicking gestures was something she'd learned was another way to get people to continue talking. "Are the police investigating his disappearance?"

"We assume so. No one has been up here to question us, so that's kind of strange. If they did, I'd tell them about the tense meetings in Doctor Wilson's office with our board president, Carson Moore. The last one was two days ago. Carson stormed into his office. There was yelling and when he came out, his face was beet red. Dr. Wilson came out not long after. He smiled at me and said he was going for a run after work, and that he hoped I'd have a nice evening. That was the last time I saw him."

She'd investigated many things for her son-in-law's law firm: cheating husbands, marathons where supposedly house-bound people ran twenty-six miles, and even a clothing company that gained their flammable cloth from an illegal vendor. Never in her sixty-nine years had she investigated a murder. It almost made her excited. She thought about it all the way home; how she could fill her time with the facts of the case instead of worrying about Leo.

"You're on my lawn."

Gemini jumped when she heard the deep, snarling voice. She looked up to see a tall man in a red-and-yellow checkered shirt and a wide-brimmed hat to shade his eyes from the late afternoon sun. He was holding a hoe in one hand and his gardening gloves in the other.

"Oh! I'm sorry. I was deep in thought. I'm your new

neighbor, Gemini Reed." She shaded her eyes with one hand and offered the other to the man. He chose not to take it.

"Gemini Reed," she repeated. "I always liked to know who my neighbors were back in Fassetville. In case I had some sort of late-night emergency. I didn't want that to be the first time I met the person, when I was begging for their help."

He turned around abruptly, staring hard. She reasoned he was about seventy years old, with a salt-and-pepper beard, green eyes and a good head of hair. His dark, bushy eyebrows made him appear menacing. "Heard you the first time. Didn't think it required a response."

Gemini began walking toward her driveway.

"Fassetville, you say?" he asked, leaning his entire body weight on his hoe.

Gemini stopped and did an about face. "Yes. Lived there my entire adult life. It's a lovely community. You'd love the city gardens and–"

"My ex lives there. Horrible woman. She took everything I knew I had, and even some I didn't realize she'd hidden away. Ran off with our real estate agent. They're running some kind of pot farm now. Hope they smoke themselves like a brisket on a long Saturday."

"Yes, I'm sure they are fine." Gemini ran through the people she knew from Fassetville who farmed marijuana. There was one family who came into the law firm looking to sue someone for stealing their Mac the Marijuana Farm logo. But they were young and upbeat, clearly nothing like this man.

"Name's Howard Beachmont." He bent down to his flower bed and put his gloves on, laying the hoe beside him carefully. "In case your house is on fire. Now you know."

"Well, thanks then!" Gemini said with false happiness. "I won't be one of those neighbors whose always lurking around. My husband is taking part in a drug trial, so his needs are my main focus." She maneuvered to the other side of him and up his brick walk, where a multi-level flower garden displayed blooms of all shades.

"Your petunias are gorgeous. I've never seen that color before. Sunset orange?"

Howard huffed and followed her. "Regal Orange, they call it. I've got all four varieties of petunia. Two in the front garden, two in the back."

"We're only here for six months, or I'd consider planting something. It would sure brighten up this depressingly brown exterior." She pointed a thumb at her front door. "Who would choose something so dour?"

Howard grunted. "Going inside now." He stood up and moved toward his front door, then paused. "Take care to keep quiet. Last neighbors took it upon themselves to have a party on a Sunday. I have powerful friends in this town. Got 'em kicked out by the following weekend."

Gemini shook her head. "Nice to meet you, Howard!" she called over her shoulder as she walked up the three steps to her front door.

That night she tossed and turned, wondering if they'd made a terrible mistake. Esther C., the nurse she'd spoken with, was obviously a gossip, but would she allege Dr. Wilson was murdered without at least having some evidence? Someone else came to the desk just then, so the conversation ended.

When Gemini woke the next morning, she had a new attitude. Things were going to be okay. She was sure of it. As she walked out the front door, her phone buzzed in her pocket. Charming General

CHAPTER 4

"I don't understand. He was just fine when I left last night." Gemini looked tearfully at her husband, whose chest was moving up and down with the help of a respirator. "He was here for his treatment. There was only a minor risk. That's what Dr. Wilson assured us."

Dr. Natchez, a beefy, balding man with no sign of personality, cleared his throat. "Your husband was ill when he arrived. We knew there would be some risks involved–"

"Is this because Dr. Wilson wasn't here? Did someone do something wrong?" she asked accusingly.

"No, I can assure you, Mrs. Reed, that everyone here is doing their job to the utmost of their ability. Your husband received his first dose of the medication last night. He seemed fine until early this morning, when his heart stopped briefly. We got it restarted, but he's comatose now. He's not in any pain that we know of. Mr. Reed is resting comfortably now." Dr. Natchez had a strangely calm expression on his face. "We're going to do some tests today and get this figured out."

"Can I get you something? Maybe a coffee?" Denise, the

nurse from the day before, asked. She rubbed Gemini's back lightly.

Gemini nodded. "Two sugars, please!" She turned to Dr. Natchez. "How long will he be like this, Doctor?"

He shook his head. "I can't answer that yet. We'll know more soon. I have to finish my rounds, but Denise will take good care of you." He turned and left the room abruptly, leaving Gemini to listen to the whirring and pumping of the machines keeping Leo alive.

She brought Leo's hand to her lips. "This wasn't the way we planned things, but since when has our life worked out according to script?" She could call their daughter Sophia. She really should call her. But that wasn't a thought she relished.

Sophia and her husband, Brandon, had been against this move from the start. Sophia liked to be orchestra leader, not the last person in the room to get the music. The decision to move to Charming had been abrupt, at least in her eyes, and things hadn't been good between her and her parents since.

Esther C. the charge nurse, came in and hugged Gemini. "I'm so sorry about the turn of events."

Gemini was grateful for the affection. "Thank you, Esther. I'm still in shock. Even through his illness, my Leo has been strong."

Ester patted Leo's hand. "It was a shock to all of us. Poor Denise was so upset, she had to leave the room. Stood at my desk and made a very tearful phone call. Glad she had the support of whoever was on the other end. Nursing can be tough on the soul." Esther moved to the door. "Let me know if you need anything, Mrs. Reed. I'm always right here."

Gemini waved to her as she left.

"Here's your coffee." Denise returned and set the cup on Leo's nightstand. "I know this is difficult. And not having family nearby to support you makes it harder. The woman who was in the room before your husband had to leave seven grandchildren behind. She missed them terribly."

"I have one; He's a terror." Gemini took a sip of her coffee. "What happened to her? The woman who was here before Leo?"

"Oh, she hated the view. She said there was no way she was going to get better if she had to look at rooftops all day. Yesterday, the charge nurse had enough and put her in a different room. I can introduce you, if you like? You'll be here so much, it would probably be nice to have a friend."

Gemini smiled. "That's where you're wrong. Leo only agreed to do this study if I promised him I wouldn't spend all of my time sitting by his bed. My husband firmly believes in community service, and I assured him that's how I would spend my time in Charming."

Denise looked taken aback. "Okay, well, I can get you a list of–"

"That's alright. I can find my way around. Leo always says, find the least likely place of need. That's where your minutes are best spent."

"What a lovely idea!" Denise put her hand to her chest. "You're an amazing woman, Mrs. Reed. You remind me of my grandmother. She always did for others." Denise folded her arms over each other and walked to the window. "I was lost when she died. Fell down a dark hole, you might say. If I hadn't found Rodney, I'd still be there."

"Husband?"

"Boyfriend. Of seven years. He's not interested in marriage, and that's fine with me. He's a drug rep, so he's gone much of the time. We have a comfortable routine."

Gemini shifted her weight and tilted her head to the side. "Denise, can you tell me what you think happened to Doctor Wilson? I've been hearing differing stories and I'm very concerned for him."

Denise turned to face her, and Gemini noticed her cheeks were bright red. "There's always gossip in Charming. If this town could turn that into fuel, we'd all be rich."

"Oh sure, sure. I know how that is," Gemini agreed. "I guess people are worried because Doctor Wilson and Carson Moore had some public spats. That got the old gossip mill churning."

Denise was silent.

It was Gemini's turn to fill in the space. "I'd like to bake some cookies for the staff and patients on this floor. Can you give me a head count? It's therapeutic for me."

"Twenty-four. No, wait. We're one down from last night."

"Did something–happen?"

Denise shrugged. "It is a hospital. That's, unfortunately, the nature of things here."

Gemini gulped, feeling like the walls were closing in around her. She struggled when confronted with too many hardships at once. Leaving their hometown, a new drug trial without the doctor they trusted and a strange neighbor were already too many this week, without thinking about Leo's condition. "I need to go for a walk," she muttered, pushing her way past Denise. She didn't breathe until she reached the ground floor. Leo always said she should put that skill on her job applications.

She hurried outside, where she drank in the warm, spring sunshine. A short walk would clear her mind, at least giving her space for any ideas about what was happening up there. Leo's condition couldn't be connected to the death, could it?

Gemini and Leo planned to travel during their retirement. Leo jokingly called it, "the big astrological adventure." After Leo's diagnosis of bladder cancer, their wide world of adventure narrowed down to the city of Charming, Oregon, sixty miles from their home of Fassetville. The drug trial at Charming Regional Hospital offered them hope, something the local doctors hadn't been able to provide. Though it came with risks, it seemed worth it to both of them; to have a chance at a few more years together.

A bronze plaque sat on a pedestal at the corner of the scenic part of town. Main Street, Charming Oregon. Re-envisioned 2018. She made her way down the refurbished main street, where remodeled building fronts gave it a uniform, colonial style. There were cute little shops down this maple tree-lined cobblestone street. A tea room, a candle store, and a hair salon. She caught her reflection in the window of the candle store and remembered she'd skipped her last haircut. Maybe she should make an appointment to get her hair done.

As she opened the door to Feather Works Salon, a bell attached to the top jingled. There were several people standing and sitting in the small waiting area, and all looked at her, annoyed another person had stepped into their increasingly small space. The scent of perms and hair color was intoxicating to Gemini. She'd thought at one time about becoming a hairdresser.

"I've been here almost thirty minutes!" one woman yelled. A stylist, blow-drying and cutting hair looked up, and then resumed her work without comment.

"This is crazy! I'm not sticking around anymore!" the annoyed customer huffed, pushing her way past Gemini and out the door.

A short, sturdy woman with dark brown roots and fuchsia tips put her scissors down and walked to the front counter when she heard the door jangle. Gemini could see her eyes were a bright blue as she came closer. She was wearing a torn leather jacket over a bright yellow t-shirt, and fluorescent pink leggings, their skin-tight material tucked into her black combat boots.

"What's going on?" She asked. "Who's causing trouble?"

"Lottie. You know how grumbly she gets when she has to wait," another customer called out.

The stylist shook her head and then looked at Gemini and grinned. "I'm Feather Jones, the owner. I'm so sorry. We get backed up sometimes. I'd be glad to reschedule you if you don't have time to wait."

"Oh, I was going to make an appointment. It looks like you're at capacity today." Gemini replied cheerfully.

"I'm sorry. We call it 'wash and dish.' We're known as the best hair washing salon in town because people use that time as therapy. It really gets us backed up sometimes. Can I schedule you for tomorrow?"

The woman who stormed out a few minutes earlier came back through the door with an equal amount of gusto, pounding her fist on the counter. "Hi Lottie!" Feather said enthusiastically, as if nothing had happened.

The disgruntled customer looked around her. "I'm not here to see you. My appointment is with Theresa. Tell her I'm here. She's probably ready for me."

Feather turned around and bent forward, stretching to view one of three rooms in the back, where several stylists were washing hair. "It looks like she's still busy."

"It shouldn't take this long," the woman protested. She walked to the back of the store when Feather put her hand out, holding her back.

"She's with a woman who had a recent family trauma. She'll be with you in a few minutes, I'm sure."

Lottie strained her neck to see who was sitting in the chair. "Oh, her. I heard husband left last week. It's all anybody's talking about in the hospital cafeteria." She reluctantly returned to the waiting area.

. . .

Lottie motioned to Gemini. "Can you believe they would treat me like that? This Feather person is going to lose a lot of potential clients if they treat everyone so badly!" She huffed and walked out for the second time, the jingling bells on the door protesting loudly as she opened it with a flourish.

Impulsively, Gemini walked to Feather's chair. "I can help with your line," she offered.

"Huh?" Feather continued blow-drying through her customer's thick blonde hair.

"Your backlog. I can help. I'll come in and shampoo clients for you. I'm a good listener and an excellent problem solver. They're my best two qualities, if I'm being honest." When she worked at the law firm, the other secretaries knew to send the complainers in her direction.

Feather put her brush down and turned off the blow dryer. "Why would you want to do that? I can't pay you."

"My husband is getting treatments at the hospital. Experimental. We've had to move here temporarily and I need something to do while he's at getting better. It was a deal we made. I suspect he knew I would get myself into trouble if I spent all day by his side." She smiled, thinking about the embarrassment she'd caused Leo when she asked personal questions every time they were at one of his appointments. "Can't you just sit still, Gem? These people are trying to do their jobs."

"I don't need any pay. I'd like to help." She smiled, her eyes crinkling slightly. "That's what I do."

Feather pulled her lips together and bit the inside of her cheek. "Okay, I guess that's fine, if you really want to. You'll need to ask the girls what kind of shampoo to use for each client, though. And you can't spend all day shampooing." She picked up the brush, turned on the blow dryer, and began rolling her client's hair as she ran the dryer up and down each piece. "You can come tomorrow morning. It's going to be a busy day. We've got a big festival coming up and everybody wants to look good. Maybe we can squeeze you in for a cut. The color of your hair is gorgeous. Natural?"

Gemini touched her hair absently. "Yes. I went grey last year. It drove my daughter nuts. She feels we should all pretend to be something we're not. She's married to a lawyer and–" She put her hand over her mouth. "Oh dear. I'm talking too much. I guess I'm a little lonely since we moved here."

Feather smiled, moving to the other side of her client's head and combing a new area. "That's okay. What's your name?"

"Gemini Reed. Retiree and enthusiastic volunteer." She stuck her hand out and Feather stopped what she was doing to shake it. Feather's relaxed expression tensed.

"What did you call yourself?"

Gemini shrugged. "I enjoy volunteer work. I'm enthusiastic about it, one might say."

Feather gulped. "I've owned the shop for six months after the previous owner passed away. I'm still learning as I go. Also enthusiastically."

Her client gasped.

"Sorry, Mrs. Windover. I thought you knew. It was unexpected for everyone, most of all, me." Feather shrugged her shoulders. "Nice meeting you, Gemini. I'll see you in the morning!"

She was looking forward to focusing her energy on something besides her husband's frail condition. Leo was seldom wrong about things. By encouraging her to find a meaningful way to stay occupied, he demonstrated, once again, how attuned he was to her needs. "Today I'm really hating that you're so noble, Leo Reed," she said out loud as she walked home. She daydreamed about his large, distinguished nose, full lips, and square jaw. They'd forgotten to book a haircut for his salt-and-pepper hair before his hospital stay, and it was now almost down to his collar. It reminded her of the young, wild Leo she'd met thirty-four years ago.

"Two astrological names. It must be fate," He'd said to her when she'd come into the hardware store the first time, flashing her the dazzling smile that melted her heart immediately. Cedar Green was the color she'd purchased to paint her kitchen, against his advice. When he called the next day to see how she liked the paint, she told him it was much too dark and dreary. He offered to repaint it for her and instead they went on their first date. Gemini and Leo were never apart after that.

WALKING in the kitchen door of the mud-brown rental, Gemini realized it was time to do the thing she dreaded most. She took her phone out of her pocket and found the number, pausing for a moment before dialing.

CHAPTER 5

Feather met Tug at the gym on a rainy Thursday afternoon. Just another pretty face and body who was more a nuisance than a potential mate, she thought. That day, she was on her 4th set of squats. She was feeling especially pumped up, now beginning her second month of gym membership. She had been off the drugs for three months and her body was thanking her in ways she couldn't believe. If only her family could see her now. They would be proud of the person she'd become, or at least the person she showed to the world.

"You don't seem like the average gym rat. You haven't looked in the mirror once and really focused on your squats." He was so handsome he took her breath away: hair the color of brown sugar, muscular tanned arms and green eyes that had no end. He looked like something out of the clothing catalogs she used to peruse as a child for images of her fake husband.

"Are you for real? You seem like you should walk down a boardwalk somewhere with a sweater over your shoulder and a blonde on your arm." Feather returned to her squats, unconcerned. Whatever his game was, she wasn't playing.

"More than usual. Sweaters make me itch, and I've given up blondes. They only lead to trouble. Now brunettes, they're another matter." He winked, something she would normally find creepy and off-putting in a man. "Ever since my heart attack, I've devoted myself to honesty and being an all-around good guy."

She set the bar down and turned to him. "You had a heart attack? But you're so young and fit; that doesn't seem possible."

"The Muehler genes. They cursed me. They gave me my sickeningly studly good looks, but they also gave me some ugly cholesterol, which led to a heart attack. It's all under control now, though. My name is Tug, by the way. And yours?" He extended his hand for her to shake, but changed his mind and folded both of them across his chest.

"Feather. Feather Jones." She looked him up and down, still on guard, still certain someone like him would have some ulterior motive for speaking to her.

"That's an interesting one. I suppose you get that a lot. People wanting to find out where that came from and why you haven't changed it yet? I have a similar issue with my name. Tug is not something you hear every day. But Thaddeus Bartholomew Muehler the Fourth is a mouthful. Tug works better for everyone. My dad is Tag. We're an obnoxious family."

He was charming. She'd give him a point for that. "My parents didn't think too hard when they named their kids. My mother thought she saw a bluebird on the window after my birth and decided that the Feather in her room was a sign. Kind of ridiculous, but there it is."

Tug chuckled. "I like Feather. It's a name that makes me want to know more about its owner."

They stood, looking at each other but trying not to stare. "Miss? Are you about done?" A beefy-looking man in far too short shorts asked Feather.

"I've got a few more sets to do. Just give me five minutes, okay?" She spoke to the man, but her eyes were still on Tug.

"I suppose I should finish too, or I'll talk myself out of the rest of this. Still need to do my cardio. Are you into boxing class?"

"Never tried it." Feather began lifting the heavy bar again. "I've always wanted to, though." She concentrated on keeping her knees behind her toes as she dropped into the squatting position. Whoever this Tug person was, he would watch her form for mistakes. That was how his type always worked.

"Boxing starts in ten minutes. I'd love to see you in there, Feather. A Feather and a Tug in the back row. Now that's a class!" He winked again, and they both giggled.

She decided, with some hesitation, she would join him in the class. They went for beet juice afterward and sat for three hours talking about every mundane detail of their lives. Tug was in business school, taking classes online so he wouldn't have to leave his ailing grandmother. He sold Doctor Whipley Health Products and Safe N-Secure Self Defense, both multi-level marketing companies, on the side. Although he never admitted it, he was a disappointment to his family, too. He'd started and stopped college four times, always finding something to stand in his way. His heart attack was the latest -using his rehabilitation time as an excuse to avoid school.

From that day on, they were inseparable. Tug was her everything, especially because she had no family to rely on. Even her brother, who worked at the hospital and sent his friends in for haircuts, had nothing to do with her. She was the family disappointment, no matter what anyone said.

CHAPTER 6

"Sophie? It's mom." Gemini's insides tensed up.

"Mother? You promised to call me every day. It's been three." Her high-pitched voice alerted Gemini to the fact that it was a stressful day for Sophia, like most seemed to be. "I tried Daddy's phone, but it was turned off. It's completely irresponsible to leave me in the dark. I need to know everything that—"

"You're absolutely right, Soph. I dropped the ball." Gemini had just recently discovered this tactic of "cutting her off at that pass," as Leo called it.

They assumed they couldn't have children after twelve years of trying. Painting their baby girl's room with a bold, Luscious Lipstick Pink was the right move. Sophia was a force to be reckoned with from the age of one when she began speaking in full sentences.

They were by far the oldest parents of any child in the school. It didn't bother Leo, but Gemini hated feeling out of place. Sophia sensed it too. She didn't want her parents around when other kids were engaging with their much younger mothers and fathers. Each volunteer opportunity at school meant assigning her parents to areas where she wouldn't have to associate with them. She gave them each a list of parents they could communicate with and the questions they should ask. Sophia was the boat captain on their untraditional parenting cruise.

It seemed like the right decision to encourage her to be the most outspoken person in the room. They relished having a bright and driven child. She was everything they weren't. Sophia Reed wouldn't spend her life in Fassetville; she was going places.

"Good grief, Mother." Sophia put her hand over the phone. Gemini heard her daughter lecturing her grandson. "You know where to put your shoes. Ask Lucie to help you. Tomorrow she'll organize your closet and you can decide where you want everything." She uncovered the mouthpiece. "Sorry. I can't wait until you come back and he's with family all day. I don't like the idea of a stranger raising my child."

Gemini felt a tightness in her throat. When she retired from the law firm, she promised Sophia she would babysit. Sophia took this as an explicit contract to be their nanny. She and Leo were figuring out how to tell her they were planning to travel and wouldn't be the only care providers for their grandson when Leo became ill.

"I've been too busy to call. Your father's first treatment went well. He felt fine and was telling me jokes."

"Paint store jokes, not funny ones," Sophia replied tersely. "We had a very clear agreement that you would let me know right away how things were going. We haven't spoken since you moved."

"I know. I'm sorry. We've been settling in." Gemini looked around the room where Leo had patiently directed her while she unpacked every box. "Charming is a cute little town."

"Brandon and I drove through when we did our coast trip last year, remember?"

Gemini rolled her eyes. "Yes, I remember."

"So? Do we think these drugs are going to work? Don't keep me guessing."

Gemini squeezed her free hand into a fist and released it. "Great! So far, he's had no adverse reaction. He'd talk to you himself, but he's exhausted." Not that she relished lying to her only child, but it made life so much easier when she didn't have to explain things. Sophia would call the hospital making impossible demands of the staff, and it would make their time at Charming General even more difficult.

There was a loud squeal and Gemini pulled the phone away from her ear until it finished. "I'll continue my conversation in the other room until you're done, darling," Sophia cooed. A door shut, and she heard the squeak of bedsprings. "I'll just wait in the bedroom until he's done with his moment of reactivity."

"He'll need to learn manners at some point. You don't want reactivity happening in public spaces." Her grandson needed discipline and, at the very least, some direction. Sophia believed in neither.

"What are you finding to entertain yourself, Mom? Is there a knitting club or something?"

Gemini snorted. "You know I don't knit. I don't have the patience. Your ideas about retirement are outdated."

"You don't need to snap at me. You had lots of friends who knit. I just thought, you know, that you might need something to do besides sit by Daddy's bed. Is there a support group you could join?"

"I didn't mean to snap, dear. I've not been getting much sleep. New bed and all." It was the familiar routine they fell into: Sophia trying to force her version of Gemini's life upon her. "No, but I've found activities to keep me occupied." She pushed the ruffled pink curtain to one side, where she could view her strange next-door neighbor working in his flower garden.

"We'll come visit you soon. I'm sure Daddy would love to see his grandson."

"No!" she answered quickly. The thought of her wild grandchild barreling through the hallway of the second floor made her shudder. "They don't allow children on your father's floor. We'll do a video call soon, when your father is a little stronger. I have to go now."

"Don't get yourself into trouble, Mother. I know how much you like to stick your nose where it doesn't belong. Brandon has told me stories–"

"Your husband appreciated every minute of my work for him," Gemini said defensively. Everyone else in the law office refused when asked to investigate. She did it happily and willingly.

"It's just that you get carried away. We'll be eager to receive updates. Don't wait so long to call next time."

"I love you, Sophia. Give my grandson a kiss." Gemini hung up the phone and looked around the kitchen for something interesting to eat. She and Leo had gone to the store before he entered the hospital. They stocked the refrigerator full of green vegetables and sauces that he loved.

She reached into the cupboard and grabbed the peanut butter jar then found a spoon in the drawer. It was almost like being a child, home alone for the first time. She felt a little guilty, enjoying her time by herself.

The next morning, she arrived at Feather Works Salon shortly after 8 a.m. She'd had little sleep as the drug trial and strange hospital happenings competed for space with Sophia's judgement in her head.

She peeked in the window when the door wouldn't open. "Oh, you're here early!" a voice from behind her stated.

She stepped out of the way so Feather could unlock the door.

"I can stay for a couple of hours before I go sit with my husband. He's not doing well."

"That's too bad." Feather set her things on the counter as they walked in. "You never know when your jig is up. I have experience with death and it's not as bad as you'd think."

Gemini tried not to be offended. "Yes, I suppose you're right. He's going to be fine, though. It's just a minor setback. The nurse assured me of that today." She pushed away the panic and sadness trying to creep into her mind. Leo would never approve.

Feather turned on all the lights and adjusted the heat for the chilly space. "I turn it off at night to save money," she explained. "Come back here and I'll explain."

Gemini followed her past an empty room to the room. "What used to be in here?" she asked, pointing to the space.

"Oh, that's where we had a nail technician. There are so many in town, I decided it wasn't in my best interest to find a replacement." She leaned in close to Gemini and whispered, "I think maybe the former tenant died in there. It's got a bad vibe, if you know what I mean."

Gemini nodded.

They entered a room with four black sinks next to a full wall of hair care products. "Here are the shampoos and conditioners–four different types. You'll ask the stylist which one they recommend. As I mentioned yesterday, people really unload on us. We're almost like counselors. You'll learn some pretty hairy stuff. Just keep it to yourself, if you can. I mean, unless you just have to unload; then you can tell your husband or something."

"He's in a coma," Gemini said matter-of-factly. "The doctor thinks he'll come out of it soon." As soon as she said it, she realized there was no "we" right now.

"Oh! That's—wow." Feather glanced around the room. "I'm so sorry. Though some days, it would be pretty great-sharing my deepest, darkest secrets with someone who couldn't respond." She ran through the unique set of worries in her head and quickly pushed them aside. "Although my boyfriend, Tug, is pretty wonderful. Near perfect."

"My Leo is pretty great too."

Feather pushed by Gemini again and put her lunch in the refrigerator opposite the hair washing stations. She stood up and looked at Gemini. "I've never met anyone like you before. You know, wanting to be nice for no reason. Not sure I trust that, but we'll see."

Gemini took her coat off and hung it on the coat tree in the corner. She rolled up the sleeves of her green flower-print top and stood, waiting for her first customer.

CHAPTER 7

"The staff will be so grateful you baked cookies. They look amazing!" Denise gushed, taking a large plastic tub from Gemini. "What did you say these were again?"

"Oatmeal chocolate chip. Leo's favorite." Gemini gazed at her immobile husband wistfully.

Denise set the cookies on the nightstand and glanced at Leo's vitals before writing them into the chart. "The powers-that-be will review these events carefully." She patted Leo's leg and smiled. We won't let anything happen to your handsome husband, I promise."

Gemini took little comfort from that familiar statement. Staff uttered it regularly during every hospital visit they'd made. She scooted her chair closer to the bed. "Doctor Wilson said he'd had lots of success with this drug. 'A miracle,' he called it. Now I'm wondering if this was a big mistake. Maybe my Leo should be removed from the program."

Denise shook her head. "No, that would be premature. Let's see how the next few days go."

"How is the other lady doing? The one who moved to

another room?" Gemini took a cookie from the container on the nightstand and began munching nervously.

"She's fine. I can introduce you if you'd like." Denise pushed her dark hair behind her ear and looked out the window. "Sunny again today. I should have been a lifeguard," she mused. "So I could spend my time in the open air and not feel trapped inside."

"Why do you stay? You should go do what you really want. Leo wanted to spend his retirement traveling and instead, he's stuck." Gemini stared out the window, trying to understand what Denise found so appealing. It was a flat roof with several air conditioners.

"We're saving up to move somewhere tropical," Denise continued. "Rodney's always wanted to live in luxury. As a kid, he was shuffled between his parents and grandparents and he felt like he never got to enjoy life."

"You mentioned your plans. How nice you can move on so young!" Gemini nodded her head absently. "I worked far too long at the law firm. My son-in-law's business. He took advantage of my skills and never really thanked me. I'm glad to be out of there."

Denise took a cookie of her own from the container. "From our first day together, Rodney promised he would move us somewhere tropical. He's always looking out for me. "She moved to the doorway, brushing cookie crumbs from her scrubs. "But for today, I'm here, happily, of course."

"No word on Doctor Wilson?"

Denise sighed. "You certainly are persistent. Maybe he was tired of bickering with our board president." She stuck her head outside the door, making sure no one was walking down the hall before continuing. "He and Carson Moore fought over their differing visions for the hospital. Carson wanted a major expansion and Doctor Wilson, along with the rest of the board thought that would be a mistake. Carson pushed the Atomycin drug trial and Doctor Wilson wasn't interested. You can see who won that argument."

"That doesn't sound like the man we spoke with on the phone. Doctor Wilson told us it was wonderful! Said he'd give it to his own family member if they needed it!"

Denise shrugged. "He probably saw the benefits once he was on board." She looked at the clock above Leo's bed. "I need to check on my other patients. Thanks for the cookies! We'll enjoy them!"

Gemini took Leo's hand. "There is something going on here, Leo. I will not rest until I know exactly what happened to Doctor Wilson. I promise you that."

After an hour with her husband, she returned to Feather Works Beauty Salon.

"What's your deal again?" The round, elderly woman asked, as Gemini gently lowered her head into the sink.

"I'm helping Feather. I saw she needed help, so I jumped in and volunteered. Those are the best kind of volunteer activities, the ones that you—"

"Not that." She snapped. "What's in it for you?"

"My first job out of high school was washing hair for a local beautician. I did that for a summer and got acquainted with many interesting people." She squeezed a small amount of shampoo into her hands and began massaging it gently into the woman's scalp. "It's a pleasant diversion for me, if you want to know the truth."

"Oh? Why's that? You get yourself in some kind of trouble? I know all the gossip in town. Never heard about you before."

Gemini smiled. "No, my husband is in the hospital. He's part of a drug trial and yesterday he had a complication. He's in a coma."

The woman frowned as Gemini ran the warm water over

her scalp. "And you're here? Why in the dickens would you choose to wash my hair instead of sitting beside him?"

"You'd have to understand my husband." Gemini squirted some conditioner onto the woman's head. "He didn't want me sitting in the hospital. He was adamant about that. I'm honoring his wishes by doing something I enjoy." She pushed the back of the chair to the upright position and rubbed the customer's wet head before wrapping it in the towel.

"Sugar, that makes no sense to me. None t'all." The woman shook her head as Gemini tried to keep the towel in place. "That hospital is a dark place. He shouldn't be there without you."

"If we're getting into serious business, I should introduce myself. I'm Gemini Reed." Gemini wiped her hands on a brown stained towel and offered the driest hand to the skeptical woman.

"Olive Thomas." She shook Gemini's tanned hand. "Sure is a strange name. You some kind of hippie?"

"My parents were. I was lucky—they named my brother for the day of the week he was born. Friday hates his name to this day and goes by his middle name Hadley."

Olive huffed. "Parents didn't have any common sense, I'd imagine."

"It was my grandfather's name." Gemini crossed her arms. "What was it you were saying about strange goings on at the hospital?"

Olive leaned forward. "There was a drug trial last year and more than one person died. The hospital, of course, said other things caused their deaths. There are rumors, but no one really knows for sure. I asked my grandson about it. He's one of those drug reps. His girlfriend is a nurse there, and she says–"

"I'm ready for you, Mrs. Thomas," Feather walked into the shampoo room and smiled warmly. "Are you scaring our newest resident away with horror stories?" She winked at Gemini. "Wait for me at my station, Mrs. Thomas. I'll be there in a jiffy."

After Olive left, Feather touched Gemini's arm. "She's the biggest gossip in town. Half of what she says is pure bull. Don't let her scare you. Ask me first before you assume what's she's telling you is true."

Gemini nodded. "I'm ready for my next customer." She filed the story away in her head for future use.

A young mother with two loud toddlers at her feet sat in the chair. "I've had no one other than Feather wash me," she remarked." Are you her grandmother?"

Gemini gulped. Not that many years ago, people would ask if she was in her forties. Since she let her hair naturally gray, and she'd gone through the stress of Leo's illness, she'd aged some. "No," she replied. "I'm just a volunteer here. Tell me about yourself. I'm new in town and need to learn the ropes." She leaned the young mother back into the seat as one toddler ran his toy truck over Gemini's feet.

"My husband is an x-ray technician at the hospital. They hired him a few years back during a big shakeup, when they fired someone having an affair with the CEO's wife. You'll find drama is a common theme there. I stay home with my boys for now, but I'm planning to return to nursing as soon as they're old enough–Daniel! Stop pinching the poor woman's leg!" She snapped her fingers. The toddler was standing next to the sink, staring innocently at his mother.

"That's okay," Gemini said as she massaged shampoo into the harried mother's head. "I have a grandson myself, so I'm used to a little abuse. He's two-and-a-half." She smiled as she thought about the precocious tot who always got into trouble. He'd gotten two more teeth and learned a nasty word since she'd seen him last.

"Mm-mm. That feels so good. I haven't been able to relax

for months. Ever since my sister got fired and took another job in another town. I've been a ball of knots. She never even called me to let me know she was leaving. I felt so betrayed. Now I'm never sure when someone will make a nasty comment, you know? This town is so full of gossips."

"I've been told. The last woman I shampooed said there were rumors of bad things happening recently at the hospital. Has your husband heard anything?"

The mother opened her eyes and looked up at Gemini. "What rumors?"

"Oh, I don't know. Something about Doctor Wilson's sudden absence." Gemini cocked her head to the side.

"I–you'll have to ask someone else about that," she snapped. She was quiet for the rest of her wash. When she got up to leave, she paused for a moment. "I didn't mean to be short with you. I promised my husband I wouldn't tell anyone. We're all a little on edge because no one at the top is saying anything. It's like he vanished into thin air."

"I understand," Gemini said with a fake smile that didn't give away her frustration.

The next person who sat down in the chair had lots to say. "I'm Wendy from down the street. I own Wendy's Handcrafted. Everything in our store is made locally. We do soaps and candles and honey and–"

Gemini drifted off. Leo must experience wonderful dreams of their life together. The paint store they owned for thirty-two years. The many times they'd repainted their home together, after laughing at all the different color options. "What is seashell white? Why would I choose that over eggshell white? Why not linen white?" They'd laugh as they painted each wall a different color until they found something unique. On one occasion, it was Oceanberry Blue. "Now that's a color with a story inside," Leo proclaimed. "Where in the world might you find a shade of pale blue like that? It's a shade the screams 'adventure.' Every day of our lives together is Oceanberry Blue, if you think about it."

"Gemini? Are you alright?" Feather was shaking Gemini's arm. "There are several people here with doctors in the family. If you need medical attention."

"Huh?" Her mind jumped back to the present day, where she was standing with shampoo -covered hands dripping on the floor. "Oh, I'm fine, thanks. I'm just a little tired. I didn't sleep much last night, thinking about my husband."

"What's wrong with your husband?" Wendy asked. "I've been blabbering away and haven't asked a thing about you."

"He's in the hospital. In a coma," Feather informed her. "Gemini is just working here to keep her mind off things. Isn't that sweet of her?"

"Oh, I'm so sorry. I went on and on about my business and I didn't even think that you were dealing with your own stuff," Wendy said, hopping out of the chair and grabbing her own towel. "Really sorry–Gemini, is it?"

"Yes, Gemini Reed." She looked at Feather, her face flushed. "I think I need to quit for today. I'll be back tomorrow morning." She put the towel she was holding on the counter and walked out.

"Thanks for your help!" Feather called after her.

"Come back for my wash next week!" Olive hollered from Feather's chair. "I have more to tell you!"

As exhausted as she was, it had been a good day. Eventually, someone at the salon would tell her what she needed to know. She sat down in the recliner with her mystery book, Doris Drama, Amateur Sleuth, and a cup of orange blossom tea. Because of everything that had been going on, she had to re-start the book at the beginning four times.

As she turned the page to chapter one, her phone buzzed.

"Mrs. Reed? This is Olive Thomas. You washed my hair at the beauty salon."

"Yes! I remember. Beautiful, thick hair. Bob cut." And the town gossip, if one person can claim that title.

"I got your number from Feather Jones. Remember, I told you about my grandson, who is a drug rep? Well, I've just come across some very disturbing information. Would you be able to meet me tomorrow?"

"Tomorrow is a busy day for me, but I'll be at the salon from eight a.m. until ten. Could you meet me there?"

"Oh, no. We can't meet so publicly. I believe there is a killer in the hospital. I'm worried about your husband."

CHAPTER 8

Feather walked into the house and threw her keys into the empty candy bowl. "Tug? You here?"

There was no response. Feather experienced a sense of relief, knowing she'd have the place to herself for a while. She needed to research further and as much as he tried to help, this was something that she needed to do in private. The old laptop she'd bought from a sketchy antique dealer in Piney Falls took a good ten minutes to warm up. While she waited, she made herself a sandwich - hummus, turkey and vegan cheese. A twisted mix of personalities, just like Feather herself.

When the laptop stopped its furious whirring, she sat down and typed in her search terms. There were seventeen-hundred results on the topic. "I won't have time for all of this," she grumbled.

"Just do it a little at a time then," a voice from behind her suggested.

She jumped up and snapped, "Don't do that! You know I'm the last person you want to scare!"

Her brown-haired boyfriend chuckled. "What? You'll send them after me? I'm still skeptical. Not about you, babe, but this is a little strange."

"I know, I know. You've told me a million times." She sighed. "But I'm glad you don't discourage me. I was just getting ready to do some research and—"

He leaned down over her shoulder, the musky mix of sweat and his body spray swirling around her. He kissed her neck lightly and then looked up at the computer screen. "Holy crap! All of that? Do you need my help?"

She looked at him appreciatively. "Would you? Just take notes and tell me later if anything pertains to my, whatever you'd call it."

"Business. It's going to be a business, babe. We're going to be rich some day from your side gig." Tug stood back up and pulled his shirt off, revealing a muscular trunk with no excesses.

"You'd better not do that in front of the window. The neighbors will bang down the door wanting a better look at you." Feather smiled and pulled him in close, kissing his belly button. "How would it look if you were the cause of women overheating?"

He kissed the top of her head. "Okay. I'll get in the shower and then be out to help you. Don't do anything strange before I get back!"

She turned around to the computer and continued her work. As she pulled up the first page and began reading, she felt the hairs on the back of her neck rise. "Tug?" she asked hopefully.

The bathroom pipes squeaked and she could hear him singing. He was definitely in the shower. "What is it? What do I need to know?"

She pulled a sticky note off of the pad that had Buzby

Beauty Supply printed across the top of each one. She wrote furiously on one and then pulled off another. When she finished, she shoved it away and stood.

Feather Jones had quit nothing in her life. In the fifth grade, all of her friends joined a workout challenge. Seven days a week for four weeks, they had a series of ten exercises to do before jogging three miles. In the last week, Feather was the only one still taking part.

Now was not the time to quit this task either, no matter how much it frightened her. She breathed in deeply. "Okay, okay. I got it." One of these days, she would adjust. Everything was a matter of adjustment, as her cigar-smoking grandmother used to say.

Her strange journey required constant adjusting. Once, when they were on a camping trip in the Yellowstone National Park, she saw a grizzly bear. She decided the best thing to do was to distract it so her brother and sister could get away.

When they told their parents what had happened, they were furious she'd put herself in danger. The bear, as it turned out, lost interest in Feather. After a minute or two facing down the spikey-haired teen, he must've decided there were easier ways to find dinner, such as the young deer standing within striking distance.

As much as they chided her, her parents saw it as an opportunity to make a name for themselves. Every news outlet within one-hundred miles did a story on Feather's bravery, her parents happily accepting each offer without asking her if she really wanted to tell the tale one more time.

The incident became a part of family lore, a story told any time there was an audience. Soon, expectations for Feather rose to a ridiculous level. "She's going to be president one day, mark my words," her Uncle Carl bragged. Her tobacco-scented grandmother told everyone, "the only people who look a bear in the eye and live to tell the story will become rulers or serial killers."

"You shouldn't think about The Great Bear Incident anymore, Feather," her mother said randomly one day.

"No one else feels that way, Mom. Any time I try to talk about my life, people look at me like I'm crazy. I wish you wouldn't have made a big deal of this. I'm stuck now. Probably for the rest of my life."

"You're being overly dramatic," her mother replied dismissively. "The rest of us never bring it up. Last weekend we went to Great Aunt Nora's ninetieth birthday, and no one said a word about The Great Bear Incident."

"You weren't listening, Mom. It came up twice at dinner. Cousin Morgan said we should eat bear patties next year."

When Feather became a hairdresser, her entire family expressed their shame that the one person in the family to find fame squandered her good fortune.

"It takes a lot of talent to cut hair," she protested. "You should recognize that, Mom, because your hairdresser spends four-plus hours on your hair every month and you're still not satisfied. This is what I want to do with my life, and nothing that you or Dad say is going to change that. Maybe you don't really see who I am. Deep down, you still think I've got magical powers, but I'm just average, ordinary Feather Jones."

Her mother made a clucking sound and turned her head. It was only when she entered beauty school that she learned how deeply wounded her relatives were by her choice of career.

Little by little, her large extended family cut off contact with Feather, including her mother, brother, and sister. Her father had, by that time, taken a job with an engineering company far away and he and her mother were planning to move soon. In an act he would later call, "a slight mis-judgement," he didn't bother saying goodbye to his youngest child.

When she graduated from beauty school, there were no familiar faces cheering her on. It was only Feather's sheer determination that got her through the next months. That and the drugs she used to dull the pain. There was also the matter of the urgent whispers in her head.

Tug got out of the shower and dried himself off before returning to the living room. "I'm ready to help you," he announced.

Feather glared at him. "Well, I'd be more interested in your help if you were wearing clothing. This is very distracting–this whole look." She turned away, not willing to engage in anything beyond her troubling circumstance right now.

"I take it you've got something else on your mind or -this would be very appealing to you." Tug replied, trying not to appear hurt.

"It happened again."

He raised his eyebrows. "Did you write it down?"

"Of course I did. I've got a lengthy list. Not really sure I know what to do with it though."

Tug walked across the room, unconcerned about displaying his unclothed body in front of the uncurtained window. He looked at her papers and read them over several times. "Are you sure? Are you positive this is what they said?"

She nodded. "Positive."

"What should we do, babe? We're in this together now. I'm with you no matter what you decide. You know my feelings about this; there is a reason for everything. It's not just random."

Feather was grateful once again for the man she'd unexpectedly found in the gym. Tug called it "intervention at the fittest level." She touched his arm. "It's been happening more and more. I can't ignore it, Tug. I have to acknowledge this is real. These people need my help."

CHAPTER 9

"I'll take a hot tea and an oatmeal with extra brown sugar and granola on top. You'll make sure the granola is fresh?" Olive touched her expertly curled hair and stared at the server.

"I'm sure our granola is the freshest. We get a truck in every Thursday." He didn't bother looking up from his pad. "What about you, ma'am?"

"A bagel, toasted with peanut butter, and a coffee with two sugars," Gemini replied. She looked at her watch. Exactly one hour until she was due at the salon. At least that was the schedule she'd set for herself.

"You don't go for the fancy coffee either? Never understood what was wrong with plain old cream." Olive glanced around the dining room of the Boastful Elk, where two other tables had couples who weren't paying any attention to her.

"No, my Leo always says if you want to dress up coffee in a different outfit, you really should call it something else." She let out a loud sigh and, realizing that she'd allowed herself to do that in front of a stranger, she put her hand over her mouth. "I don't make those noises in public."

Olive shook her head. "Not to worry. I know you're fit to be tied over your husband. I lost my Chester seven years ago this March. He was finally taking down the Christmas lights when he slipped off the roof. Impaled himself on the Santa display our son made us the year before," she said matter-of-factly. "Landed right on Prancer's antlers." She took a sip of her water.

"Oh, Olive! That's awful! I'm so sorry! What a horrible experience for you." Gemini reached forward and patted her new friend's gnarled hand.

"Christmas isn't the same without him. Never did like those lights on the house, anyway."

The server brought their dishes and set them down, pausing after leaving Olive's oatmeal. "I asked," he announced pointedly. "The granola is from last week's shipment. But we have not used it until today. So it's fresh from the package."

"Well, thank you, young man." Olive nodded. When he walked away, she leaned forward. "They think they can bamboozle an old lady. I realize it's the same box they used last month when I came in. I keep them on their toes or they'll be serving me stale bread before you know it."

"I'm pressed for time today, Olive. It surprised me you wanted to meet here. It's not very private. Can you give me more details?"

"More private than the hair salon. Some of those ladies possess ears like radar." Olive stirred her oatmeal and then looked around the large space once more. "Well, you remember my telling you about the deaths at the hospital from the last drug trial? I have it on good authority that they aren't being reported for what they are."

"What do you mean?" Gemini cocked her head to the side.

"What I mean, dear woman, is that for every cause there is an effect. They featured doctor Wilson in the paper for his success after the last drug trial—all roses and accolades. What I heard was entirely different—he didn't think it had gone well and he and Carson Moore argued in the hospital parking lot every night during that time. When people tried to intervene, they both shut up immediately. Suddenly, they start a new drug trial and Doctor Wilson vanishes? Cause and effect."

"That's pecul–"

"Doctor Wilson wasn't any too happy to start another drug trial, no siree. Not if it meant spending more time with Carson Moore."Olive wiped the corners of her mouth, leaving thick-berry-colored lipstick on the napkin. "I know well and good that Doctor Wilson is dead. No one has heard a peep since he disappeared. Not one tiny peep."

Gemini thought back to the first day she and Leo got to the hospital. The staff were very calm, no one seemed at all concerned about Doctor Wilson's absence. "How do you know he's not on vacation somewhere? Family emergency? I have found no proof that he's dead."

Olive took a sip of her tea. "One thing you'll learn about me, Gemini Reed, is that I have my finger on the pulse of just about everything going on in this town." She smiled with satisfaction. "I've lived here my entire life and I know them all – young and old. I have sources at the hospital who tell me strange things have been happening there. Everyone who works there has a secret of some kind, most aren't good. I thought you'd want to know, given your husband is in Doctor Wilson's trial."

Gemini felt uncomfortable. Feather told her that Olive was nothing but a gossip. "What does your grandson say? Doesn't he work at the hospital?"

"Oh, he thinks I'm a crazy old lady," Olive scoffed. I don't bother telling him what I learn. He'd find a way to discredit me before I spit out the first sentence. 'You're crazy,

Grandma. Those things don't happen here.' I love the boy, but he can make me so mad."

Gemini tapped her fingers on the table. "Have you heard anything about Doctor Wilson's personal life? Is he seeing someone?"

"He's a randy one," Olive commented, rolling her eyes. "Went through most of the staff last year alone. Married or single, it didn't matter. I heard he was seeing an older woman for a while. One nurse you wouldn't expect would catch his eye. " Olive stirred her tea absentmindedly. "Of course, finding one that lasted more than one night might take you some time."

"What about his relationship with Carson Moore? What made things so contentious?"

"They were golfing buddies, mostly. When Moore's wife left him, that's when the two men started spending more time together. Maybe they became sick of each other's company, or they fought over who was the better golfer." Olive chuckled. "Neither one of us believe that t'all."

Gemini looked at her watch once more. "I really should–"

"Do you want to learn my secret? How I get everyone to confide in me?" Olive asked with a hint of a smile.

"Okay, sure."

"Tell them you understand how hard things are for them. You have four kids? Oh, how tiring? I had four kids. I barely slept for ten years."

"You had four children? You must've been exhausted." Gemini replied.

Olive shook her head. "No, I had three. Doesn't matter. You meet them at their level and then you sit back and let them release everything. When the air has gone out of their sails, then you go in for the kill. 'Say, can I ask you about your neighbor? Seems like he's doing something shady.' Works every time."

Gemini thought back to her days as a legal secretary. Just as it was in the hair salon, people always wanted to unload their personal business. It didn't seem like she'd 'met them at their level, but they always wanted to confess their secrets. "I found a nice batch of cookies can also do the trick. Food is a great way to open the door." She tilted her head. "And Doctor Wilson? Were you able to get information from him that way?"

"Didn't expect things would take such a turn," Olive sniffed. "Otherwise, I would have gotten all of his secrets at the last Charming General charity event."

"Is there anyone besides Carson Moore who might benefit from Doctor Wilson's disappearance?" Gemini pushed the last bite of bagel into her mouth.

"Many people. Running a drug trial made him the darling of the hospital board. I'd imagine folks were jealous. Then there's the matter of all of those women he loved and left; you mark my words, they're going to find that poor man's body soon."

Gemini pulled a twenty-dollar bill from her pocket and set it on the table. "I must run. It was such a delight to visit with you."

Olive grabbed her hand as she set the money in the middle of the table. "No, it's my treat. I insist. Next time will be your turn. You'll want to hear more, I'm sure."

"Thank you!" Gemini stood, pulling on her baby blue windbreaker. "I'll see you for your wash on Thursday!"

Olive waved as Gemini walked out the door. She hurried down the street to her car, where she had two plastic-wrapped plates of baked goods sitting in the front seat. She took one out and carefully walked half a block to Feather Works Hair Salon.

CHAPTER 10

Feather was sitting at the front desk, reviewing her appointments, when Gemini arrived. She smiled and looked up when her new friend walked in. "Oh, hey there! It's a light appointment day for me, and there's only one other girl working this morning. You don't have to stay if you don't want."

"I'm just here to drop these off." Gemini set a plastic container full of frosted brownies covered in festive sprinkles on the counter. "Leo and I used to paint something when we felt stressed. When he got sick, the smell of paint made him nauseous, so I started baking as my stress reliever. Luckily, baked goods didn't bother him. I won't bring them here if you'd rather I didn't."

Feather came around the counter to view Gemini's thick, fudgy creations cut in uniform squares. "Those are impressive! I'm sure the girls and all the customers will love them!"

Gemini admired Feather's current look: a lavender headband decorated with a large flower complimented her spikey fuchsia hair. She was wearing matching lavender lipstick and dark eyeliner. As little as Gemini understood this generation, she had to admit Feather was an attractive girl. Nothing at all like Sophia, who always wore the latest fashions and looked like a runway model, but attractive in her own way.

"Can I ask you about something?" Gemini asked.

"Sure!"

"You mentioned the other day that Olive Thomas is the town gossip. Do you think there's any merit to the things she says?"

Feather laughed and shook her head. "Last month, she was sure there was a grocery store coup. She saw some kids hanging out in front and decided they were going to block the entrance and prevent people from going in unless they paid each kid ten dollars. It turns out the kids belonged to one of the new employees. They were waiting for their mom to get off work."

"Alright. I just wanted to make sure. I met her this morning for breakfast. She's full of information."

Feather set the brownies on the counter in a back room and returned to where Gemini was standing. "She wants to find conspiracy everywhere. She's mentioned several times now that the ear, nose and throat doctor, who moved to Tucson last year, was taken against his will. This is a small town. I'm sure someone would talk if that were happening." The door jingled and a customer using a cane walked in. His eyes traveled from Gemini to Feather and then back to Feather again without saying a word.

"Morning, Buster. I'm ready for you if you want to get settled in my chair."

The man nodded at Gemini as he walked by her, pushing her out of the way with his cane.

"Good morning, sir. I'm sure you'll have an excellent cut with Feather!"

He kept walking without acknowledging her words. Feather followed, turning around to shrug her shoulders at

Gemini. He sat down in her chair with a thud and dropped his cane beside him.

Gemini watched as Feather wrapped a black and red cape around his neck. "I'll be in tomorrow morning."

"That's great! I have a full schedule and I'll need you here!" Feather pulled her scissors from the drawer and paused. "I don't know why you walked into my shop, but I feel like it was a stroke of good luck for me, Gemini Reed. Women with unusual names need to stick together, don't we?"

"We sure do!" Gemini waved as she left, feeling a strong connection to this young woman.

She strolled to the hospital, engaging in a deep internal discussion about whether to take Olive's claims seriously. Instead of going straight up to the fourth floor, she paused at the half-moon desk in the giant, open lobby.

"Beverly B.? I was wondering if you could answer a question for me?" She hadn't noticed the first day, but this young woman appeared to be about Sophia's age. She immediately felt guilt for snapping at her.

"Yes ma'am? I'll help you if I can."

"I'd like to find out which cases were Doctor Wilson's before he, you know, went on vacation. How would I get that information?"

Beverly's perfect smile faded quickly. "There's no way the public can access that. I'm sorry."

"I'm doing research for a... story I'm writing for Red Hot Retirees magazine. They want me to chronicle my journey here, and I wanted to speak with some of his other patients." She was quite proud she came up with that so quickly. Gemini had read that magazine out loud once to Leo, both of them chuckling over the silly quizzes like, "We can tell your age by how you fix your potatoes." She tilted her head to the side, a move that normally gained her access to deep secrets.

Beverly B. pushed her thick glasses up her nose. "Well,

you could request information from the health department, I suppose. We don't give out that kind of information here, though. Patient confidentiality, you know."

Olive's words filtered into her head. Connect with her. "You must be about twenty-five. I bet this job is very taxing," she responded sympathetically. "My daughter is your age. I know how much pressure you face these days. Not as easy as things were in my day."

Beverly's upper lip quivered. "I barely see my son," she began. "Sometimes he's in bed when I get home. Between work and trying to find time to exercise, I barely have any life at all." She explained she was taking courses to become a court reporter. Gemini listened intently until she'd finished.

"I'm so sorry, dear. You have so many challenges. I'm facing some myself, trying to get this article finished. Few people will hire a woman my age, you know. I really have to prove myself."

Beverly B. wiped her tears away with a tissue and smiled at Gemini. "Tell you what. Sometimes information changes hands without it being a whole formal thing." She wrote a suite number, along with a brief message, and slid it across the desk. "Go to this suite. Ask for Miranda and tell her I sent you. She should have the information for you. Don't tell anyone else; I could lose my job for this." Beverly B. cocked her head to the side. "There's just something about you, Mrs. Reed. You make me feel safe. Thank you for listening."

Gemini walked through the door of suite 229 and to the reception desk. "I'm looking for Miranda?" She straightened her pink top and set her face to its most pleasant expression.

The young red-headed woman stifled a yawn with one hand while shuffling papers with the other. "I'm Miranda. How can I help you?" Her voice was as dull as her appearance.

"Beverly from the front desk sent me. I'm a friend of the

family. She wanted me to pass along this note." Gemini pushed the note across the counter, watching nervously as Miranda picked it up and read it. When she finished, her eyes jumped to Gemini's face. "Are you serious?"

"As a heart attack," Gemini replied, hoping she wouldn't be asked to elaborate, since she did not know what the note actually said.

"Hold on a minute. I could get into so much trouble. She typed furiously into her computer, her brows furrowing as she concentrated on the information she was getting.

Gemini let a small giggle escape. This young woman had no expression in her arsenal other than concentration.

"I'm going to the printer. Don't talk to ANYONE until I get back. Got it?" she asked.

"I promise." Gemini crossed her heart. "I'll stand silently awaiting your return."

Miranda stared at her uncomfortably for a minute, before rising from her chair and walking down a long hallway. When she was out of sight, Gemini reached over the counter and picked up the note she'd brought from the young woman at the main hospital desk. "Calling in my favor today. Give this lady all the case files for Doctor Wilson. You know I have those pictures."

Gemini shuddered. She didn't want to think of Beverly B. as a blackmailer. She quickly returned the note to its spot and stood back up, scanning the room to make sure no one else had seen what she'd done.

When Miranda reappeared, she shoved a folder across the counter. "There. I paid my debt. You can't tell anyone where this came from." She was back to her lifeless demeanor.

"I saw and heard nothing. In fact, I wasn't even here today." Gemini took the folder and turned to leave. She paused and looked at Miranda. "It occurs to me that what she needs the most is a good friend. If you took her out to lunch and offered to hear her stories, you both might get past whatever issue this is between you."

Miranda stared at her.

"You don't know anything. If Carson Moore found out about my second job, he'd fire me in an instant. He's made it very clear he doesn't allow employees to tarnish the hospital's reputation. Bev has been holding that over my head for too long."

"I'm sorry, dear. I hope you two will eventually work things out. "Gemini paused, waiting for a response, but Miranda resumed her work. She fled the office, stuffing the folder into her large turquoise bag. Gemini let out an enormous sigh of relief when she reached the elevator. She would study these tonight when she was home alone, but for now, she needed to spend some time with her husband.

Leo was resting as comfortably as he had been a day earlier. She kissed his cheek, drinking in his familiar scent. "I made the brownies you like with chocolate chunks on top, love. I'm going to share them with your nurse. You always say honey catches the biggest flies."

As she rested in the tan recliner in the corner of the room, Denise walked in wearing sky blue scrubs. Her dark hair was high on her head in a bun, surrounded by a white scrunchy. "Good morning, Mrs. Reed. I was hoping you'd be here today," she said warmly.

Gemini reached into her bag and pulled out an ornately decorated cellophane bag of frosted brownies and handed them to Denise. "I made these for you. I used to bring them when we had Potluck Fridays at the law firm. Everyone thought of it as a competition, and my egg salad was no match for Mary's."

"Oh, you're such a doll. You're really spoiling us!" Her brown eyes lit up as she took the package. "My boyfriend loves brownies and I never have time to bake for him." She took the bag and set it on Leo's nightstand. "I've been thinking about you and Leo. What an incredible love story you have. I hope Rodney and I will be together just as long."

"The days aren't always wonderful. The good part of aging is that the darker ones fade from our memories. Shortly after we married, Leo and I bought our first home together. We'd both been adults enough to have set up households of our own. How we struggled to find just the right place with a big kitchen and a large garage shop area. It only had one bedroom and a small office to make up for the size of everything else." Gemini chuckled at the thought of how absurd that very first purchase actually was.

"We fought over everything. We couldn't agree on colors for each room, so we made a line down the middle and each painted our own half. Every room was a strange color combination, and neither one of us would give in and let the other paint the entire room in their color. Kind of ridiculous."

Denise laughed, almost-inappropriately loud-for-a-hospital-setting. "How did you resolve the striped walls issue"?

Gemini crossed her legs. "One day, Leo stood in the middle of the Burstin' Berry Blue and Grassy Hill Green living room and said, 'we're never going to resolve this as long as we live here. Let's move.' And that's just what we did. We never fought over paint colors again."

"You're just a doll. I can see why Leo thinks you're special." Denise crossed her arms and sat down beside Gemini.

"Did he tell you that?" Gemini asked with surprise. Leo was a loving man when they were alone, but he was very self-conscious in public, always the consummate professional.

"Oh yes. After you left that first evening, he wouldn't stop bragging about you. He said his wife was best cook in the Northwest and he'd invite us all for dinner once he finished his drug regimen." Her eyes fell on his still body. "And I'm sure he will. He's a vigorous man. I know he'll be back to normal soon."

Gemini diverted her gaze from her husband, not wanting to let herself feel emotional about his condition when there was so much to accomplish. She remembered her earlier success using the Olive Method to sweeten up the front desk lady.

"Tell me about your life, Denise. Your boyfriend sounds like a peach. How did you two meet?"

"I was sitting in a bar, actually. The Fuzzy Martini across the street." Denise crossed her legs. "I have the worst luck with men. I'd just been dumped by Al after two years of living together and promising we would marry. He came home that day and told me his wife had found out where he was living and he had to move. That was the first time I heard he was married!"

Gemini's mouth dropped. "How was he living with you and his wife at the same time?"

"He told her he traveled on business. Instead, he drove sixty miles and lived with me. He'd done this before, I later discovered. That was one week to the day after my grandmother died. Anyway, I was in the bar drowning my sorrows. This guy plops down beside me and says he'd like to buy me a drink. Well, I've heard that one a million times."

Sophia did her research before going to bars: Who hung out there, what their income was. Gemini and Leo were oddly proud of her for never ending up in that type of situation. She always knew the clientele. "How did he win you over?"

"Rodney said I looked like I'd just lost my best friend. He'd move to a different part of the bar if I wanted. He just wanted to do something nice."

"How lovely!" Gemini replied enthusiastically.

"I was putty in his hands after that. We talked until the bar closed that night and haven't stopped. Going on eighteen months now. He really saved me." Denise looked at the clock on the wall. "I've got to finish up my rounds before our staff meeting. Maybe we can visit again tomorrow?" Denise stood and took the brownies from the nightstand.

"I'd like that." Gemini nodded. "Oh, Denise, I heard a rumor at the beauty shop. There is talk that Doctor Wilson was in the crosshairs of some women he dated; that one of them may have done him harm. Do you know anything about that?"

Denise shook her head. " Unfortunately, the people who come to us are very sick. When they spend so much time with our doctors, they begin to believe they have an intimate relationship with them. Someone probably had a crush on Doctor Wilson and was upset when he didn't want to date a patient." She smiled again, a professional, well-rehearsed smile. "I have to run, but if you need anything, just ask Esther at the nurse's station."

As hard as it was, she didn't allow herself to remove the other patients' information from her bag while she sat beside Leo. "You won't believe the crazy day I've had. I'm nudging closer to answers and I'll figure this out for you, Leo. When you come out of this, we'll sit in the kitchen eating my homemade cinnamon rolls while I tell you everything I've done. You'll get a real kick out of the whole thing."

She watched her husband's emotionless face as his chest moved up and down. It seemed unnatural for him to depend on a machine. He painted houses with the stomach flu and only stopped for water when his fever reached 101.

. . .

Gemini walked home that evening, unsure of her next step. "Am I crazy for even considering this?" she asked out loud.

"If you're asking me, I'm gonna say yes, you are. Don't talk to yourself outside. That's my rule if I want to be taken seriously."

"Oh, hello Mr. Beachmont," Gemini said absently, turning the key in her lock. "I didn't see you there."

"Then you're blind," he barked. "I'm here every day at the same time. Evening watering begins at seven. I keep to my schedule."

"I'm sorry. I'm just feeling a bit out of sorts. Usually the right steps just come to me, but my mind feels like a big multi-flavored ice cream cone—swirls of everything mixed together. These ideas may be a waste of my time or they may save my husband's life."

"Well, those are serious worries. Talking to yourself might not be such a bad idea." He returned to his task, focusing on one flowering plant at a time while just a trickle of water ran from his hose.

Gemini put the key back in her purse and walked over to his lawn. "Can I ask you something, Mr. Beachmont?"

"Ask away."

"What would you think if I told you there was a big coverup happening at the hospital? That a doctor has disappeared, and no one seems to care? Would you think I was crazy?"

Howard Beachmont set the hose down in the grass. "That hospital has a dark underbelly. No craziness assumed to believe that. For a time, I had close ties to Charming General. Coverups are what they do best."

Gemini stared at him with wide eyes. "I can understand why you'd be wary of them. You must've felt betrayed."

Howard Beachmont went over and shut off his hose. "Anything else, Mrs. Reed?"

"No," she replied disappointedly. "I'm just consumed with that."

"Follow your instincts. You'll come up with a good plan. Oh, Mrs. Reed? You had a visitor earlier."

Many possibilities raced through Gemini's mind. "Was it our next-door neighbors from Fassetville? They promised they'd stop when they came to town for groceries."

"I didn't ask."

THE DOOR to Gemini's house opened.

"Mother?"

CHAPTER 11

These dead people weren't making predictions for the future or wanting to express their love; they had embarrassing comments they wanted her to share. Feather was starting to wonder if she was crazy.

Thankfully, Tug was always there to assure her she wasn't. "The only test of your sanity will be if you keep ignoring them. There's obviously a reason the entities are contacting you and we need to deal with it."

"They've been whispering in my ear continuously, like I'm their voicemail. It's getting worse every day."

"If they're not going to leave you alone, then you can insist they cooperate. That's how it works, right? You're in charge?" Tug asked, rolling to his side on the floor in front of her.

The other side, apparently, is filled with smart alecs. I don't know if I can force them to be sincere." She thrust a foot toward his belly, which he immediately picked up and began massaging.

"You're in the driver's seat, Feath. They have no voice without you."

Feather sat taller with that realization. "I am in control."

* * *

"What are we doing today, Agnes?"

"Well, I think I'd like to go short. I haven't done that since I was in high school and maybe it's time to buzz my hair."

Don't let her do it. She looks like a mushroom with short hair.

I'm not passing that on. Give me something I can work with and I'll tell her. Be nice.

I want her to look respectable when she goes in for her job interview next week, and she won't get hired with a mushroom head.

"What if we just take it slightly shorter for now?" Feather lifted her hair from the underside, stopping an inch from the end. "And then if you like that, we'll shorten it up more. Lots of people get carried away and then they really hate having short hair. I don't want that to happen to you, especially with the job interview you have coming up next week."

Agnes stared at her. "I didn't tell you about my job interview!"

Feather blushed. "I'm sure I heard it somewhere. You know how small towns are. People like to gossip."

"I have told no one," Agnes said, looking puzzled. "It is a job that I'm sure I'm not qualified for and I didn't want to sound like I was bragging and then fall flat on my face. Double humiliation."

She'll get the job as long as she doesn't go on and on about her dog. That's why she failed the last job interview; she yammered about Flufflybottom for almost an hour. Never once did she bring up her years of experience in the electrical field.

"You have a dog, right?" Feather would have to approach

this gently. "I mean, if you do, I've heard of people who talk about their pets in job interviews and then lose sight of the fact that they have great qualifications to share." She trimmed a small amount from Agnes's thick, brunette head.

"You're an excellent listener. I don't think we've talked much about Fluffybottom but somehow you remembered. I have about 3000 photos of her on my phone-I had to buy a phone with more storage. Would you like to see one?"

Feather glanced up at the enormous clock with scissor hands. "I've got another client coming soon, but maybe next time?"

The next time she heard an otherworldly voice, it was during an appointment two days later. Jesse had lost a friend in a motorcycle accident two years earlier.

She was wrapping a cape around his large body when it began. Tell him to stop remembering me by snarfing down a tub of ice cream. He's resembling his Grandma Beegus. That's not a compliment.

Feather shook her head and furrowed her brow as she snapped the cape around his thick neck. "Jesse? I remember you're telling me about your friend who died. Do you still ride motorcycles? I think you said he was going to some sort of festival and you hadn't been back since."

The man opened his mouth, stunned. "I'm not sure how you remember that. I told you that the very first time you cut my hair and we haven't talked about it since. But yeah, I did. My buddy Todd died in that motorcycle accident and it was way too traumatizing for me to think about going to the Berry Bird festival again. My bike's been in the garage, covered in a drop cloth ever since. I should probably just sell it."

Tell him to go to the festival. He needs to get over my death. If he doesn't do that, he's going to be dwelling on this one time in history for the rest of his life. Just lay off the butter brickle!

"It would probably be very healing for you to go to the festival. I bet your friend would really like it if you went in his honor. Maybe you could even do something while you're there that he enjoyed doing."

"I guess I never thought about that." Jesse stroked his thick beard with a tattoo-covered hand. "He loved the beer garden, and we always bought ice cream before we went bird watching. That was the main event and also his favorite thing to do. I've never even considered going back."

Jesse tapped his fingers on his pants while she finished styling his hair. Feather noticed for the first time the tattoo on the back of his hand was a large ice cream cone.

When she was done, he smiled a big, toothy grin. "You know what? I'm going to take the bike out to the festival, maybe for half a day, and see how things go. Thanks, Feather!"

"I hear ice cream isn't so popular at that festival anymore. Someone got food poisoning last year."

That night, over fried rice and shrimp dumplings, she spilled every detail. "And then Jesse hugged me and gave me a $100 tip. I tried to refuse, but he insisted."

"I knew they had a purpose for talking to you," Tug said enthusiastically, shoving an entire dumpling in his mouth. When he finished, he wiped his mouth and stood. "It's time we make this official. In my marketing class at college, I'm learning that you go where your market is. When my grannie died, I was crushed. I remember looking at the community board at the grocery store, just staring at it for the longest time. Looking for an answer."

Feather and Tug only dated six months before his beloved grandmother died. She didn't understand how deeply it hurt him until many months later. "Did you find one?"

"No. That was the day I came home and asked if you'd consider buying a used piano. The point I was making is that we should make flyers and hang them everywhere. Discreet, not overly showy."

Feather's eyes lit up. "I'd like that very much!"

I'll hang some up at the college too, when I sign up for next semester's classes."

"You're taking another semester? I'm so proud of you!" she jumped up from the table and hugged him tightly. "Tug, you're wonderful. I don't tell you that enough."

He shrugged. "Yes, you do. But I always like to hear it. I wish my family still thought of me like that. 'Tug's never going to settle down and accomplish anything. He's a big talker with no follow-through.' They don't understand me the way you do."

"You don't quit." She gazed at him with admiration. "They should be proud that you always get up and start over."

They spent the next four hours designing an eye-catching advertisement. "Do you have unfinished business with a relative? Let me help!" At the bottom of each sheet, they made tear-away phone numbers so people could call or text. She and Tug placed her signs on every public board in town.

The next morning, she went to the salon with renewed vigor. She wasn't crazy and these voices were real. Nothing happened for five days. On the sixth day, she received a text message from an unknown number while she was coloring Norma Buttry's grey roots.

Saw your number on the college bulletin board. Are you the lady who talks to dead people? I need some help!

"We'll let that really soak in for a few minutes, Norma. I need to make a call." Feather patted Norma's shoulder before heading out the backdoor, leading to the alley behind her salon. She pulled out her phone and texted back.

Yes! I can help you, or at least I can try. When would you like to meet?

You can come to my home at 7:00 this evening. 414 Derry Lane. Please don't tell anyone!

Feather laughed. The very last thing she would do is tell anyone about this experience.

Don't worry, your secret is safe with me.

That evening after work, Feather headed to the house, armed with a pen and paper, unsure what other materials paranormal investigators usually carried. Tug offered to come with her and wait in the car, but she thought that may not be wise. If the client looked out the window and saw someone there, she'd automatically distrust Feather.

"I'll be waiting to hear what happens!" he said enthusiastically.

As she pulled up in front of the house, she took a deep breath. If this didn't work, it wasn't the end of the world. She had a job and a life. She didn't need this. But somehow, she did.

She knocked on the door and a short, round woman with curly dishwater blonde hair and red-framed glasses opened it.

"Come in!" she said warmly.

Feather walked into the living room and immediately began hearing a voice.

Don't sit on the couch. The cat peed there last week, and she didn't get it cleaned up.

"Would you like to sit down?" the woman asked, motioning toward the couch.

"It works better if I stand," Feather replied. "Can you tell me what you'd like to know?"

"Well," the lady began, crossing her arms over her ample chest, "I lived here with my aunt and uncle for over twenty years and we were very close. My uncle passed away last July and my aunt died in August. I miss them so much and I feel like they're trying to talk to me every day, but I just can't understand them. I feel it in my gut; they have a message to share about our time together." She sniffed, holding back tears.

Clean up my furniture! I never agreed to pets!

Feather closed her eyes and took a deep breath. "Your aunt wasn't a fan of your cat?"

"She hated pets. I got Tortoise after she died," the woman said sheepishly. "She's mad about that? That's why she won't leave me alone? Because she doesn't like my Tortoise? Tell her to forget it. I'm not giving him up. Sorry I wasted your time today. I thought it was something–

We buried money in the backyard under the shed. She needs to dig it up now or she'll lose the house to the bank.

Feather's eyes popped open. "Do you have a shovel? If you have two, I'll help you. Your aunt says there is money buried in the backyard."

CHAPTER 12

"Come see Gammie, Baby T!" The chubby toddler threw his arms up in the air and Gemini picked him up, smothering his face with kisses.

Sophia Floris scowled at her mother, placing her thin body between the screen door and the wooden one. "I wish you wouldn't call him that. You know his name. He's going to be confused if he never hears his proper name from his own grandmother."

Gemini looked over at her neighbor with embarrassment and then back at her daughter. "Your father and I purposely gave you a normal sounding name so you wouldn't have to go through the questions and odd remarks. So you could start a conversation with something other than, 'this is why I have a unique name.'"

Sophia folded her thin arms across her designer dress and set her chin, the one that resembled her father's. "It's a family tradition. Taurus is just carrying on what his grandparents began."

"How did you get in? I left the doors locked. At least I thought I did. "Taurus squirmed and slapped at Gemini until she set him down. "Let's go inside to discuss this, please," Gemini insisted, grabbing Taurus's hand and tugging gently. "C'mon baby boy. I'll get you a cookie." He immediately stopped struggling and followed her obediently inside.

"You brought your hollow rock from Fassetville. If you didn't paint it fluorescent green, it might be less noticeable to a burglar."

Gemini went to the cupboard and opened a box of cookies, Sunny Day Shortbread, Sophia's favorite as a child. Gemini didn't dare give him one of her brownies. He would have it smeared all over the wall before she even sat down.

Once Taurus was chomping happily on his cookie, she sat down at the table and motioned for Sophia to join her.

"I called the hospital, and they said they couldn't give me any more information, other than that he was stable." She flipped her long, curly hair behind her shoulders and sat down on a kitchen chair. "So, of course, I called Brandon and had him pull some strings. Imagine my surprise when I discovered my father is in a coma!" She wiggled her shoulders like a cat, ready to pounce, her normal behavior when she was about to attack one of her parents. "When were you going to share that with me?"

"You're busy with Taurus. I didn't want to concern you if it wasn't warranted. Doctor Natchez said he'll come out of this soon," Gemini displayed her fake smile, hoping Sophia didn't see through it. "I knew it would upset you to know your father was in this condition, so I was hoping to wait until he came out of it to tell you."

Sophia huffed and crossed one leg tightly over the other. "I'm just deeply hurt, Mother. It's like you've punched me in the stomach. I'm a part of this process too, you know. I've been struggling so much with Daddy's illness and the fact that you chose to have treatment so far away from your family–" her voice trailed off.

Taurus took his cookie and rubbed it on his face before smashing it onto the floor. "More!" he demanded. "More! More! More!"

"Of course, darling," Sophia responded in a softer voice. She got up and retrieved two more cookies from the cupboard, handing them to her son and kissing him on the head.

"Your father signed up for the drug trial because he wanted to recover from this illness. It wasn't available in Fassetville. You know all of this." Gemini steadied herself for the next round. Sophia always had to be right, no matter what the circumstance. Sometimes, her daughter just wore her down.

"You promised to become Taurus's nanny. You said when you retired that taking care of your grandson was all that mattered. Then you and Daddy made this rash decision."

What I said was, I'd enjoy spending more time with him, not become his nanny. "You have a nanny. I'll be able to see him when we return." Gemini tapped her fingers on the table, one at a time.

"We have other expenses and paying for a nanny isn't something we expected to do long-term. He should be with family." Sophia pulled her fake-gemstone-covered phone from her purse and looked at it absently.

Gemini stood, trying to keep her anxiety at bay. "You and Brandon have plenty of money. He's a partner in the law firm. I'm not having this conversation again today, Sophia. I have too much on my mind." She turned around to witness Taurus rolling on the carpet, spreading cookie goo all over everything.

"How long are you planning to stay? They won't allow Taurus on the fourth floor, so if you're going to spend time with your father, I'll need to babysit. I do have lots on my schedule."

Sophia guffawed. "What kind of schedule? You're retired!"

"I've been volunteering," she began, and then paused. If Sophia knew she was washing people's hair, she would ridicule her, and that was a rabbit hole she didn't want to go down. "At the hospital. I hand out mail."

"Oh," Sophia's tone softened. "That's nice of you, Mother. I'd think your time would be better spent sitting by Daddy, though. What happens if he wakes up and you're not there? Because you're out 'volunteering?' He'd be devastated. And to answer your question, we're going home in the morning. Taurus has a toddler yoga class and I don't want him to miss it. He's the best student."

Gemini watched as her grandson stuck a bit of cookie up his nose. "No, Baby T. Let me get you something else to play with." She jumped up and grabbed some plastic storage containers before returning to her grandson and removing the cookie from his nose. "These kept your mother entertained for hours."

Taurus fussed as she wiped his face clean, then took what was left of the cookies from him before he screamed in protest. He shoved her hand away and bit her. "No! We don't bite!" Gemini yanked her hand back to find a drop of blood on her finger.

"We don't say the word 'no' in our house. Negative words lead to negative thoughts." Sophia stood up. "Do you have any decent tea?"

Gemini looked up from cleaning her grandson. "Second drawer on the left. You really should get up to the hospital and see your dad. Visiting hours will be over soon. I'll feed my grandson."

Sophia put her hands on her slender hips. "Yes, I should do that. When I get back, we can discuss moving Daddy home. He would hate to waste away in a strange town."

Gemini shook her head, but said nothing. "Pick your

battles, dear," Leo always reminded her wisely. They thought they were raising her to be a strong, confident person. Instead, she'd become a self-centered woman with no empathy for others.

After Gemini fed and bathed Taurus, she sat down on the floor to read him a book. Her mind wouldn't stop drifting. She got up and removed the files from her bag and began sifting through them as her grandson banged a wooden spoon on the pans she'd given him. That her daughter had brought no toys shouldn't have surprised her.

She opened the folder and read the first file. "Peter Boyd. Age 60. Drug trial participant died on the 28th of November. A Tuesday. Cause of death: pneumonia." She thought for a moment. Esther, the charge nurse, whispered they'd all had stomach problems. Gemini cocked her head to the side and listened sympathetically. She'd never heard of that being a symptom of pneumonia before. The next file was a Marilyn Jasper, age 49. She also died on a Tuesday, three weeks prior. Were they as full of hope for the future as Leo and Gemini had been? Did Doctor Wilson fill their heads full of good things, too?

She scanned to the bottom of the page. "Pneumonia. Again."

Taurus flopped a pan in her lap. "Pay Gamma!" he insisted.

She kissed his wet, curly head. "In a minute, sweet boy."

Quickly, she thumbed through the rest of the deaths. There were four in total. All of them listed pneumonia as the cause of death. All were in the drug trial and all died on a Tuesday. How curious.

Gemini pulled Taurus onto her lap and put his chubby hands in front of him. "How many fingers do you have? Can we count?"

"No! No! No! No!" he screeched. Sophia's reluctance to use that word didn't prevent her son from learning it.

The back door swung open, and his mother appeared. "Did you miss me, handsome?" she asked, bending down and opening her arms to greet her son. Taurus slid off Gemini's lap and ran to his mother, slapping her in the face.

"He's going to think that's okay," Gemini spurted before she could stop herself.

"We never shut down emotions. He's joyful, and that is something to celebrate."

Gemini looked at her grandson with skepticism.

"You're a joyful boy, aren't you, my son? Taurus Floris is the best boy in the universe!" Taurus pulled on her curly hair until she gently removed it from his hands and she set him down.

Gemini rolled her eyes. "Did you have a pleasant visit with your father?"

"Yes, I did. I spoke with the night nurse. She said she's never met you. You really should be by his side at all times." She stood and smoothed her dress. "The nurse said they're optimistic that he'll recover."

"I told you. That's why I didn't want you bothering to come. We'll be back before you know it."

Sophia set her large lambskin bag on the table. "I certainly hope so. I'm going to give the nanny her notice soon. She's been trying to teach Taurus alternate meanings for words. It will confuse him if he doesn't learn the proper meaning first." She sighed. "So many challenges. I'm going to go into the spare room and call Brandon. He wanted me to let him know after I found out about Daddy's treatment plan. Brandon has a client in Seattle at one of the big hospitals there. He thinks we can get him in to their drug trial as soon as he's off the ventilator."

"We're not moving him!" Gemini snapped. "You have no

right to make those decisions! It's up to me! And that's even farther away, Sophia!"

Sophia ignored her mother and kept walking. "We'll see." She closed the door behind her.

"Your mother is infuriating!" she said sternly, looking in Taurus's general direction. She returned to the files to study them further. More pneumonia deaths.

"What's that?"

Gemini jumped, unaware that her daughter had come out of the room and was standing behind her. "Good gracious! Let me know when you're lurking behind me! I thought you were calling Brandon!"

"He's busy with a client right now. They're having a working dinner. You didn't answer my question. What is that?" She reached over Gemini's shoulder and picked up one sheet. "Oh my god, Mother, you've stolen people's medical information! How did you manage that? And why? Are you being nosy again?"

Throughout the years she worked for Floris, Fealgood and Flem, Gemini wanted the clients to know she cared. She couldn't help it: everyone seemed to confess their deepest concerns, and she wanted to offer support. Once a client was suing her former employer for harassment. This poor woman told Gemini her boss came to her home at night and stood outside, watching her from the street. There was no evidence other than this woman's word. He disappeared every time she tried taking a photo.

Gemini decided she would follow him after work. She turned on the recording device on her phone and approached him, asking why he was in that neighborhood. She made up a story about being a neighbor who had seen him frequently. He said he was in love with the woman and confessed everything to Gemini. The woman won her lawsuit.

"I have concerns. But if you don't want to be involved, don't ask questions." She slammed the folder shut and stood up, grabbing the paper from her daughter. "It's really better that you don't know what's going on. I'm going to bed. I'd ask if you want dinner, but I know you don't eat."

CHAPTER 13

*G*emini watched the front door of the salon impatiently. It was almost ten-thirty. Olive was a half-an-hour late.

"Like I was saying, I don't have enough money for a new car, and this one will barely get me around town. If my mother-in-law takes the car, we'll be in a hard spot." The soapy-haired woman gazed up at Gemini, waiting for a response.

"Huh? I'm so sorry, dear. You need reliable transportation. Is there someone else in your family who might be willing to help out?"

"No, I just said a few minutes ago that my family has all moved away. My mother-in-law took my car and moved to Texas."

Gemini rinsed her hair, squeezed the water from the thin, straight strands, and then wrapped her head in a towel. "It looks like your stylist is just about ready for you. I brought snickerdoodles today. They're sitting at the front desk for when you're finished. Would you excuse me, please?"

Gemini walked up to the front where Feather was checking out a customer. "Did Olive say that she was going to be late today?"

"She hasn't said anything to me. But that's the way she is. Sometimes she shows up and sometimes she doesn't. I told you, she's not a very reliable person."

Gemini wasn't sure what to believe at this point. All the information that she'd gained so far had led her to believe something untoward was happening at the hospital. If Olive didn't have the answers, Denise would be her next option.

Gemini sat down and began thumbing through a magazine of hairstyles from 1997. The door to Feather Work's Salon jingled and Olive walked in, looking harried.

"A woman who thinks her work ends at retirement hasn't retired. I'm so sorry, Gemini." She touched her hair as she caught her breath. "I got a phone call this morning about strange goings on out at the Country Club. I had to hear all the details before I left."

Feather caught Gemini's eye. "See what I mean?" she mouthed.

"Olive, can I take you back and shampoo you?" Gemini gently touched Olive's back and guided her to the far end of the salon.

When they reached the sinks, Olive sat down in the chair with a thud and Gemini leaned over and whispered in her ear. "I got the charts of Doctor Wilson's patients for the last year. Quite a few have died, and strangely, they all died on the same day of the week. The other thing that I found odd was that it listed their cause of death as pneumonia. Every single one."

Olive picked up her head and turned it towards Gemini, flicking water all over the floor. "I told you there was something fishy going on. Everyone has a secret up there. Back when my husband was still alive, the board president was siphoning funds to buy himself an airplane. Can you imagine? An airplane in this small town. Like nobody was going to figure that one out."

Gemini gently guided her head back into the sink.

"I want to know more about Carson Moore. "She massaged Olive's scalp slowly, making tiny circles with her thumbs.

"He's a loner. Doesn't spend his time at the country club with everyone else. I know his wife left him months ago, but nothing more."

"I was thinking of asking my husband's nurse. Maybe she could help me understand why no one has questioned these people's deaths."

"Oh, don't do that!" Olive lifted her head again, splashing wet hair all over once more. The woman in the next station over gave her an angry look and wiped soapy water from her face.

"There's too much gossip at that hospital and we don't know who to trust. You need to get into Doctor Wilson's home. That's our plan."

Gemini wanted to giggle. Now they were doing this together? "My daughter is visiting right now, but when she leaves, I'll see what I can do." She thought about their supposedly clandestine meeting at the Boastful Elk. "Should I meet you in a dark alley somewhere after she's gone?"

Olive scoffed. "This isn't a spy movie, dear woman. We can find somewhere to meet together, like maybe my house or yours."

"I'll have to mull this over and come up with a plan of action. After Sophia is gone. I can't think with her constantly judging me."

Olive shook her head, causing the towel wrapped around her head to come loose and fly into her lap. "Sorry to hear that. I had a son that way. My grandson's father. The two of us did not get along, but I developed a close relationship with his children, and for that, I am eternally grateful. Someday maybe she'll appreciate you."

Gemini laughed. "Doubtful. You don't know my Sophia. We raised her to be headstrong, but we didn't realize that, in the process, we forgot to teach her that other people have feelings too. I think Feather is ready for you."

She helped Olive over to Feather's chair, and they exchanged glances.

Her mind was swirling with possibilities, nothing good, as she came up the walk of her mud-brown rental. Sophia was sitting on the cement step dressed in a formal-looking sleeveless white dress while Taurus played in the driveway. She glanced at Gemini with a scowl on her face.

"What took you so long, Mother? I wanted to be on the road by now. I have Taurus on a schedule. We have yoga and he must read his book at approximately 2:00 PM or his nap will be ruined. Did you want to ruin his nap? Do you want me to be up all night? Would that make you happy?"

"Cheese and biscuits, Sophia. I was delivering the mail at the hospital, remember?" There was no use in arguing with her, as usual. "What did you think when you saw your father last night? He still looks good, right?" She sat down on the step beside her daughter and grinned at her grandson, who pulled a handful of grass and threw it in her general direction.

"For a man who's in a coma? Honestly! I can't believe you would ask me that question, Mother." Sophia leaned forward, folding her hands in her lap. This was her serious talk pose. "Mother, I want you to think about moving Daddy to this drug trial in Seattle. Brandon's acquaintance can get him in. The hospital is much bigger and much better."

She took a moment to flip her hair behind her shoulder

and clasped her well-manicured fingers together. "When you're finished with that, you can move in with Brandon and I. We've discussed it and we're going to renovate the guesthouse for the two of you. That way, you'll be right there to take care of Taurus and there will be no running back and forth for you. Won't you love that?"

Taurus came over and kicked his mother in the shin as if on cue. "Soft touch, not hard, Taurus!" She whispered. He paused for a moment before kicking her other shin.

Gemini took a deep breath. "I don't think I want to live in your guest house. It's a perfectly lovely place, Sophia. But your father and I have come to enjoy our privacy. I appreciate your offer, but for now, we're going to stay right where we are."

"We need to think of Daddy," Sophia said sternly. "If you're living close to us, we'll be able to check on him when needed. You're getting older and you may not be able to care for him much longer." Sophia's face softened. "This is my father's health we're talking about. Don't you understand?"

Gemini patted her daughter's leg. "I do, dear. I'm just as scared as you are. You have to trust that Daddy and I know what we're doing. This is all going to work out, you'll see."

"If I feel things are out of hand, Brandon is prepared to go to court so we can have guardianship of him. I don't believe you fully understand the seriousness of this situation." She took Taurus's hand and stood up, walking beside him to where the toy trucks Gemini kept for him sat in the driveway. She bent down and picked one up, offering it to her son. He took the truck and threw it onto the lawn. "Honestly, Mother, I just can't understand why you'd want to stay in this awful little town. There's nothing here for you."

Gemini stood too, choosing to go inside and avoid the challenge. Maybe someday she could be like Olive and have a closer relationship with her grandson. That day wasn't today.

It was a relief to see them pull out of the driveway later that day, though it was strangely quiet without Taurus's high-pitched screaming or Sophia constantly berating her. She wasn't sure if she missed them, or if it was just a big change from her new life here without Leo.

She poured herself a cup of coffee that Sophia had made earlier. She reached into the fridge for her cream, filling the mug to the top to dilute the taste of the thick brew. Sophia only drank organic coffee made from a specific bean that came from a specific region of Africa in a specific jar. It was supposed to give her youth and vitality. Sophia already had both, so there was really no purpose in torturing herself to drink such sludge. Right now, what Gemini needed most was something to help her think. And maybe this fountain of youth would offer just that.

She thought back to her days working as a secretary at Floris, Fealgood, and Flem. She learned so much from the clients who came in. Not only from their cases, but from the things they divulged while they were waiting for their attorneys. One woman was convinced her husband, a former doctor, was following her. She saw him coming around the corner when she went for her evening walks, but she had nothing with her to record that he was there. So she set up a sting operation.

"Not that hard, Mrs. Reed,," the muscular woman told Gemini as she leaned across the desk as if they were more than acquaintances. "I had my friend invite him out for dinner. Mutual friend, that is. I said nothing about his following me. I just told him that my husband was most likely lonely since our split. They went out for Chinese. Sweet and sour pork was always his favorite." She moved so close Gemini could smell the mint gum on her breath.

"I hid myself in the booth behind them, put on a new outfit and bought myself a wig. Nobody was the wiser. I just leaned back and listen to them talk. He spilled everything about how he was following me home from work at night, how he knew my routine and my mailbox code. It was just that easy."

"It's just that easy." Gemini repeated to herself. She decided not to tell Olive of her plans. Whether Feather was completely on target about Olive's motives or whether Olive knew what she was talking about, she didn't want to take any chances. Sophia was right about one thing: it was Leo's life they were gambling with.

The next day, she asked Feather if she had any wigs she could borrow. Feather kept many in her shop for people who'd lost their hair or those who just wanted to try a fresh look.

"Wow! You're so trendy!" Feather said enthusiastically. "I thought you might be open to something different. I could tell when you came in here the first day that you weren't like everybody else. There's got a purple one here–"

"No, dear. I don't want anything crazy. I just need to change my look a little. Please don't ask me why."

Feather gazed at her with curiosity. "As you know, clients like to tell us their deepest secrets. I've heard them all, and nothing surprises me." Feather searched through a metal locker before pulling out a short blonde wig and a brunette one parted on the side.

Gemini pointed at the brunette wig. A complete departure from her lifelong blonde hair.

"Great choice! I'll show you how to put it on and make sure it stays attached."

"I appreciate that, Feather. Thank you for all of your help. And thank you for allowing me to come in here when I need somewhere different to direct my thoughts."

Feather smiled. "About that. People have really been saying good things about you, Gemini. They love having someone to talk to. I didn't realize what a service we were to the community. I mean, I know people feel better when someone does their hair. But we're almost like unpaid counselors. I had a-let's call it a premonition-about something good coming in to my life. I think it was you. Here, let's try these."

CHAPTER 14

A case that stuck in Gemini's mind was the Bartles. The Bartles were a warring couple who had two children. They had been happy together, owning a successful chain of dry cleaners. When their twins were born, Mrs. Bartles stayed home and worked from there, doing the books and only coming into the store occasionally. Mr. Bartles saw this as his opportunity to find extra sources of income, namely selling illegal diet pills to his customers.

Gemini offered to go undercover, posing as a potential client to catch him in the act, thus giving his soon-to-be-ex-wife the upper hand in the impending divorce. Gemini's boss, her son-in-law Brandon, said absolutely not. "Mom, we can't have you putting yourself in danger for this client."

"I'm not a frail, elderly woman, Brandon," Gemini said defiantly. "I'm perfectly capable of getting the information we need and reporting back."

Gemini took it upon herself to go undercover without Brandon's knowledge. She found some clothing that fit her tightly and applied her makeup abnormally thick. For the final touch, she splashed her face with water until the makeup looked streaked.

"I need to speak with Mr. Bartles. I've heard he has a 'special deal,'" she said tearfully, standing at the dry cleaning counter and wiping her nose.

After some hesitation by the clerk, she retrieved a stocky man with curly hair. He looked annoyed by her very existence. "I'm Gene Bartles. What can I do for you?"

"A friend gave me your name. My husband threatened to leave me unless I get this weight under control. I've been told you have something that might help me. Not laundry, not mending. Something more. I'm prepared to pay whatever you're charging."

Gene Bartles eyed her suspiciously. "What did you say your name was?"

Gemini thought about her shopping list. " Mrs. Cinnamon Plum. My friend told me not to mention her name, though. I need to respect her privacy."

Gemini followed him through the rotating racks of clothes. They wandered in and out of the noisy machinery until they reached a small mint green office in the back. He gave her the bright orange pills.

"First two are on the house. After that, it's three hundred a week. Those clothes will hang on you by next month." He smiled, displaying four gold teeth on the bottom and two missing on top.

"Are these legal?" she asked innocently. "Like a multi-level marketing thingy?"

Gene shrugged. "Nothing worth your time ever is FDA approved. You know how the government works. It takes years to approve something. By that time, your husband would be on a beach with some twenty-year-old sipping pina coladas."

When she came back to work the next day, Brandon

exploded. "What were you thinking, Mom? This was so reckless. And now we only have your word against his."

Gemini pulled out the recording device she'd kept in her purse. "If you'll stop yelling, I'll play the entire conversation." It was the biggest divorce settlement Floris, Fealgood, and Flem had negotiated in their entire history. Gene Bartles went to prison for three years.

One of the other legal secretaries, who had previously worked for the firm Mitt and Glove, encouraged her to ask for a raise. "You've earned it!" she insisted. When Gemini asked her son-in-law, he told her they had a tight budget that didn't allow for expenses like extra raises. He finished the condescending conversation by asking her to call the country club and move his dinner reservation to eight. That experience still rattled her.

Instead of walking up her walkway, she went one house further. "Be brave, Gemini," she said to herself. She knocked on the door and braced herself for a slurry of insults.

The door swung open. "What?" he barked and then softened his tone. "I'm in the middle of something."

"I–um–" She'd never been quite this close to Howard Beachmont, and it surprised her to discover that he was an attractive man. His red-and-black flannel shirt was unbuttoned two buttons, a touch of curly grey hair peeking out. He hadn't shaved yet today, and the hint of a beard on his powerful jaw reminded her of the lead characters in the many romance novels she read while waiting for Leo in the hospital.

"I wanted to ask you a question. You said you had some experiences with 'the underbelly.' I need some of those contacts. Someone who is on the inside at the hospital."

Howard growled, "Come in."

Gemini was in for her next surprise. As her eyes adjusted to the dim light of the heavily paneled home, she stepped inside into a whole different world. Light radiated from the multi-tiered chandelier over the table, lit the room enough for her to make out the massive colorful tapestries covering the walls.

A stately china hutch sat in the hallway. Ornately etched glasses and crystal pieces decorated the glass shelves. His home looked like it had come straight out of a magazine that she kept in the lobby of the law firm. There were multi-colored flowers from his garden featured in another crystal piece on a small table in the front hall. He guided her to a Naugahyde couch. Matching chairs sat on a rug that looked to be something from the Orient or somewhere far away that she had never visited. There was an intoxicating smell coming from the kitchen, like rich soup and bread baking in the oven. Classical music played from some sophisticated sound system. He sat down on the chair facing her and crossed his legs.

"Your home is exquisite, Mr. Beachmont," Gemini said without a hint of jealousy. She noticed a large bookshelf full of books on the Civil War, Leo's favorite topic after paint and home improvement supplies.

"Did you think I lived in a dump?" he grumbled. "You can have a seat if you like. I was in the middle of a jigsaw puzzle. It's the Tower of London in 3000 pieces."

She glanced over at the ornately carved Maplewood kitchen table, where a gigantic puzzle sat halfway completed. One thing she thought she'd have time for in retirement was a puzzle. So far, her life was far too full for any kind of puzzle work.

"And it smells like you're making something wonderful for dinner. I certainly don't want to impose." It seemed like he liked to keep life was private in every single way. "I just don't know where else to turn. I don't know many people in this town. And those I do, I've already asked for favors. So now I'm asking you—how do I get inside information on that hospital?"

"I kind of figured you were the snoopy type. I'm usually right about those things." Howard folded his arms across his chest.

"Yes, I've been called a snoop before. My son-in-law said he expected it would get me into trouble more than once. But usually it suits me well." She sniffed. "There's nothing wrong with that."

"No, there's nothing wrong with that," Howard agreed. "In fact, that's how I found out they betrayed me. So you need a contact at the hospital? Someone who might know the dark side? I think the person you're looking for is sitting right in front of you."

CHAPTER 15

Feather opened the door to the salon and hurried to the thermostat to turn up the heat. "Put my things on the counter, Tug," she instructed.

She heard voices murmuring as she walked back up to the front of the salon where Tug was chatting with the mailman. When she reached the front desk, the mailman walked out the door. Tug turned to her and smiled, holding a package in his arms. "I know you were expecting a delivery. This isn't your supplies."

She furrowed her brows and took the box from him, ripping it open as quickly as she could. She pulled out a brown leather jacket that looked suspiciously familiar. "Is this the same one I was admiring in the window of Dressed in Decadence last week? Oh, Tug. That was so expensive!"

He smiled, both of his dimples visible. "They were out of your size, so she ordered one. Try it on!" He encouraged, slipping it nimbly over her arms.

She walked to her station and admired herself in the mirror. It wasn't Feather Jones, the weird girl in high school, staring back. This was a successful career woman. "But Tug, you're a student. We should send it back and spend this on books."

"I have a trust fund. If I can't spend part of it on the woman I love, then what's the point?" He walked over and wrapped his arms around her. "Besides, once your second career takes off, you'll be taking me out for lobster every week." He kissed her gently on top of the head.

She rested her head on his chest. "I still don't understand why you aren't looking for the perfect blonde ski bunny to make a matching set."

"I don't want perfect. I want interesting. And that's you."

Someone else came through the door, this time from a delivery service. "Heather Jones?" he asked, holding a gigantic bouquet and a box of candy.

"It's Feather," she corrected him. "Tug? You didn't have to do this!" She set the flowers on the counter and took the box of candy. "Although, you know I'm not big on candy. Did you buy this for yourself?"

"You don't eat candy? Well, that's a game-changer." Tug winked. "I'd like to take credit, but this didn't come from me." He plucked the card from the flowers and read it. "It's from the lady you saw the other day with the money buried out back. It says, 'Thanks for all you did. I can pay my bills and I'm getting another cat!' Wow. Your first client visit was a successful one!"

"Yeah. I guess I'll need to find more clients. Though the dead seem to come to me regardless of whether I invite them."

"They do. You just haven't allowed them much space before. I've been taking that marketing class and I'm going to figure out how best to market your skills. This is going to be big." Tug's eyes widened. "You're offering a service no one else in town does. I can say I was in on the ground floor."

Feather smiled and grabbed his hand, bringing it to her

mouth to kiss. "I still pinch myself sometimes. I think you're going to disappear. Feather Jones never has this kind of luck."

"You're not getting rid of me. Even if you decide you're sick of my handsome face and push me out a window, I'll be back competing with the others for your attention."

They both laughed before kissing passionately. Feather pulled away from him abruptly, her face filled with concern.

"What is it?" Tug asked.

"Someone's here," she whispered.

"Who is it? What do they want?"

Feather put her hands on her hips and walked around in a circle. "It's the former owner, Angie Bard."

"I can't believe she hasn't been around sooner. Talk to her. Maybe she has some friendly advice for you," Tug encouraged. "I'm gonna take off. I have an online class in an hour." He kissed Feather lightly on the cheek. "Don't be afraid to hear what she has to say."

Feather waved at him and continued pacing. She hadn't been completely honest. This voice had been coming to her for months. It was the only one that frightened her. After he was gone, she replied to the voice in her head. "Mm hmmm. You're upset about your death. Weren't you sick for a long time? I found the alcohol in your place. Many bottles. And the letter about your liver test."

Gemini walked in the door, humming her favorite tune. "Gracious, what lovely flowers!" she said, smelling the multi-colored bouquet of lilies and hydrangeas. "Do you need a vase?"

"Shhh–" Feather hissed in her general direction.

Gemini nodded and tiptoed to the break room, where she set a plastic container full of peanut butter sandwich cookies and her wig supplies on the cabinet. She began wiping down the table and then the chairs.

"I'm sorry, Gemini. I was in the middle of a–"

"Affirmation? I could tell you talked to yourself. I do it all the time and it helps me to make sense of everything swirling around in my head."

"No, this is something a little different. A message." Feather stared at her solemnly.

"Not too many people your age would willingly listen to their inner voices and act on them. What is your better self telling you to do?"

Feather shook her head. "The message wasn't for me. It was for you."

CHAPTER 16

"Let's sit down for a minute and talk." Feather pulled a chair out from the table and gestured for Gemini to do the same. When Feather sat down, she immediately jumped back up. "Yuck! That's wet! Is there a leak in the ceiling again?"

"No, dear. Don't worry." Gemini sat down in the chair next to hers. "It's just slightly damp because I cleaned everything. This room needed some attention. I hope you don't mind."

Feather blushed. "I've been meaning to find someone to help with that. The women who rent stalls from me complain about doing it and I never find the time."

Gemini patted her arm. "That's alright. I'm here to help. What was it you wanted to tell me?"

Feather clasped her hands together in front of her. "I need to tell you the story of how I came to own the salon."

"It's none of my business, really," Gemini said, though she had been wondering how someone so young came to be the owner of a thriving business.

Feather sat back in her chair. "I got out of beauty school

and thought no one would want to hire me. I've got a unique look, and I wasn't interested in changing that to meet someone else's standards." She ran her fingers through her magenta-and-black-striped hair. Last night's new creation. "I was sitting at the burger place down the street one day, reading my favorite steampunk mystery book–Ride the Ramp by Benedict Round.' Someone tapped my shoulder and I turned around to see this beautiful woman with honey colored hair and a killer body standing there. She said that was her favorite author too. We talked for over an hour."

"She died and left you money?" Gemini asked.

"She said she owned the salon down the street. I reminded her of herself in her younger days–a non-conformist. I said I was looking for work in a salon and she hired me right there on the spot."

"That was an enormous leap of faith for her."

"Huge. I explained I had never worked in the business before, but she had a 'feeling' about me. She said she had some rough edges, too."

"That's lovely, Feather. I'm still not sure what that has to do with us here today." Gemini tapped her fingers on the table, one at a time.

"She died last year. Her liver gave out or something. It devastated me. When they called me to say she'd left me something in her will, I thought maybe it was her magenta sweater. Imagine my shock when it turned out to be this place."

Gemini's mouth dropped open. "Really? You must've been very close."

"We were friendly, but she spent her off-hours with people her own age. I thought she'd leave this place to her family or someone she knew better than me." Feather wiggled in her seat uncomfortably. "This next part is weird."

"I've heard it all. As a legal secretary, people told me all of their deep—"

"I—hear people; dead ones. They tell me things the living need to know. I used to ignore them, but recently I realized their messages can be very important. Today, my former boss spoke to me. She said you are in danger."

Gemini grabbed Feather's hands and gripped them. "I believe the dead communicate with us. What an amazing gift you've been given. I'm so glad you told me; I'm sure it wasn't easy."

"Did you miss the other part? About you being in danger?"

"Yes. I can't worry about trouble. That's how you attract problems, my Leo always says. I've got to figure out what happened to Doctor Wilson, and then I'll worry about myself." She looked impatiently at Feather. "Can we get going? I won't discuss this any further."

"You're frustrating, Gemini Reed." Feather took the wig cap from Gemini's hand and began tugging it over her head. "And stubborn."

"Reminds me of panty hose," Gemini commented as she watched the process in the mirror. Feather applied a heavy layer of hairspray to secure the wig. Feather fitted the short, curly brunette wig over her silver hair. When it was secured, she applied powder to match Gemini's skin tone.

Feather spun her around to look in the mirror. "Does that seem okay?" She adjusted each curl to make sure it looked just right.

Gemini had always been proud that her hair remained thick even after she went through her life change. Now that was coming back to haunt her.

"It feels a little tight." She looked in the mirror, pleasantly surprised by the outcome.

Feather applied a little more powder to her part line. "It

will feel uncomfortable until you get used to it. I'm assuming you won't be wearing this all day. Just be careful when you remove it. This is one of my best wigs." She touched the sides and looked at Gemini in the mirror.

"I have to wonder why you haven't been a brunette your entire life. It really suits you." Feather's face fell.

Gemini grabbed her friend's hand again. "Don't worry, hon. Everything will be fine. I've done this before. I really appreciate your confiding in me, and I'll want to learn more about it later." She walked toward the door and then stopped. "Was there mention of specific trouble? Or just in general terms? I don't know how these things work."

CHAPTER 17

Gemini attached her new identification to the aqua smock she'd acquired from the local medical supply store. The details make the disguise, she'd remembered from her law firm days.

"Maureen Johnson, Mail Room Volunteer." Gemini read outlaid, describing the identification Howard acquired for her. "I once knew a Maureen Johnson when I was working at the law firm. She was the uppity type and didn't think that she should spend her time conversing with a lowly secretary like me. She would waltz through the door and when I said, 'Can I help you?' she wouldn't even look at me as she brushed past my desk and said, 'I'm not paying all this money to speak with the help. I'll be in his office."

Howard glanced at her with no expression on his face. "I'm sure you have quite a few stories. Just as I do from my time at the hospital. Maybe when things quiet down, we can have some tea in the garden and discuss that. If your husband would be amenable. And he could join us when he's out of the hospital."

Gemini smiled. "Yes, I'd like that, thank you. We must

remain positive. And thank you for helping me. I'll let you know how my detective work goes. Unless you want me to pretend like we never spoke?"

Howard shook his head. "Doesn't matter to me one way or the other. I'm done with that place, other than the few people I stay in contact with. As you can see by that badge there, maybe I shouldn't be in contact with anyone." He chortled. "Let me know how your spy work turns out!"

After the success of the Bartles case, Gemini went on many undercover missions. She observed Morris Willoby at his place of employment, Chopped Figs, to see if he was really as ill as he claimed to be. Their client, corporate franchise owners, Goodness in a Can, was paying him thousands of dollars because he allegedly grabbed onto a fryer and slipped and fell. Morris claimed the defective fryer caused his accident and as a result, he could no longer bend over.

Gemini went into the restaurant several times, wearing a colorful scarf over her head, thick, black glasses and torn jeans. She wore a hidden camera and recorded him lifting heavy boxes, eating several French fries off the floor and even leading a co-worker in a bend-and-stretch routine.

Catching him in the act was a thrill, and she wanted more. She offered to do it again, and one of Brandon's partners asked her to record someone pretending to have amnesia. Brandon warned her it wasn't a good sign she took to deceiving people so easily.

She adjusted her wig as she walked up to the hospital and paused when she caught sight of herself in the door. Whoever this woman was, she was confident. She didn't look like a mild-mannered legal secretary who kept to herself. The bright red lipstick may have been overkill, but it was definitely not a shade Gemini Reed would wear.

Walking to the elevator, she didn't look anyone in the eye, just in case she ran into someone who knew her.

"Excuse me?"

Gemini recognized that voice and turned slowly. "Yes?" she replied in her most un-Gemini-like voice. Beverly B., the lobby receptionist who had bared her soul to Gemini recently, studied her face.

"I just need to check your credentials. I've never seen you here before and you can never be too careful these days." She held out her hand expectantly.

Gemini removed the lanyard from around her neck and handed it to Beverly. The receptionist examined her identification carefully before clicking her tongue in disapproval. Gemini gulped, ready to make her way to the front door as quickly as possible.

Beverly shook her head. "Your picture is fuzzy. Ever since they had a staff shake up, that department has gone downhill. You'll need to have it retaken." She scanned the back of Gemini's large, square identification tag with a scanner and the scanner flashed green. "I can call down there now and tell them you're coming, Ms. Johnson?"

Gemini shook her head. "In a hurry," she said in her gruffest voice. "Don't want to be late for the first day." She grabbed her lanyard and pivoted away from the desk.

"Maureen?" Beverly called.

Gemini stopped. "Yes?"

"You're going to enjoy working here. It's full of interesting people."

Gemini waved over her shoulder and headed to the elevator.

Once inside, she relaxed. The elevator doors opened on the third floor and she made her way to the cafeteria. In a glass case beside a croissant, overfilled with cheese, was a cinnamon roll the size of her head. She purchased that, along with a coffee and two sugars, and found a centrally located booth. She took tiny bites of the enormous roll, thankful for its size. This could very well take her all day to eat. The key to good undercover work was patience. It wasn't long before two doctors came in and sat in the booth behind her. She recognized one from the second floor and turned her head to the wall as he walked by. Once they sat, she leaned back to hear what they were saying.

"My kid wants to go to an Ivy League school. Going to cost me fifty grand a year." His voice was high-pitched and tense.

"How are you going to cover that? Will Carson Moore let you wash his car on the weekends?"

They both chuckled.

"Do you remember him at the last Christmas party?" The high-pitched voice asked.

"The life of the party. Can't believe his wife stayed with him after that. Wilson's a bad influence. My wife told me if I went for drinks with him, she'd take the kids and I'd be lucky to see them on holidays."

They laughed again, establishing an easy rhythm. "The rumor mill cranked up to level ten. The nurses are all gossiping that something happened to him. Can you believe that?"

"Wilson? He's always been a loose cannon. Remember the year he took off to Europe with two days' notice? Can't believe the board didn't fire him after that stunt."

"He and Moore have always been tight."

"I've never liked that guy. He reminds me of a traveling salesman; he's always got something hidden in the other pocket. Can't quite put my finger on it, but Carson Moore has some heavy secrets."

The two men changed the topic to football, losing her completely. Gemini sipped her coffee slowly as she digested what she heard. This didn't explain their parking lot spats.

OCEANBERRY BLUES

"How's this drug trial going without him? Have you heard?" the high-pitched voice asked.

"Things are going smoothly. Better than the last one. Wilson lost several patients at that time. They called it 'pneumonia.' Only one patient on a respirator this time, but it's unclear whether it's Atomycin-related. He's responding well to the treatment."

Gemini breathed a sigh of relief. It was good to hear that Leo was recovering, just as she'd believed. One doctor got up and retrieved a spoon before returning to his seat. She kept her head down until he'd passed.

"I heard a nasty rumor, though. There is another drug study trial going on. Up in Seattle, the Tandor Company has had positive results with their drug. I heard a crazy one the other day: one nurse told me there are rumors they messed with our last drug trial to make us look bad. They actually think this hospital is competition!"

Both of the doctors chuckled. "It's hard to imagine someone would have that kind of access. But we don't call this place 'Soap Opera Central' for nothing. You ready? I've got to get out of here by five tonight. My kid has a baseball game. Last time I missed it, he actually hit the ball."

The men got up, and Gemini was alone with her thoughts. What if someone were really doctoring the study for their own benefit? Who would benefit from changing the results? Maybe Olive would know. Or Denise. She decided from now on she would keep her conversations and suspicions to herself inside the hospital.

The next people who came and sat down were a couple who were visiting their first grandchild.

"You're going to make a lovely grandma," a male voice said. "We're going to be the best grandparents."

"I know, dear. Won't we have fun buying things? Aren't we lucky to live down the street, where we'll be able to pop over whenever we want? And when she goes back to work, we'll be seeing the little sunshine every single day! It's like raising our child again, but without the worries."

"That's what I thought too. I retired from my job as a legal secretary at a law firm, and I had this idea in my head that I would take my grandson to the park and buy him ice cream. But that all changed. Soon it was, 'you're going to babysit while I get my nails and hair done. I might go out for a drink after.' From there, they expected I would care for him whenever they felt like it. I didn't have a life. My daughter thinks that my life is still about her. Well, it's not. I'm done raising her. It's time that I think about me. And my Leo. We're not at her disposal. We're going to enjoy our retirement!"

Gemini didn't realize how much this had been building up inside her. Nor did she understand how badly she'd wanted to tell her daughter what she really thought about becoming their nanny. "I'm so sorry. That was more for me than you. You'll enjoy your granddaughter, I'm sure. Have a lovely day." She walked away before the confused couple could respond.

Having that revelation in the middle of her day wasn't quite what she'd planned, but there it was. She stopped in the bathroom and removed her wig, spending time fixing her hair nicely before continuing to the fourth floor. As she walked into Leo's room, she bumped into Denise.

"Oh, Gemini! It's so good to see you." She smiled the welcoming smile Gemini looked forward to seeing every day. "My boyfriend and I really enjoyed your cookies. You're so thoughtful."

"Thank you." She touched her natural hair, her head feeling strange since she removed the wig and cap. "How is Leo today?"

"He's doing well. The doctors think they might try to wean him off the ventilator soon."

"That's great!" She worried it was too soon, but didn't want to tell Denise. "I hoped that would happen. And how is he doing with the Atomycin? Is he still getting his regular doses?"

"Yes, he sure is. I can pull up his chart if you like? So you can see?"

"No, that won't be necessary today."

"Okay. Well, it was lovely seeing you. Just push the buzzer if you need anything while you're here." Denise turned to leave.

"Oh, Denise, I was wondering if you could answer a question for me. Do you all work a set schedule, or do you rotate your days off?"

"We are pretty firm on our schedules for now. Until the drug trial is over. The doctors want us here at the same time on the same days. You know, for continuity."

"Okay. So if someone is here on, say, Tuesday, they will be here next Tuesday as well?"

"Yes, that's right."

"And the same for the doctors?"

"Mm hmm." A voice came over the hospital intercom, asking for help in room 409, three doors away from Leo. "I've got to go. I'll check back later!"

Gemini sat down beside Leo, her mind whirring. Now she would also need to get ahold of the weekly schedules to find out who was always there on Tuesdays. That wouldn't be too difficult with her new hospital identification.

"I've had such an adventure today, Leo. I wish I could tell you about it, but I'll make note of it in my diary and we can talk about it later." She leaned forward and took his hand, bringing it up to her face to kiss. "Oh, these powerful hands. It was something that attracted me to you early on. Did you know that? I was madly, deeply in love with your hands."

There was a knock on the door. A nurse Gemini hadn't

seen before walked in. "Mrs. Reed? It's nice to meet you. I was working the night your daughter came in to visit your husband. Lovely girl. She mentioned you might move Mr. Reed to another hospital?"

Gemini sighed and placed Leo's hand back by his side. "No, I'm afraid she was mistaken. Leo is staying right where he is for now."

"Okay. I was just wondering." She stood uncomfortably in the doorway. "That's a good idea, keeping him here. Atomycin has every chance of returning Leo to the man he was."

CHAPTER 18

She debated whether she should tell Howard about her day. He might think she was being paranoid. She walked up the path to her own home and then changed her mind and went over to Howard's door and knocked. He opened it before she finished her second knock.

"More undercover work, James Bond? I could probably get you explosives, but it would cost a pretty penny."

Gemini blushed. "No, I'm afraid my actions would embarrass a real detective today. I sat in the cafeteria listening to conversations. I didn't take my new alter-ego up to the break room."

Howard crossed his arms over his chest. "Did you learn anything?"

"Yes, I did. In fact, two doctors sat behind me and talked about Doctor Wilson. They said he and the board president, Carson Moore, are very close. They also mentioned some competition between Charming General and a hospital in Seattle. Maybe someone is trying to change the results of our studies to make them look better."

"Then you did your detective work for today. Doesn't matter if it ended differently than you'd planned."

"It's just that—well, usually I don't lose my nerve. I've been in some very sticky situations and never backed down. I'm rather ashamed, if you want to know the truth."

"Never too late to change, is it?" Howard leaned against the door, seemingly unwilling to ask her in.

"No, I suppose it isn't. You're right, Howard. Today was a success. Tomorrow I'll go back and do something different. Thank you!" She spun around.

"I'll be awaiting your update!" he called after her.

The next morning she entered the hospital again, waving confidently to Beverly B. as she walked by. Since she had a badge that got her into the mail room, she retrieved a cart and began delivering mail to the second floor. Only once was she stopped by a staff member. "Haven't seen you around before. Are you new to our hospital?" He asked in a friendly tone.

"Yes, just started my volunteer work today. Running behind or I'd chat more!" She kept walking quickly, hoping he wouldn't follow her. He didn't. She slowed her pace as she passed the nurses' station. They were gossiping about who had the better first date. She paused, thinking of her next move.

"I'm wondering if I could ask you ladies something," she began. "I'm a new volunteer and I've noticed that the staff seems very unsettled and I'm not sure why? Everywhere I go, faces are tense and people are jumpy. If you'd give me some idea of what's going on, perhaps I could be supportive."

The nurses looked at each other, trying to gain reassurance that it was alright to speak to this stranger. "A doctor disappeared from the fourth floor. We're wondering if something happened to him, which of us is next?"

"If you ask me," another nurse began, "that creepy nurse

who started last year is involved somehow. She refuses to speak to most of the staff, and won't use a locker here because she thinks that they have recording devices in them." She crossed her arms. "For whatever reason, Doctor Wilson took a liking to her. I can't explain it. His taste generally leans toward the younger nurses." They all nodded knowingly.

"She and Doctor Wilson had intimate conversations, always exchanging packages," the third nurse agreed.

"Oh, I know who you're talking about," the first nurse said. She turned to Gemini and explained, "She's a floater, so she goes from floor three to floor four whenever she's needed."

Gemini nodded. "What's her name? It sounds like someone I should avoid."

"I think it's Billie Jo or Billie Beth. Her last name is Jansen. And she won't allow you to call her anything but her full name, so if you're going to speak with her, you need to be ready to address her as nurse Billie Ray Jo Beth Jansen." All the nurses giggled.

"What does she look like? I want to be prepared in case I encounter her during a mail delivery. Polite but distant."

"She's a very serious-looking woman in her 50s. She's got short, brown hair, a bowl cut. And she only has one eye. She wears a white eye patch. Billie Jo usually works days, so she's lurking around somewhere."

"Thanks for the tip, ladies!" Gemini/Maureen tried not to be obvious as she read name tags and watched people who were walking by on floor three. Just as she was about to give up, she passed the nurses' lounge. Out of the corner of her eye, she noticed a woman sitting on the windowsill with her feet propped up on a chair. She was reading a book and eating an apple. This nurse had a white eye patch over one eye.

Gemini knocked on the door frame. "Nurse Jansen? I was told I could find you here."

"You may speak to me only when you address me properly." She pointed to her name tag and then looked at Gemini expectantly.

"I apologize." Gemini squinted to read the badge from across the room. "Nurse Billie Jo Jansen. You're the first person I've seen with their last name displayed on their badge. I like that. Tells me the entire story." Gemini smiled and tipped her head to the side.

Billie Jo returned to her reading and shook her head. "I'm not the conversational sort."

"I was told I could find you here. I would like to ask you for some help with something."

Billie Jo Jansen dropped her feet to the floor and slammed her book on the table. "Why would I help you? I'm medical personnel and you're a volunteer. Don't even work a full eight hours, I'm sure." She got up from her reading spot and began examining Gemini closely. It was almost as if she were trying to sniff out her fear. "I'm certain I've never seen you before. And usually when someone new starts in the mailroom, they send us notification. I've received nothing today."

"Well," Gemini cleared her throat. "Be that as it may, I'm here. And I was told that I should come and talk to you about Doctor Wilson."

Billie Jo Janson's face tightened. "You have to go through proper channels for that. I am not the proper channel. Whoever told you that I was is confused." Billie picked up her book once more, moved back to her window spot, and picked up her book.

"What I was told was that you are the person on the inside. You can do special things for people that others can't. Because of your relationship with Doctor Wilson."

Billie Jo's face turned crimson. "Who would say that?" She

squinted her eye. "I want to know who is passing this around. This gossip is out of control. I can get small things for you, but if you're asking for Doctor Wilson-sized things, you'll need to go through the proper channels, as I've already told you. That's high-end and complicated."

"I'm willing to take whatever you have. Because I have many needs. Gemini gazed at her with steely eyes. "I've heard you can hook me up with just about anything. Maybe even something for a special project."

"How much do you have? How much do you want? These are questions that need to be answered before I can help you in any way. And are you wearing some sort of a wire? You look like the type that might." Billie Jo eyed her up and down and back up again.

"I have one-hundred-and-fifty with me right now." Gemini had been planning to buy groceries with that money. It was pure luck that she had cash on her. "I can get you more later if you need. Depending, you know, on what you offer. I can assure you I wouldn't know the first thing about wearing a wire. People my age aren't keen on fancy electronics."

Billie Jo's face tensed further. "He never said he was bringing someone else in. Why wouldn't he tell me that directly? He drops out of sight and then sends me new people? He knows the deal we made."

"I–"

"If you're wanting to start top of the line, we can do small amounts. But it will take me some time to get it all together. Can you come back tomorrow? We can meet in here, or we can meet somewhere more private. One-hundred-and-fifty gets you started. There is a room that isn't in use at the end of the hallway—room 344. I've been meeting my clients in there."

"What time? I can be here whenever you need me."

"Let's say 10:30 on Thursday? Unless there's some sort of

emergency. You know how that goes, working in the hospital. Things come up and we have no control."

"10:30 it is then. I'll meet you in room 344."

Gemini took the cart and walked out of the room, letting out a gigantic sigh when she was out of earshot of Billie Jo Jansen. When she worked the Bartles' case, she had a plan of action. Buy the diet pills and get out. She knew exactly what she was purchasing. With Billie Jo Jansen, she had no idea what came next.

There was always someone at the law firm whose field of expertise covered whatever she did. Feather, Howard and Olive weren't quite the same, but they would have to suffice.

Instead of going to see Leo like she'd planned, Gemini walked to the beauty salon. Her hands shook as she waited patiently for Feather to finish with her client.

"Gemini, you're flushed." Feather gasped. "Did everything go alright? I've been worried about you ever since you left. To be honest, I was also worried that what I told you scared you off, and you'd never come back."

"No, I don't scare that easily." Gemini smiled weakly. "I want to know more about your special gifts. This is about the hospital. I just contacted a woman who is selling what I assume is Atomycin under the counter."

CHAPTER 19

Feather was a lifelong resident of Charming, Oregon. She loved her town, and only wished once that she lived somewhere else. When she was thirteen, she had a cousin visit from the Midwest. The cousin showed her pictures of golden wheat fields and wide-open skies.

Feather imagined moving, but she couldn't bear the thought of leaving her parents, brother, and sister. That, and the secret she shared with no one, kept her in Charming.

That's why Donald's proposal made so much sense: he was safe. The tallest boy in her class, he always felt out of place just like her. They bonded as outcasts.

Donald had a secret, too. In four generations of Drabler Brothers Trucking, not one member of the family worked anywhere else. If you didn't want to drive a truck, you did the books or learned how to be a mechanic. It was that simple.

At sixteen, Donald quietly applied to work at a construction company. When his mother discovered his torn pants and dirt-covered shirt, she confronted him. He refused to quit.

Feather's family had already disowned her, too. They assumed she would become a faith healer, bringing celebrity and a large quantity of cash into the fold. She refused their demands. It seemed like the logical progression to take the next step in disgusting them by marrying someone in her senior year of high school.

Donald found her exciting and bold, at least at first. He knew she was smarter than he was, and by persuading her to drop out of high school with him, he ensured she wouldn't find anyone or anything better. After one year of wedded semi-bliss, Donald found exciting wasn't what he wanted. She talked too loud and laughed at things he didn't find funny. She dashed any hope of reconciliation with his family when she showed up at the family Christmas party with red and green striped hair. Everything she did set him on edge.

Feather struggled to change to his liking, but wasn't sure exactly what that was. She offered to buy him headphones with her next paycheck, so he didn't have to listen to her, but he refused. Instead, she spoke in hushed tones, afraid of what might set him off next.

Feather worked at The Q-T Mart. She convinced herself it wasn't so bad, even though every morning she thought about ways she might die while walking to work. Getting hit by a car would not only end her work day sooner, but suing the owner of the car might make her transition to a new life easier.

She came home one evening, completely unscathed from her walk, and announced, "I'm going to beauty school. If I don't change my life soon, I'm going to go crazy."

Donald nodded enthusiastically. "You'll be gone more, right?"

On graduation day, Donald went out to get beer to "ease the boredom" of sitting through a ceremony. She did her hair perfectly, coloring the ends a bright orange to match the branding for the beauty school. Feather put on makeup, using the expert techniques she'd learned in two years of cosmetology school. When she looked in the mirror, she saw a successful entrepreneur.

When she came out of the bathroom, she called for her husband. There was no answer. He'd been out for almost two hours. She called his phone, and it went directly to voicemail.

Feather walked into the kitchen and found a room temperature generic six pack of beer sitting on the table with a card on top. Inside, it read, "Good luck with your graduation. Not working out anymore. I paid the rent till the end of the month. I'll see you around."

She walked into the Charming Inn and Convention Center and noticed the other students enjoying their family time. She could've called her mother to come, she supposed. But her mother read the papers and must've seen the picture of Donald being arrested for ramming a series of cars last month because he thought they were driving too slow.

She had a persona she used as a stylist at Cutz Hair Salon, and she was quite good at it. She put on her fake smile and cheerily asked clients about their lives, never revealing her own loneliness. At night she'd go home and sit in a corner, giving in to the darkness of depression that nagged at her all day. She hated being different.

Drama marked her six-month tenure at Cutz Salon. Three of the girls had a party and didn't invite the other three. From then on, each group refused to talk to the other and Feather straddled the center line.

Still new to the business and adult friendships, she didn't want to take sides. There was also the matter of her clientele. Any of the other girls who'd been there longer could ruin her business by word of mouth. She didn't know where the clients' loyalties laid and whether they would be interested in staying with her if she lost her job and had to move to another salon.

Things became so contentious at the salon that two of the girls put tape around their stations and made it known the others were not to cross it. The clients, including Feather's, were placed in an impossible situation.

She moved to the back of the salon, away from everyone. It was a relief. She could hide her true self and no one was any the wiser. The voices she'd heard as a child were growing louder. She couldn't quite make out the words, but they were definitely trying to tell her something.

One day, after a two-hour attempt to remove an entire pack of gum from the head of an unruly client, she went outside to breathe. It wasn't her normal break time, but she needed to clear her head. Standing next to the large dumpster in the alley was a beautiful woman with honey-colored hair. She was leaning against the brick wall, in a passionate embrace with a well-dressed man. The couple seemed out of place.

Feather realized that it was her boss, Angie Bard, with a man who looked nothing like her current boyfriend pressed up against her. If Feather opened the door quietly and returned to her station, they would never know what she'd witnessed. Her feet refused to move.

"Darling, we've only got a few months and this will all be over. You and I can run away." The man ran his fingers up and down her shirt.

"I know," she answered breathlessly. "It's hard thinking about the sacrifices you're making, but we'll be together forever. You're sure no one is going to get hurt?"

"Cross my heart," he replied.

Feather felt the sneeze coming and did her best to suppress it, but instead, caused a louder, more pronounced sound. The couple looked up, startled. Feather slammed the door shut and went back to her station, her heart pounding.

When Angie returned, she whispered in Feather's ear. "What did you hear?" she asked.

Feather shook her head and continued organizing her drawer.

"You don't have to worry. I'm going to be fine. This isn't dangerous for me at all."

Feather looked up, startled. She hadn't thought about this being dangerous. Just that her boss was carrying on, most likely with a married man. Otherwise, why would they be in the alley?

"Ms. Bard, I'm not sure if it's my place or not. But I'm concerned about you. You don't seem like yourself, and as you know, this salon is a war zone."

"You're a love, Feather. I'm fine. My friend and I were just discussing a trip we're taking together soon. Purely platonic."

Feather looked at her, incredulous. "Okay."

Each day when she came to work, Feather tried to push that scene from her mind. Her boss's life was none of her business, but she began noticing that Angie couldn't concentrate. She'd start cutting someone's hair and then ask what style they'd asked for.

Her hair, normally perfectly coiffed, was often messy and tangled, like she'd gotten up and lost her brush. One day, she left the perm solution on someone's head too long and it burned the client's scalp. A shoulder-length style had to be converted to a short bob.

The bickering in the salon had only escalated during this time. Feather approached her one day. "I'm worried about you, Angie. Are you alright?"

Angie smiled. "Never better." She picked up the sizeable chunk of mail that had been piling up on her desk.

"What can I do to help you?" Feather asked with concern.

Angie stopped sorting the mail. "You could do something. Why don't you tell those ungrateful witches that you're buying the salon and if they don't shape up, they're out the door?"

Feather was stunned. "What?" She asked. "I'm new to this business. I know nothing about managing a salon."

"What if I taught you? It won't take that long for you to learn the business. I promise. And when you've learned everything I have to teach you, then you can decide if business ownership is for you. That will also keep you out of the path of those warring factions out there." She pointed her thumb at the empty stations where, within a few hours, the other women would come in and the chilly atmosphere would resume.

"I suppose. I'll try. But really, I'm not any good at the financial stuff. I'm not sure I can do it."

Feather caught onto the system quickly. It had only been a month, and she was doing all the bookwork.

"You realize I'm bribing you, right?"

Angie said one afternoon, as Feather went over the previous day's profits.

"Huh? What do you mean?"

"For what you saw. I want you to keep to yourself."

"I don't know what you're—"

"Of course you do, love." She tousled Feather's hair in a way that made her uncomfortable. "You're a smart girl. Don't worry, things are going to work out fine."

The next day, Feather came in to the salon and picked up the mail. She was thumbing through the bills when the phone rang.

"May I speak with Heather Jones?"

"I'm Feather Jones. How can I help you?"

"I'm calling from Charming General Hospital. You're

listed as next of kin for Angie Bard. I am sorry to inform you she passed away this morning."

Feather dropped the mail. "There has to be some mistake. I'm not next of kin; she's got to have some family somewhere." Feather searched her memory for any conversations the two of them had shared about relatives. She realized, with sadness, that she'd never asked about Angie's family.

"What am I supposed to do now?"

"I can't really tell you that. You can come and pick up her personal effects any time, though. We have a purse and keys. The EMTs brought those in with her when they picked her up early this morning."

"What happened? How did she–"

"She usually helped an elderly neighbor bathe each morning. When she didn't show, he called the police. She never made it out of bed. They'll perform an autopsy to determine just what happened."

Feather went up to the hospital and retrieved her boss's purse. It didn't feel right taking something so personal, and yet that was all that was left of the person who she'd come to admire. She took the keys and went into her apartment, where she found a sparsely adorned space. It was the exact opposite of the salon, where Angie filled every inch with dried flowers from the discount store and movie posters of dead stars from the forties.

She walked into the bedroom, trying not to stare at the bed where her friend had taken her last breaths. On top of the dusty dresser sat a long-expired package of birth control pills and a collection of ten porcelain dolls, each with a different facial expression.

She began opening drawers, looking for any explanation for this tragedy. There was an empty pill bottle with the label removed, and a picture of Angie standing on a sailboat in a tiny bikini. She posed with one hand on her hip and her head cocked to the side, her long hair draped around the other shoulder. Angie looked like she was trying to impress someone. In the top drawer of the desk, Feather found a will that was notarized the week prior.

Angie left everything to Feather; the salon, her personal effects, her car, and all of her savings. It shocked Feather to think she might have been the only friend that this woman had. She always seemed so outgoing, so friendly. But she never once talked about going out after work and having any kind of life. She was just like Feather.

The next day, the hospital called to say they had mistakenly sent Angie's body to be cremated before they performed an autopsy. "You can pick the ashes up at the funeral home over on third street. They'll have them ready in time for your service."

There was no way she would plan a funeral for someone she barely knew. "You should contact her boyfriend about those. Hal or Harry, something like that."

"You're the next of kin. It's up to you to find Hal or Harry. Have a good day, Miss Jones."

Funerals and Feather Jones didn't mix. She decided instead to ask the girls at the shop to each stand up and say something. They got into an argument about who should go first and all stormed out.

Sitting alone in the salon, she heard a voice telling her this was her opportunity to start over. Sometimes she couldn't make out the words clearly, but today, there was no mistaking them. "Be your own person. I've given you the tools."

CHAPTER 20

"Billie Jo Jansen and Doctor Wilson were doing drug deals. He gave her Atomycin, and she sold it to people. Doctor Wilson told Leo it was a miracle drug and those taking it felt years younger. He was probably taking it himself," Gemini shared with Feather excitedly.

Feather frowned. "I've got twenty minutes until my highlight and trim comes. You can't just throw that one out there and expect me to walk away. Let's go sit in the empty room and talk."

Gemini followed her to the space that used to house a nail salon. Now all that remained was a brown reclining chair and two tables. "You should know that Olive's information turned out to be legitimate. I found out from other employees that this woman had fights with Doctor Wilson and that she may have been the last person to see him alive."

"Oh, Gemini! This is scary! Are you sure you want to go through with it? Maybe you should call the police instead."

Gemini touched her wig, still getting used to curls where straight hair normally hung. "No. My neighbor used to work at the hospital. He told me the police do whatever the hospital management tells them to do. If I call them now, before I have all the evidence I need, they'll have no reason to believe me. I need to meet with her first."

Feather crossed her legs and leaned against the table. "How can I help?"

"I'd go to my neighbor with this problem, but he's already gone above and beyond to help me, and I don't want to get him in trouble. You mentioned your boyfriend, Tug, has access to all sorts of gadgets? I'm wondering if he could get me a recording device that isn't openly visible? The law firm where I used to work got them from a former client who still owed them money."

Feather smacked her lips nervously. "The Listen Right Now 2400. Tug recorded our upstairs neighbors' arguments to check it out. It even records through the ceiling. I'm worried about you, though. This seems like a dangerous undertaking for someone who is–"

"Elderly? Cheese and biscuits." Gemini guffawed. "You have no idea. I've been going undercover for years. I'm the perfect person to use, because no one would suspect me. I'll be fine. Can I drop by your place later and pick it up?"

"No," Feather answered quickly. "I can drop it off tonight after work. I think you told me your address."

"414 Elderberry Lane. It's the only dreadfully brown house on the street."

"Okay. I'll be by around seven. The horrid brown house." Feather's next client walked through the door a few minutes early.

"Is anyone here? I'm ready for the new me!" she hollered.

"I'll be out in a minute, Phyllis!" Feather called.

Feather glanced at Gemini with a worried face. "I'm afraid this is more than you have dealt with in the past. You had the law firm backing you up before, and now you're on your own. This lady could be very dangerous."

Gemini patted Feather's arm. "Not to worry. As long as I have a recording of what's going on, I'll be fine. And I promise I will come and talk to you as soon as I'm done." Seeing that Feather still wasn't convinced, she squeezed her shoulder. "Don't worry, dear. I've been in much worse scrapes than this. I'll be in a hospital. There will be lots of people around."

Gemini stood up alongside Feather, and they hugged for a moment. They walked together to the front of the salon where Phyllis was waiting.

"Oh, Mrs. Reed, that color really is perfect for you. Feather, can you do my hair exactly like hers? She looks stunning!"

Gemini felt a tinge of pride. "Thanks. I thought so too."

"I can certainly try, Phyllis. I'll see you tonight, Gemini!" Feather waved at her as she walked out the door. As she meandered four blocks to her home, she wondered to herself if maybe she wasn't in over her head. Whatever this nurse had to share with her tomorrow, she needed to be prepared. Maybe she should go to her neighbor and ask for his advice. As she walked up towards his door, she changed her mind and went home. Maybe another day.

When she went inside, she realized she'd left the ringer off on her phone again. The sound was such a nuisance she hated it to interrupt conversations. She longed for the days when there was silence, when people were speaking and there wasn't the constant buzz or chirping of some electronic device. How could you have a meaningful conversation when you were constantly being distracted?

Sophia would not understand, and it was her calls that she had missed once again. She took a moment to center herself before dialing her daughter's number. "I know what you're going to say and you're right. Your mother should always keep her phone on. I am elderly and you never know when—"

"Mother, I'm at the hospital with Taurus. He's fallen down and we're having him examined. I won't know anything until the doctor comes in." The sound of Taurus shrieking in the background wasn't a good indicator of his current state. He always shrieked.

"Is there blood? Is something broken? Did he have some sort of liver laceration? I've seen those on TV shows. Those can be nasty. I hope you're keeping him still." Gemini knew she wasn't. Sophia and Brandon always felt like he should be a more "free range" kind of child.

"No, there's no blood, Mother. He was playing on the playground with his nanny and she must not have been paying attention. She says that some other child screamed, and she snapped her head away just for a moment. I don't believe that. How can you miss a child falling off the monkey bars? Pure negligence. I've asked Brandon to look into a lawsuit against her. Clearly, we will not need her back again. I'll have to hire someone else temporarily until you get here."

Gemini stomach sunk. "I'm not so sure that this nanny was bad. Accidents happen, Sophia. I remember when you were three, and you fell while we were painting the fence. I just looked away for a moment and you crawled on top of the gate. When I went to get you down, you decided that's where you wanted to be and we had a little tug-of-war. I lost my balance and off you went. It was no one's fault. And you're just fine now."

"Well. I had that scar between my eyes. It only took two-thousand dollars in cosmetic work to remove it. I guess you could call that fine. But, I choose to raise my child with a little more care. Oh, the doctor's here. I'll have to call you back." Sophia hung up before Gemini could say anything else.

She felt guilty for not being more understanding to her daughter. When she called back later to check on her grandson, she would tell her she was sorry. She also felt concern for Taurus. This would have to be the time that he really hurt himself seriously.

There was one thing she hadn't done today, and that was talk to Leo. She called the hospital and asked to have the phone put next to his head.

"Leo, I want you to know that I am doing everything I can for you. When you wake up, I'm going to have all sorts of information for you. You'll be so proud of me for everything I've done. We can get back to painting and traveling and doing all the things that we planned. I love you!"

She made herself a supper of leftover roast chicken and a green salad. Just as she was sitting down to eat, there was a knock on the door. Gemini was pleased to see Feather standing on the porch.

"Hello, Feather! Come on in. I was just about to eat. Can I make you a plate?"

Feather stepped inside. "No thanks. I've got to get home. I just wanted to drop this off for you." She handed Gemini a stylish black pen. "Tug sells amateur detective supplies on the side. Along with supplements. He dabbles in lots of areas, you could say."

"This is it? It doesn't look big enough to record anything!" Gemini marveled.

"You can put it in your purse or your pocket. When you're done, bring it into work and I'll show you how to retrieve the information. Tug says to tell you that he has extra time tomorrow. He also wanted me to give you this." She handed Gemini another small item, this time it was octagon-shaped and looked like a ruby necklace on a silver chain. There was a raised portion in the middle of the stone. Gemini examined it. "It's beautiful. What does it do?"

Feather pointed to the center. "The gem in the middle is actually an emergency contact button. When you push it, a text goes to Tug's phone. He's a brown belt in karate and he isn't afraid to defend you."

"That's very kind of him, but I'm perfectly capable of getting help myself. Your Tug has a stereotype of the elderly that isn't necessarily true." She sniffed, trying to hand it back to Feather.

Feather closed Gemini's fingers around the necklace. "It may come in handy one day. You'll hurt his feelings if you don't at least wear it for a day or two."

Gemini shrugged and put the necklace in her purse.

"Are you sure you won't stay? My grandson was here, so I have a house full of food I'll never touch again. Green things and brown things. I don't know what these young mothers are thinking. Might as well let their children just graze in the yard."

"Maybe just a few minutes. It's been a long day and I do have a project to finish." Feather walked into the living room and looked around. "This is a cute little place. Have you thought about buying it?"

"Yes, I have." It just slipped out of her mouth. "Actually, no. We're moving back to Fassetville once Leo finishes with his treatment. I'm going to be a full-time nanny for my grandson. You know how grandmothers love to dote on their grandchildren? I want to be that kind of grandma. But my daughter insists that I be his care provider instead. Following all of her silly rules. Poor Taurus is going to grow up to be a weird kid. Yes, I said it. He's going to be weird. And she wants me to be a party to that. Isn't it awful?" It wasn't like she'd just thought of these things, but it was the first time they'd slipped from her lips.

"Gemini, it sounds like you don't want to do this at all. Why don't you tell your daughter what you just told me? She's got to understand that you're retired, and this is your time to do what you want."

"You'd have to meet my Sophia to understand. We raised her to be her own person. We just didn't realize that person was going to be a bulldozer." Gemini looked down at her feet. "But it will be so nice to see Taurus every day and watch while he grows!"

The phone rang, an obnoxious sound that made her shiver. "That'll be Sophia now."

"I'll let you talk. I really should go." Feather scurried to the door. "I'll see you tomorrow. Please be safe, Gemini!"

Gemini waved to her as she answered the phone. "Sophia? How is he? Anything broken?"

"No. He appears to be alright, other than the nasty bump on his head. We're to watch him tonight and come back if there are any changes. Brandon says we should hire a babysitting service for the next week, just to be safe."

Gemini was glad Sophia couldn't see that she was rolling her eyes. "I need to talk to you about a few things. The drug trial in Seattle, for starters."

"Not now, Mother. We're taking Taurus home and giving him a protein shake. I have to focus on my son's needs. We can talk tomorrow."

CHAPTER 21

It was all Gemini could do not to throw the phone in a rage. "You have no grounds. I'm not incapacitated. Besides, your father made it very clear he didn't want to leave this area. I have that in writing."

Sophia sighed heavily. "Oh, Mother. I was hoping I wouldn't have to bring this up. But you're forcing me now, aren't you? When you were working for Brandon, there were several times when you acted irrationally. One might say without common sense."

Gemini squeezed her fists tight. "Isn't that what irrationally means? We all have our moments." She thought back to her years at Floris, Fealgood, and Flem. She did nothing to embarrass her son-in-law; in fact, it was quite the opposite. There were several cases they had won for their clients because of her detective work. This was another one of Sophia's exaggerations.

"Brandon reminded me of the time you took it upon yourself to do a stakeout. You followed some man around for weeks, abandoning Daddy and living out of your car. By the time you returned to work, the workload had doubled and

Brandon had to hire someone to meet deadlines, putting them in a bad spot. That's not someone who should be in charge of the health of another."

"You're twisting things, Sophia. Your father joined me several times, and I only spent one night in the car. We hired an extra person because a partner had a big murder case. Brandon told me he'd grown to trust me and only me for undercover work. So did the other partners."

"That's where you're wrong, Mother. Brandon trusts no one."

Gemini had a queasy feeling in her stomach. "That's what he told me."

"I hold all the cards, Mother. Just keep that in mind. Daddy is leaving in two weeks, with or without you."

Gemini hung up the phone, feeling so much rage she didn't know what to do with herself. How could her daughter and son-in-law betray her like this? If Leo were awake, he would put her in her place. He was the gentle parent, the one who rarely found fault with his daughter. But when he did, he dealt with it abruptly. She was so used to his compliance that when he put his foot down; she rarely argued.

Gemini looked out her front window to see her neighbor in his yard working on his garden. Impulsively, she walked outside and over to his property.

"Do you have children of your own, Howard?"

Howard stood up and scratched his back. "I have a son. Haven't seen him in a decade. Why do you ask?"

Gemini thought about whether she should press him further. Sophia would say she was being nosy. "My daughter is trying to get my husband transferred to another hospital. She doesn't believe anyone knows what they're doing here. I haven't told her anything about my suspicions with Doctor Wilson. But Sophia can sniff out bad news from one-hundred miles away. I'm afraid there's nothing I can do."

"There are always answers, Mrs. Reed. You just have to be willing to look in every crevice. Your daughter is going to go to court then? Force you both up there? I've seen that happen several times. Do you think that he'll get better care?"

Gemini shook her head and squeezed her fists again. Her hands developed marks from her fingernails." It's not about better care. It's about Sophia being in control. Don't I owe it to Leo to figure out what's going on? He needs to finish his treatment here."

Howard wiped the sweat from his brow. "So, are you asking for my help, or are you just using me as a sounding board? Either way, I'm not sure that I'm the right man for the job. You know I have strong feelings about that hospital and goings-on there. It's not a stretch to believe someone is up to no good. Maybe you'd want your husband away from that. He'd be a lot safer."

"True." Gemini thought for a moment. Was she being selfish? Was this all about her boredom since retirement and needing something to occupy her mind? "What about Doctor Wilson's strange disappearance? If I don't discover what happened to him, I'm leaving the other patients in the study vulnerable. Wouldn't I be responsible for whatever happened to them?"

"I'm guessing that means you need to stay and fight. You got a battle on two fronts as I see it. Your daughter wants to have say so, and then there's the shady business with Wilson. You need to have a battle plan for both. Do you have a good lawyer?"

"We always used our son-in-law or their firm," she lamented. "Just for contracts and such. Leo and I are very boring. We never had a need for anything else."

"There's someone I can contact for you. I'll call them in

the morning. So that battlefront is taken care of for now. How about the other one?"

"I'm meeting with a nurse tomorrow. I think she may have something to do with Doctor Wilson's disappearance."

Howard squinted. "Do you have a plan to go about this? Or are you just throwing spaghetti at the wall and hoping something sticks?"

"I'm open to your suggestions, Mr. Beachmont. Apparently, your expertise runs deeper than I knew?"

"Ruling people out is what I'd suggest. Since you've got that fake ID and wig and all that, I'd go to scheduling and get the names of everybody who works on that floor. Start making nice with all of them, one at a time. And you can scratch them off your list as you go. It may take a little while, but you'll get to figure out who's doing something shady and who is not."

She felt silly now. "That's an excellent idea. You really know what you're talking about." Gemini moved forward automatically, leaning in to embrace him as she would any time she felt gratitude.

He put his arm out. "Don't assume that everybody wants a hug. I don't like affection."

Her face turned crimson. "It's my natural impulse. I meant nothing by it. I should go home and make plans for tomorrow. Thank you again!" Gemini walked back over to her house with a little spring in her step.

After all of this was done, and Leo had recovered, they would have to figure out a way to deal with Sophia and Brandon. Their behavior was just atrocious. Somehow, she needed to find common ground so she could still see her grandson. And she needed to tell them once and for all that she would not become the new nanny.

CHAPTER 22

Gemini tried remembering not to touch her smock as she walked down the hallway. She did not trust this pen to pick up all the words from her purse, so she stuck it behind her ear like a carpenter's pencil. When she reached room 344, she took a deep breath before she pushed the door open. It was dark inside. "Nurse Billie Jo Jansen?" she whispered.

"You're two minutes late." The light switched on behind her and Billie Jo locked the door before she could change her mind.

"I was nervous," Gemini replied truthfully. "But I'm here now."

"So you are, Maureen Johnson, mail room volunteer." Billie Jo observed her momentarily before going over to the corner and reaching inside a box. She pulled out a package wrapped in brown paper and sat it on the bed. "One Doctor Wilson Special." She held her hand out. "Cash?"

Gemini fumbled for her purse and pulled out the cash. "It's all there, but you can count it if you need."

Billie Jo took the roll of cash and held it in one hand, and then the other. "No, this is correct."

Gemini put the package in her bag. It was lighter than she expected. Drugs on television shows always took a big brute to carry. "Before I go, can you tell me anything about Doctor Wilson? I mean, this is a great way to make money on the side and I can't wait to try the product. But he's kind of a mystery to me."

Billie Jo's entire face transformed. Like a light bulb had turned on inside causing her to glow. "At first I thought he was just like all the other doctors—arrogant, selfish. One day last winter, we left work at the same time and walked together to the employee parking lot. The wind was howling, and the rain was coming down sideways. When he got to his car, it had a flat tire. I offered to give him a ride home, and he said only if I'd let him buy me a drink on the way."

"He was your—lover?" Gemini asked uncomfortably. "It's perfectly fine if he was–is."

Billie Jo smiled, displaying crooked yellow teeth. "Yes. We spent many nights in a passionate embrace. He was so stressed about this secret project and he told me I was the best kind of release. I'm kind of legendary here for my 'abilities.'"

In the law office, many men and women confessed their sexual adventures to Gemini. Nothing surprised her anymore. "You must be very proud of your skills. You helped him, but did he help you too?" She cocked her head to the side.

Billie Jo's eyes narrowed. "Are you for real? Isn't that the point of your visit with me? You don't strike me as the type to engage me for other reasons. I guess I could be wrong about—"

Gemini looked at her purse. "The package?"

Billie Jo nodded. "Zebulon said he could move as much Wondermen's Chocolate as I could get him."

"Is that code for drugs?"

Billie Jo laughed sharply. "What are you talking about?"

Gemini forced a laugh in response. "A joke. We joke about drugs coming in to the mail room instead of going out."

"Doctor Wilson moved Wonderman's Fundraiser Chocolate for me in exchange for my help to change the chart notes."

Gemini did her best to keep a straight face. "Of course. That's why I'm here today. He told me about the chocolate."

"Black market fundraiser chocolate may not seem like much, but it put both of my kids through college. It's a big business. I'm just the middle of the supply chain."

Gemini made a mental note to find out more about this business. "He told me you helped him out, and he wanted me to thank you. I should be going. My shift starts soon."

Billie Jo raised an eyebrow. "There are a couple of questions I have for you, Maureen. First, I know that's not your name. I checked in the mailroom and they have hired no one new for the last four months." Billie a look of satisfaction like a cat who had just captured a mouse. "And second, whatever Zebulon is mixed up with, I believe they've done something horrible to him. He doesn't answer any of his phones and he's not here in the middle of his drug trial." Billie Jo moved closer to Gemini, so close their noses almost touched. "Sending someone as innocent-looking as you to check out his lovers makes perfect sense. But now the game is over and I need you to tell me exactly what's going on. Where's Zeb?"

Gemini fidgeted. "I don't know anything. He told me about the chocolate before he disappeared. I was delivering the mail one day, and I told him how concerned I was about retirement. He must've taken pity on an old woman, because he told me a way to make extra money. 'Sell it to your friends at the community center," he said. I'm planning to fund my first trip to Arizona with this stuff." She cleared her throat. "I really need to go. I'll be back for more soon." She shoved Billie Jo hard and unlocked the door quickly, scurrying down the hall without looking back.

As she approached her home, a kind-faced gentleman in khaki shorts greeted her.

"Mrs. Reed? I've been trying to contact you."

She cocked her head to the side. "How can I help? I haven't been here long, but I can give you directions to a few places."

He handed her an envelope. "You've been served, ma'am. Have a nice day."

It was the oldest trick in the book, and she fell for it. She opened the envelope and skimmed the documents.

Sophia and Brandon were petitioning for guardianship of Leo so they could move him to Seattle, just as she'd threatened.

CHAPTER 23

"Feather?" Gemini called out. "Feather, I know you've got a client coming soon. I can go get the water warmed up and be ready for their wash."

"I'm down here," a weak voice answered. Gemini walked around the counter to see Feather curled up in a ball in the corner, between a box of rubber gloves and two cans of hairspray.

It didn't look like she had been home since yesterday. Her hair was messy and flat and her normally thick eyeliner was running down her cheeks. Feather's beautiful eyes were bloodshot and worst of all, she gave a look of defeat.

"Oh, dear." Gemini bent down to her level. She put one hand on each of Feather's knees and looked her directly in the eyes. "Cheese and biscuits - this won't do. Whatever made you hide here needs to be dealt with immediately. Does Tug know where you are?"

Feather concentrated on her feet. "I get really depressed sometimes. I never know when it's going to hit me. Usually I can wait until I get home to have a breakdown, but last night, one of my clients fired me--Ursula Mein.

She complained every time I did her hair, insisting I redo the color at least three times. It was never the perfect shade. It took me six hours every time she came in to do a two-hour job and the woman never tipped or said thank you."

"It sounds like you're well rid of her. You should feel proud of yourself for taking out the garbage," Gemini said supportively.

"After she said, 'Feather, I'm never coming back here. You're not up to my standards,' she told me that Angie would roll over in her grave, knowing I'd made such a mess of her salon."

Gemini clucked in sympathy. "That's rough and completely untrue. Does that woman realize your old boss isn't in the ground? No rolling in her situation."

A smile flickered across Feather's face. "I can't bear the thought of disappointing Angie after she left me so much. It just crushed my soul to hear her say that. I sat here in the dark for about two hours wondering why I didn't notice she was sick or hurting? And then I started thinking I should call the client and beg her forgiveness, because I didn't want Angie to be ashamed of me. Isn't that crazy? I actually was going to beg her to come back and be my client. After she treated me like trash."

"You're so tenderhearted, dear. I understand you don't want anyone to hate you, and that's normal. Once you have some perspective, you'll be glad to be rid of her. Now you can fill her time with someone who appreciates your talents. You really should call Tug, though. He has to be worried sick."

"He went to visit a cousin yesterday in Tellum. He'll be home tonight. That's probably what made it so convenient to have a breakdown."

"May I give you a hug?" Gemini stretched her arms out

wide, forgetting what happened the last time she expected to hug someone.

"I'd like that very much." Feather sat forward, and the two women embraced. Gemini stroked her dark hair for several minutes. "Before we met the first time, one of my grandmothers told me my life was about to get better. I think she was referring to Gemini Reed walking through my door."

"Is she—dead?"

Feather nodded. "I have more conversations with dead people than living. Usually they're positive."

"It's okay to feel sad. It's not a sign of weakness. Do you want me to cancel your clients for today? So you can go home and wash up?"

Feather wiped her nose with the back of her hand. "No, I'll just go in the bathroom and redo my makeup. I probably don't smell wonderful, but once I spray a little hairspray and some product in the air, nobody is going to notice."

Both women chuckled. "That old trick!" Gemini joked.

Feather sat up straight. "I almost forgot: what happened with your investigation? Did you get everything you needed?"

"You won't believe what they sell undercover these days. Doctor Wilson was moving black market chocolate in exchange for Billie Jo Jansen tampering with records." Gemini put her hand under her chin, still not believing what had taken place.

"What?"

"I'll tell you more about it later." Gemini looked up at the clock. It was almost ten. " I'll shampoo your client while you're sprucing up." She offered her hand to Feather, though she wasn't sure she could pull both of them up at the same time, given her knees weren't what they used to be. Feather sat for a minute, examining everything currently at eye level.

She took a hand and wiped off the bottom shelf of the counter, which was covered in a thick coat of dust.

"You're a good friend, Gemini. Your daughter is lucky to have someone like you. I would have loved having a mother who cared what I did and where I was."

She nodded half-heartedly. Now was not the time to explain what was going on with Sophia.

The client walked in the door and tapped on the counter. "Hello? I'm here for my ten o'clock appointment."

Feather grabbed Gemini's arm in fear. "She can't see me like this!" she whispered.

Gemini reached for the top of the counter, glad she only had one person to pull up, and stood slowly, allowing her knees to crack and thanking her body for making this up and down movement with no medical intervention. She smiled as she looked at the woman dressed in a shiny red tracksuit with matching nails.

"Sorry, I was restocking some items. I'm Gemini Reed and I'll be getting you started. Would you follow me back to the shampoo station?"

The woman pulled off expensive sunglasses, revealing deep purple eye liner and a thick layer of brown eye shadow. "This is so unusual. I've never had a shampoo lady before. Is this a new service? Will she be charging more?"

Gemini put her hand out, guiding the woman to the back of the salon. "No extra charge. It's a new service we're providing at Feather Works Salon now. A chance for you to unwind a bit and enjoy a pre-pampering. I'll be giving you a head massage and you can destress. Does that sound all right?"

"It sounds divine! I'm going to tell my friends that this place has improved! You're going to have so many new clients, you won't know what to do." She snapped her gum as she dropped her sunglasses into her oversized purse and followed Gemini to the sink.

"Mm hmm." Gemini watched Feather out of the corner of her eye, sneaking into the bathroom.

"Tell me your name again, darling?" the woman asked, as she leaned her head back in the sink. "I want to rave about you to my friends."

"I'm Gemini Reed. New to town."

"I'm Shelley Natchez. My husband is kind of a big deal at the hospital. He's in charge of a drug trial there."

Gemini paused. "Dr. Natchez is your husband?"

"Yes, darling. That's the rumor. Though I don't see him much, so we mostly communicate through our checking account." She forced a laugh.

Gemini opened the bottle of conditioner and poured some into her hand. She began gently massaging, moving her fingers in tiny little circles.

"My husband is taking part in the drug trial at the hospital. They've had lots of encouraging results up there. But it is strange that Dr. Wilson disappeared right before it began. Has your husband mentioned anything about that?"

"Ohhh. I haven't had a head massage this nice since my last trip to the Caymans. Where did you learn how to do it? Are you professionally trained? I would think someone of your advancing years wouldn't have that kind of upper body strength."

"My hairdresser used to massage me every time I went. It was what I looked forward to the most. About Doctor Wilson?" Gemini persisted, ignoring the slight.

"Probably just needed a break. He hasn't been the same since he and Carson had their little dustup. They'll still get their bonus package."

Gemini stopped massaging. "What bonus package? What are you talking about?"

The woman opened her eyes. "Are you done? Already?"

Grudgingly, Gemini continued working her fingers through the woman's head. "The bonus package?" She snapped.

"For successfully completing a drug trial, the hospital gets a nice big bonus from the drug company. They pass along the money to the doctors who took part, though the results have to be favorable. It's so unfair, really. If those patients die, that's not the fault of the doctors. They're sick people to begin with."

Gemini rubbed harder. "The doctors are making money off this treatment and you're concerned about how much? Did someone get rid of Dr. Wilson so they could take his share?"

"Ow!" Shelley touched her scalp where Gemini had been working vigorously. "You're really upset about this, aren't you? All hospitals do it. We are not the only ones. Sometimes the competing drug companies can get really nasty. That's why we celebrate when we finish the trial and it has gone successfully. Dr. Wilson has taken part in many drug trials before. He knew how this worked."

"I'm ready for you now, Shelley!" Feather appeared, her face freshly washed and her hair combed.

"Your new wash girl was just telling me she doesn't approve of the way we do things at the hospital. Maybe someone should inform her that the hospital runs this town."

Gemini wiped her hands on the towel. "Looks like you're ready to go, ma'am." She patted the woman uncomfortably on the shoulder. "Every day is a new lesson. Thank you for teaching me one today."

"That was mostly nice. Just need to work on your continuity." Shelley sniffed. "Next time, take it easy and I'll leave you a tip."

Feather and Gemini exchanged eye rolls.

CHAPTER 24

"Why don't you join a knitting club, like other women your age?"

"I'm not like other women, Sophia."

She began with Frederick C., the floor nurse, for days on floor two. Gemini figured out when he took his break and sat in the floor two break room. She watched name tags as people walked by, trying not to seem obvious. She had a bag full of yarn and a half-knitted sweater that Olive was gracious enough to share. Her needles clacked as she made loops, trying to pretend she knew what to do.

A short, Asian man with dark hair and a serious face walked past her carrying a tray containing a green salad and an apple. She looked at his name tag and realized he was the person she was trying to find.

"Sir, I think you may have dropped something." She pulled a pen off the table and handed it to him.

"That's not mine, ma'am. Must be someone else."

"Oh. I volunteer in the mail room, and I needed to rest my weary bones for a bit. I could use some company, if you don't mind."

His face relaxed as he sat in the chair opposite her. "Of course. I'm always up for conversation with a pretty lady."

"I'm fascinated by the people coming in and out of here. So much drama happening and lives at various stages. You must have so many stories."

Gemini took a quick breath and clacked her needles one more time before setting them on the table. "You're the head floor nurse, correct? I've seen you several times. Have you been involved at all with the drug trial on the fourth floor?"

He looked at her strangely. "No questions about my boat or the weather? This is a very intense lunch topic." He stuffed a bite of his salad into his mouth. "It's been quite a while since I've made small talk though, so maybe this is how things work these days." He chuckled.

"Oh, you know how people gossip here. There's always some kind of drama." Gemini rolled her eyes.

"I know about the study. Everybody does. It brings in so much money for the doctors in the hospital. Of course, none of that filters down to the nursing staff. The people who actually do all the work."

"Yes, that's really a shame," Gemini agreed. "You people all deserve much more for the hard work you do and the hours you put in. Rumor has it, someone was upset with Doctor Wilson because he'd received so much money from the study. The gossipers think somebody hurt him to get his share."

"Oh, Ms.–" He leaned forward and looked at her name tag. "Ms. Johnson, you are a character. This isn't a soap opera. This is a hospital. I don't think anyone is doing anything other than what they were assigned. Doctor Wilson is the best we have. He made money from the other drug trial because he did an excellent job of administering it. Everyone knows that. I doubt very much that any harm came to him."

Gemini regarded him thoughtfully. "It just seems like an import thing to know. It could be one of us up there. Or one of our relatives. Can you imagine if your mother or sister was in the drug trial and the doctor just disappeared? Wouldn't you feel awful if something bad happened and you could have prevented it?"

Frederick interlaced his fingers together in front of him. "How about we talk about the weather? It's partly cloudy today and I think it's going to rain by five o'clock. That's what I heard on my way to work, anyway."

She wasn't giving up so easily. "The other thing on my mind is Carson Moore. I was told recently that he and Doctor Wilson didn't get along."

"I wouldn't have any idea." Frederick shoved a large forkful of salad into his mouth, trying to finish his lunch quickly.

"Because I'm a nosy old lady, I have to ask, who would stand to profit the most from his death?"

"I've had some strange lunch companions, but this has to top the list. Guess I should thank you for bringing a little excitement into my day."

Gemini, unswayed, stood up as well. "Who would stand to profit the most from his death?"

Frederick crossed his arms. "I'd say Doctor Natchez, or maybe even Carson Moore. I'm working a twelve today so I need to go outside and get some air while I have the chance." He stood. "Nothing like sea air to clear your head. Might think about that yourself."

Gemini waved him out. She picked up the half-knitted sweater and waited patiently.

A red-headed nurse with the name tag, "Alicia R." poured herself a cup of coffee and sat down across from Gemini.

The nurse sat down. "Do I know you?" she asked, bringing her cup to her lips.

"I was just thinking the same thing. Maybe I delivered

your mail recently." She kept her eyes on the knitting needles.

"Carson Moore's mail has been going to the wrong place. He was really mad about it. I guess he gets mad about lots of things." Gemini looked up briefly.

"He's not a nice man. Especially since his wife left. "Alicia R. finished the rest of her coffee with one gulp.

"Sorry to hear that. Does he take it out on other people? Like the staff or other doctors?" Gemini cocked her head to the side and smiled slightly.

Alicia looked around the room and then directly into Gemini's eyes. "My cousin is part of the cleaning staff. She comes in at night to clean the on the second floor." Alicia. leaned forward, speaking just above a whisper. "Carson Moore drinks coffee all day. I mean, his coffee budget is legendary. My cousin said when she worked in his office for the first time, he had an enormous cup on his desk, completely full. It was evening, and he had gone home for the day. She threw it away, thinking, as a rational person would, that he would get a fresh cup in the morning. The next evening she came to work and was told Carson wanted her fired for removing his cup. She begged to be given one more chance. Carson let her stay on for a cut in pay. She was barely making ends meet as it was. Horrible man. Just awful."

She clucked sympathetically.

"I can see why his wife left."

Alicia's face displayed a look of shock, and then she burst out laughing. "You're a card. Where did you work before the hospital? I've never seen you around town before. I thought I knew everyone."

"I was working at–the library before and I needed a change."

Alicia R. raised her brows. "Oh, really? My aunt works up there. Have you met Jean Lloyd? She just loves the library. I'll have to ask her about you. I bet she got a kick out of you, too."

Gemini took a napkin and cleaned the accumulated crumbs off the table, scooping them into her hand. It was easier than gazing into Alicia's eyes while she told another story. "I've changed my look dramatically since I worked at the library. You know when you get to my age, you want to be your authentic self. And sometimes that's different from the person who you've been all these years. She might not remember the Maureen who sits in front of you right now. The new woman."

"I'll keep that in mind." She looked at her watch. "Guess the fun and games are over. It was nice visiting with someone new!" she said enthusiastically.

"Oh, one more quick thing, Alicia, was Carson Moore having issues with Doctor Wilson?"

Alicia stood and straightened her scrubs. "Everybody knows that Doctor Wilson is unhappy. He asked Carson to let him out of his contract more than once. I heard a story last year about Doctor Wilson bringing a girlfriend in for an x-ray and expecting the hospital to absorb the cost. You know how Carson is with coffee. Can you imagine him with an x-ray the hospital has to pay for? I thought for sure they would fire him. They didn't."

"He is valuable to the hospital. Lucky for him," Gemini mused.

"I really have to leave now. Nice meeting you, Maureen!" Alicia F. waved as she walked out the door.

As she walked away, Gemini pulled the list of employees out of her purse and marked her off.

Her phone buzzed in her pocket. If it was Sophia, she would decide Gemini was hanging from the rafters instead of answering her call. "Hello?" She answered in her most irritated voice.

"Gemini, thank you so much for your help earlier. I feel like I owe you more of an explanation."

Gemini's posture relaxed. "Feather, that's unnecessary. Everyone has bad days. I'm just glad I was there to help."

"No, I think I need to tell you. Can you come over to the salon when you're done with your–whatever it is you're doing?"

"I'm done now. Would that work?"

"Yes. I have one more client today and he's always late."

Gemini walked out of the hospital, waving to Beverly B. at the front desk on her way by. "Have a great day, Maureen!" she called cheerily.

When she reached the salon, Feather was sitting at the desk, looking much more composed that when she'd seen her earlier in the day, despite whatever emergency she had.

"What's going on, dear? Are you and Tug having problems?"

Feather shook her head. "It's nothing like that. In fact, Tug is the reason I'm still mostly sane. I need to tell you something and it's going to come as a shock. I get a vibe that you won't freak out."

"Are you sick? Is someone threatening you?"

Feather stood up and wrapped her hands around her body. "Do you remember the other day, when I told you about my dead boss talking to me?"

"Oh, that's what this is about?"

"And now you're judging me." Feather looked away.

"No, your gift is amazing. I was expecting something different, that's all." She thought back to that morning, when she'd encountered a disheveled helpless girl behind the counter. Nothing like the confident woman who stood in front of her now. "Please tell me how all this works?" Gemini pulled a chair from the waiting area over to the desk and sat down. Feather did the same.

"They tell me things and want me to pass them along. Sometimes they don't like their loved ones' haircut. That's common, actually. Then it can be serious. That's what happened last night."

The hairs on the back of Gemini's neck stood up. "Is someone talking about me again?"

"The woman who owned the shop-Angie-died and left this place to me."

"Rather sudden, wasn't it?"

"They ruled her death was from natural causes. She didn't take good care of herself; she smoked, and she drank a lot, but it was still a shock."

Feather remembered standing with her in the alley as she blew smoke rings and talked about her lonely life, even though she'd just caught her back there with a man Feather recognized from the hospital.

"Last night I was in a bad way, as you know. I heard lots of voices and told them to go away because I could barely take care of myself. They listened, all but one. Today, I was standing at the sink, cleaning up after my last client. Just as she did before, she came with a message." Feather looked at Gemini solemnly. "It was Angie. She told me she'd been murdered."

CHAPTER 25

"...And then I went to my neighbor and asked if he would go halves with me, chopping down the giant oak. Darrell, he says, now why would I spend my own money when it's you who has the problem? And that's when I told him my secret." Darrell P. leaned forward in his chair, as if he was about to give away a matter of national security. "I got video of your wife stealing the neighbor's newspapers."

"This is very interesting, Darrell. We were discussing the staff Christmas party, though. I was wondering if we should go with punch or coffee?" Gemini pushed the corners of her mouth up as hard as she could, forcing a smile onto her face. This conversation had already gone on twenty minutes longer than she'd hoped, using every method of extraction she had at her disposal. Nothing was working.

"I've been thinking while we were talking. You don't look like anyone who volunteers in the mail room. Nobody named Maureen there."

"I just started. Maybe you missed a face or two."

"Nope." He took a bite of his sandwich and stared at her blankly. "There's a new guy named Jim, but he's the only one.

They don't like too many volunteers at once, it gums up the system."

Gemini panicked. "Well, when Jim has a day off, then I pick up the slack for him. That's kind of how it works. When you have a day off, doesn't somebody come in and pick up the slack for you?"

"That's Jean. She is my next-door neighbor's cousin." He took another large bite of sandwich and began chewing so vigorously, crumbs spewed across the table and into Gemini's hands.

"What do you know about Doctor Wilson?" She set the half-knitted sweater down and then picked it back up, realizing the potential for Darrell's food to end up on Olive's fine work.

"Oh, we all know he was murdered. You must not have been here long if you haven't figured that out."

"How do you know that?" Gemini asked casually.

"I seen him having heated conversations with lots of people: Carson Moore, a coupla nurses he never called back and then some guy dressed in fancy clothes. He reminded me of my cousin Kelvin, the drug dealer. Always dressed like he's going to a funeral."

This was the first she'd heard of a drug dealer. Gemini leaned across the table, unafraid of whatever food might hit her next. "What did this person look like?"

"Dunno. He had dark hair, I guess. Looked kind of average. I've seen him in Carson's office before, too. Looked like they were going to tear each other's throats out."

Gemini thought for a moment, trying to put all the new information in order. "Was there anyone else who might have argued with Doctor Wilson?"

Darrell let out a loud burp. He stood up and pushed his chair in. "Can't think of anyone. He had his share of enemies. That's how I know he's dead. Nice to visit with you,

Maureen. I'll tell my buddy Pete that I met you. He works the early shift in the mailroom. Always trying to one-up me with people he knows."

"I'll see you again on my rounds!" she replied cheerfully.

Someone new walked into the break room and poured himself a cup of coffee. He had earbuds in and was humming a song to himself. He sat down at the table next to Gemini and smiled. Brad W.

"Good morning, lovely people! Or is it good night? I'm just starting my shift, but you look like you've pulled an all-nighter, man."

Darrell didn't respond.

Gemini shook her head. It frustrated her that she finally might get vital information after a week of hearing about people's personal problems unrelated to the hospital, and now this.

Darrell yanked on his green scrubs, pulling them up over his enormous stomach. "I have to go. You're a nice lady. I'll look for you again. I've got lots of stories about people who work here."

As he opened the door, Gemini saw panicked people running back and forth.

Someone screamed. Gemini pushed her way past Darrell, catching the arm of an orderly as he hurried down the hall. "Can you tell me what's going on? Why is everyone so upset?"

"Someone died."

Darrell chuckled. "That happens every day here. We're working in a hospital, friend."

"It isn't just anyone. It's the president of the hospital board." He wiped the tears from his eyes. "He was always so nice to me."

Gemini gasped. "Carson Moore? Do they know what happened?"

"It looks like he came in early to get some work done. He poured himself a cup of coffee and sat down at his desk. His secretary got here this morning and thought he was concentrating on something. After he didn't respond to her messages, she went into his office and realized he wasn't concentrating. He was slumped over on his desk. There was foam coming out of his mouth—that's what happens when you're poisoned."

"I know that. You don't need to act like it's MY first day on the job," Darrell snapped.

"I'm going to have a look." Gemini pushed her way past the gathering crowd into the hallway.

"They won't let you anywhere near him!" Darrell called after her.

Gemini ignored him and continued down the hallway, following the trail of people. She reached Carson Moore's office, where police had arrived and were placing yellow crime scene tape across the doorway.

She tapped on the shoulder of a police officer. "Sir, I volunteer in this office sometimes. Can you tell me what happened? I don't want to be a nuisance, but it's frightening for an elderly woman to encounter something like this." She put her hand to her chest in dramatic fashion.

The police officer looked at her kindly. "I'm sorry, ma'am. We can't really discuss anything. I think the best idea for you is to go home."

"Should I come back tomorrow? Now you've got me frightened. You know, a doctor disappeared recently, and no one has seen or heard from him since. Do you think the two incidences are related? What if I killed him with my coffee?"

Another police officer stepped up to her side. "If you made the coffee today, we need to talk to you. I'll go get a detective and she'll be with you in a moment. Could you wait for her over there in that room? He pointed to a doorway on the other side of the hall marked, "Visitor Waiting Area."

She walked into the room and stood, tapping her fingers against her leg as she thought about what she might say. A stern woman in a dark blue pantsuit entered.

"You are the lady who made coffee this morning?" she asked.

"I pitch in wherever I'm needed. Did my coffee have something to do with his death?" She hoped the real coffee producer wasn't lurking around.

"Can you tell me your name?" The detective leaned forward and looked at her name tag. "Maureen, is it? Can you tell me what you did this morning when you got here? I need even the most minute details, even if it seems like something that wouldn't be helpful."

Gemini took a deep breath. Back when she worked at the law firm, she had to make up a story once when one partner had gotten themselves into hot water. He wanted her to pretend like she worked for his household staff when the police called her personal number. He didn't really give her much to go on, other than that she had supposedly been at his place the previous day and had seen him out by his pool.

She was the maid, Helene, who often stayed past her shift because she liked the view so much from their cliff-side home.

Helene made a dinner of polenta, pork chops, and a fresh garden salad, before making homemade brownies with her mother's recipe. All the while, her boss was beside the pool sunning himself. She could see that from her kitchen perch.

Strangely, when the interview was over, she didn't feel guilty at all. In fact, it was quite exhilarating.

Because she felt privileged to work at her son-in-law's firm, she asked no further about why the police were questioning her that day. They never came back and questioned her again, so she had the satisfaction of believing she had done a good job. That Christmas, she got a bonus of $500 and assumed it was because of her excellent performance.

"Well, I always come in early. I love the view, watching the ocean from this window is soothing for the soul. I check and see what we've got for coffee. Do you know there are so many good local coffee roasters? They donate coffee for us to use up here at the hospital. So I open whatever is on top of the pile. I think today's was–" She pretended to think. "Today's was the house blend from Caffeinated Cares. That's the new coffee place on main street over by Feather Works Salon."

"Yes, ma'am. But I'd like to move ahead a bit. You came in, you made the coffee from Caffeinated Cares. Was the package open when you saw it?"

This was going to get too complicated and yield her no more clues. "No, the package was not open. But you know, come to think of it, that was yesterday. Yes, now I'm certain I made it yesterday. I was visiting with a friend in the break room and hadn't had time to make any yet today. Sometimes I get confused." Her eyes darted back and forth as she wrinkled her brow.

"I understand. My mother does that sometimes, too. Nothing to be ashamed of." The woman relaxed her stance and looked as though she might hug Gemini. "So, you don't believe he drank any of your coffee, then?"

"No, I don't. I always clean out the pot before I go home. Someone else definitely made it today. But while you're here, did you know that a doctor recently disappeared from this hospital?"

"I hadn't heard that information." The woman viewed her skeptically. "Are you sure this doctor disappeared, or did you get confused again?"

Gemini swallowed hard. "Not confused about this. He's not here. People don't just vacation in the middle of a drug trial. They're keeping that from the police."

"I'll be sure and check that out," the woman said with little conviction.

Gemini decided to try a different tack. "Poor Carson. People at the hospital really love him or hate him. Do you think he was poisoned? It could be anyone, really."

"It's too early to know whether that is the case. He was an outstanding citizen who volunteered his time with the city council and was well known in the community. Right now we're just focusing on collecting information."

"I'm so concerned for his wife. This will break her heart. Are you going to speak with her, just to cover all of your bases?"

The detective cleared her throat. "If I didn't know any better, ma'am, I'd think you were trying to run this investigation for me." She opened the door and made a motion for Gemini to exit. "I think we've done everything we can here. Can you leave your phone number with the officer in the hallway?"

Gemini moved stealthily past the officer in the hallway, who was busy interviewing someone else. When she hit the elevator button, the doors opened immediately. Gary J, the maintenance worker who had so kindly helped them on their first day in the hospital, was standing inside sobbing.

"Gary! Are you alright?" she asked as the elevator doors closed.

"I–can't–believe he's gone." He said through tears. "That man was my idol. I never got the chance to tell him that." He wiped the tears away with a small finger.

Gemini rubbed his back. "It's a shock to everyone. I'm sure he cared deeply for you." The doors opened, and they both stepped out on the first floor.

Gary took in her new . "Why are you dressed like that, Mrs. Reed?"

She'd forgotten she was still dressed as Maureen. "Trying a fresh look. You know how women are. We like to mix things up. Next week I'll be trying out a new lip color."

The tears began welling up in his eyes again. "I'm going to Carson's house to clean up. He wouldn't want it to be messy when people are milling around. That was the kind of guy he was, always trying to make a good impression."

"I didn't realize you two were so close. You have a key to his place?"

Gary nodded. "I did odd jobs for him. Extra spending money for the wife's fancy tastes, and he pays me under the table, so it's tax free. Loved that guy so much."

"You should do that, Gary. I'd be happy to help!"

Gary stiffened. "That's nice of you, but he was a private guy. He wouldn't want you there."

They were at the front doors of the hospital now. "Thank you, Mrs. Reed. I wish I had my mother in times like this." He reached up and gave her a hug.

She patted his back. "Take it one day at a time, Gary. It's never easy losing a friend."

"BEST friend, Mrs. Reed. I would have done anything for him."

CHAPTER 26

"Feather, after learning more about your special abilities, there is something that you could help me with." Gemini glanced at Feather anxiously. Never having dealt with someone with this particular gift, she wasn't sure if it was something that one boasted about, or that they kept concealed. Her inclination was that it was something to be secret, since Feather had been so reluctant to tell anyone.

"I'll help you if I can, Gemini. But this town is funny. They don't look kindly on people who are different. And I'm different. As are you, if you don't mind my saying. I think it's a good thing to be out of the norm."

Gemini smiled warmly. "I take it as a badge of honor, but I don't like to think of it as being different. I'm distinct. Gemini Reed stands out from the crowd. I don't care what people think of me. I just want to make sure they properly care for my husband and there are no more deaths."

"Do you think you can stop it? The hospital is all-powerful. They run everything. I had a client tell me that even on his days off, he wasn't really off of work. They learned his whereabouts. People knew what he did, when he did it, and how much time he spent completing it. And if it was something that was wrong according to them, then they would tell him."

"I'm only here temporarily. I guess I don't need to worry about that." Gemini thought about Denise working hard to save up so she could leave. "I was wondering what you could tell me about a recently deceased individual. Someone who might have passed last night or this morning."

Feather looked at her with uncertainty. "I could try. I don't want anyone else to hear us, though. They might decide it's a reason to review us poorly. Can you imagine? 'Too many dead people hanging around." She moved her hands in a typing motion. "I won't go back there for my perm!" She giggled.

"Maybe we could step into the alley for a minute?"

Feather and Gemini walked outside, where their only company was an orange and white stray cat.

"Give me just a few ideas and I'll go from there. That's what I do so that people don't think that I'm faking it."

"Cheese and biscuits, Feather. This is a talent that you were given, and I trust you wholeheartedly to tell me the truth. It's about someone on the hospital board. You could say it was a drinking incident."

Feather held up her hand. "Don't tell me. I don't want you to let me know any of the details. Just give me a name and I'll go from there. First name only, please."

"His name was Carson." Gemini opened her mouth to say more, but decided against it.

Feather took hold of Gemini's hands and closed her eyes.

"Should I close my eyes too, Feather?"

"No. Don't talk."

They stood silently for several minutes. Feather's face contorted into several shapes and expressions. Eventually, she opened her eyes. "He's telling me he died violently. Unexpectedly. I don't think it was alcohol, though. He didn't like to have drinks until after a round of golf. Did he golf? No, don't tell me. He wasn't expecting this person. In fact, he had no idea this person was angry with him."

Feather put her hand up to her throat. "I feel choking. Yes, I feel a lot of choking. It's something that he drank. He's telling me he can't breathe, and he realizes who it was. Large guy down the hall who has been asking him questions for months."

"Darrell? He wouldn't have the energy to kill someone!" Gemini remarked. "I thought for sure it was his wife."

"Feather? Your 10:30 is here." Feather's new employee, Sindhora, glanced at both women questioningly. "Is there something I should worry about? You two seem like you're deep in thought here."

"I'll be there in a second, Sindhora."

Sindhora shrugged and went back into the salon.

Feather looked at Gemini. "He was a jerk. I'm just telling you that straight out. He didn't want to tell me much because he said I wasn't his caliber of people. I know who this is. It's Carson Moore. Is he really dead?"

"He's that stuffy in death?" Gemini asked, incredulous. "I thought that once we, you know, passed that everyone kind of became equal."

"They are who they are. Some people have a lot of lessons to learn before they cross the bridge. This one, well, he could be in a state of limbo for quite some time."

"Was it Darrell who poisoned his coffee? Allegedly, of course. I can't imagine why. He tried convincing me his neighbor overheard a conversation, but then there was the lost dog incident and-never mind."

"I don't know. I'm not hearing Carson's voice anymore. Often, when I get names, they are the wrong ones. I haven't quite perfected that part yet."

"Thank you so much for your help, hon. I knew there was something suspicious going on."

Feather looked at her strangely. "Yes, I think there are others in danger. But none of his caliber. If you know what I mean. He was standing in the way of something."

Gemini trudged home. She wasn't sure what to think of what had transpired over the past 24 hours. She had been enjoying this Maureen persona a little too much. It was distracting her from time with Leo. Was she trying to avoid what was going on with him? Or was she really concerned about the well-being of everyone else in the hospital?

"Looks as though you're deep in thought today, Mrs. Reed," Howard Beachmont noted as she walked up the steps. He was digging up the edging around his bright pink petunias.

"Hi Howard. You're right about that. I have quite a lot to process, it seems. Did you hear what happened to Carson Moore? Died in his coffee this morning. I have some ideas about who might have wanted him dead, but mostly they have no basis in reality."

He stood up and leaned on his shovel. "You're assuming he was murdered then? No old-fashioned 'natural causes'? Can't say as I blame you. Not a usual situation, foaming up at the mouth like that."

Gemini shook her head back and forth. "Word sure travels fast in this little town. I don't know if I'll ever get used to that."

"Indeed. But you remember I have my eyes and ears in that place."

She put her keys back in her purse and walked over to his front porch. "Yes, about that. I'd like to know more about your experiences there. May I join you?"

He motioned for her to come up on his porch. He disappeared and returned with a blue-and-white striped folding chair. "Have a seat and tell me your theories about this death while I work."

She sat down and immediately unloaded everything she'd learned from her research with all the hospital employees. "They all seem to think he had problems with Doctor Wilson. Carson Moore and Doctor Wilson were involved in something together and it wasn't stolen chocolate. Can I bring you some, by the way? I have over a hundred dollars' worth. I'd give it to my grandson, but Sophia would decide it's full of things that would make him walk backwards."

"I see you've become a bit of a conspiracy theorist." He chuckled. "Good for you, Gemini. It's always good to question authority in this small town. Especially when it has something to do with that hospital. I have no doubt the man was murdered. It's the timing and who would benefit from his death that we have to question."

"Who would have a motive? Do you know the other board members? Maybe he was sabotaging his program, and they wanted it to stop?"

"Slow down there, Mrs. Reed. I don't think you need to assume all of those things. We can look at one person at a time. Do you know his secretary? They run through them pretty quickly up there. How about any nurses or doctors that he golfs with? There's a lot of golfing that happens in this town, and what goes on the golf course is often a deal that can't be made at the hospital. If you know what I mean."

"No Sir, I don't know what you mean. The way Nurse Billie Jo Jansen talked, everything happened in the back seat of a car."

Howard displayed a look of confusion. "Let's say you're golfing with the head surgeon and he likes your company and you let him win. Well then, he may see that there are favors sent your way. Maybe the parking spot you wanted, or extra holiday time. You scratch my back, I'll scratch yours. That's how things work there."

"Oh, I see. What you're saying is this man did not agree to scratch backs. On the golf course."

"Now you're getting it. Carson Moore wasn't a scratcher. He thought quite a lot of himself and, as such, he preferred being the scratch-ee. The golf course was only the starting point. Your next step is to figure out who was upset they didn't get their back or anything else scratched."

"Yes, I will do that." They both looked up as a car barreled down the street.

"Oh, no." Gemini's stomach dropped.

"If you want to make a run for it, I can cover for you," Howard offered.

"No, she's my concern. I love her to death, but this isn't the best time to deal with her."

Sophia pulled up into the driveway and put her car in park so abruptly it lurched forward. She got out and slammed the door. "Mother! What is going on with you? I've been trying to call you for hours. You know we have a hearing tomorrow. If you don't show up, then we automatically win. Is that what you want? You scared the daylights out of me. I thought maybe you'd gone off and had yourself a heart attack or fallen, and you were stuck in a ditch somewhere."

"Cheese and biscuits, Sophia. You didn't need to make this long drive just to check on me. I've got my neighbor here who would know if I was missing and then there's Feather at the hair salon–"

"I don't know this hair salon person, and I certainly don't know your neighbor," Sophia said dismissively.

Howard turned and went inside his house.

"Mother, we need to sit down and talk. I had to find

someone to stay with my son and I made this trip to Charming because I care about you."

"You have a babysitting service to fill in until you find a new nanny, dear, so don't be giving me this sad story. I'm fine and things are going to be just fine in court."

"Can we go inside? I've been driving for an hour and I'm parched. I'm trying to drink fourteen glasses of water a day, to make sure that I've completely cleansed my system. They're saying now that your brain can't function properly unless you've had that much water. It also reduces stress."

"Yes, I'm sure it does. When you spend your entire day in the bathroom, you can't encounter much stress from the real world."

The two women walked inside, and Sophia plopped down on the kitchen chair. Gemini took her purse and set it on the counter before getting a pitcher of filtered water from the refrigerator. She poured Sophia a glass and set it in front of her before moving to the opposite end of the table.

"No lemon? I thought we discussed the importance of lemons in your water, Mother."

She wished she could confide in her daughter, but Sophia was so deep in the crevice she'd created for herself that she couldn't confide in her daughter. "I've been thinking about what you suggested. That you want Daddy moved to Seattle."

"Both of you, Mother. You would have a nice little apartment there, too. I will put it in front of the judge tomorrow."

"Maybe there isn't need for a judge. If I just agree to let your father leave."

CHAPTER 27

"Am I hearing you correctly? You're going to listen to me for the first time in my entire life? Are you ill?"

Gemini paused before saying something she might later regret. "I listen to you plenty. When you told me big flower patterns are only for women who live in Florida, I threw away both of my new blouses. Both of them, Sophia."

Sophia, for once, was speechless. It was a blessedly quiet thirty seconds. "OK, Mother. What's your game? I know you better than this. You won't give up without a fight. Even those big flower pattern blouses. I had to threaten to burn them in the driveway before you agreed to give them away. What's up?"

"I've been thinking about it and decided it is what's best for your father. Staying here in Charming would only bring us more suffering, and as a family, we've had enough of that."

"And?" Sophia demanded. "What else?"

"And, I want to set the date of his departure. Next week, on Friday or later. If you agree to that, I won't fight you."

"What's so special about Friday, Mother? Do you have some sort of voodoo dance planned?"

OCEANBERRY BLUES

Gemini laughed. "Sophia, you can be so ridiculous. Of course not. I need to keep some sort of control here. Those are my terms. Agree to them or we end up in an ugly battle in the courtroom." Gemini felt proud that, for once, she stood up to her daughter.

Sophia crossed her thin arms tightly across her chest. "I regretted keeping you at Brandon's law firm for as long as I did. You learned too much. We had several discussions about whether you should have retired sooner."

"I was the best secretary they had," Gemini replied, the hurt clear in her voice. "Besides, it wasn't up to you or Brandon. It was Brandon's father who hired me. He begged me to stay several times when I wanted to quit. You know, at one point I thought about going to beauty school."

"I didn't mean to offend you, Mother." Sophia's voice softened. "I was just saying that I thought maybe you could enjoy your life a little more. It seems like you should have been able to knit and do crossword puzzles, the things other women your age were doing. Instead, you spent your days working in a stressful office with no one there your age. It must have been terribly lonely."

There were new clients every day, and each of them had a different story to tell. She relished her time learning about different lives and those who lived them. "Someday, Sophia, I will sit down and we will discuss my life. In the meantime, I'm going to make myself some dinner. Is there anything else you wanted?"

"I'm proud of you, Mother. Doing what's right. I know that doesn't come easy for you. You like to do what you want to do, regardless of what's best for everyone else. Would you like to talk to your grandson for a minute?"

"Oh yes, please!" For the first time today, she felt joy.

Sophia picked up the phone and called the babysitter. "I'd like to speak with my son," she said curtly. In the next instant, she cooed into the phone. "Have you had your daily greens powder, my beautiful boy?" Soon after, she handed the phone to her mother.

"Gammie?" Taurus squealed. There was crying and then the phone dropped. A patient voice picked it up and told him to hang on tight. "Cookie, cookie, Gammie, Gammie, Gammie, cookie, cookie cookie."

Gemini handed the phone back to Sophia. "He's obsessing over a cookie."

"Bye for now, love. Mommy will be home soon." She put the phone back in her purse and took a long drink of water, setting down the empty glass with a thud. "I have a friend who makes spinach cookies for children and they're superb. Taurus is practically obsessed with them. I'll get you the recipe and when we visit you in Seattle, you can make him some."

"That sounds awful, frankly. But you know what's best for your child." Gemini noticed Sophia had dark circles under her eyes.

"I love you, Sophia. You don't have to worry about me. I'm doing just fine." She rubbed her daughter's thin arm.

"I love you too, Mother."

"Do you want to stay for dinner?

"No, thank you. I need to get home. I have a nighttime yoga class in two hours."

* * *

She'd only given herself seven days now to solve this mystery before Leo transferred to another hospital, where his care would be completely out of her control. He would be much safer. But there would be other people in danger and other loved ones. Someone wasn't afraid to kill, and it wasn't a leap to assume they'd be after the patients next. This was an important mission, perhaps one of the most important of her life.

"Were you able to speak with Carson any further? You know, did he come and tap you on the shoulder in the night? Or maybe give you something in a dream?" she asked Feather.

"It doesn't always work like that, Gemini. I wish it did. But these voices are people, too. And they have other things they are doing. Places to go and things to see."

"Keeping to a schedule. I'd hoped that ended in the afterlife. Is he haunting the person who killed him?"

"Oh Gemini, you are a kick. He could do that, you're right. I'll let you know if he returns. Shelley Natchez will come in for a shampoo later today. You wanted to talk to her again, right?"

"Cheese and biscuits. She's keeping her appointment after this big stir up at the hospital? What time is she coming?"

"She'll be here at one. I suggest you get here about thirty minutes early because sometimes she comes in and expects me to squeeze her in earlier. Just because she was shopping or whatever and decided this is the time for her appointment." Feather rolled her eyes. "Some of these women believe the universe goes by their clock."

"That gives me time to go see Leo and maybe interview another person on the staff at the hospital. Maybe today will be the big breakthrough for information. I'll be back at twelve-thirty!"

She walked into the hospital with purpose. Today she was wearing her Gemini Reed face as she got into the elevator, feeling determined. She hit the button for the 4th floor and smiled to herself, humming her favorite tune.

"Maureen, is that you? You got a hot date or something? I like the new hair color-silver is a good look for you."

Gemini looked up, shocked. It was Darrell, the person she interviewed right before Carson was found.

"I think you must have me mistaken for someone else. My name is Gemini Reed and my husband is a patient on the 4th floor." She looked away, hoping that Darrell would get out on the next floor. He didn't.

"No, we were talking about the staff Christmas party and my neighbor and all kinds of things. You wanted to talk again, remember? I told you I was working in two days, but I changed shifts because my me maw needs someone to take her to the doctor. And then there was a big commotion, and we found out Carson Moore was dead?"

"I'm sure I would remember you. I'm sorry I have been told many times that I must have a twin in this world. Nice to meet you, though. Have a good day." She pushed the button and got off on the second floor, breathing a sigh of relief that she could avoid Darrell. She would have to be more careful from now on. Maybe just take the stairs when she went to see Leo.

By the time she reached Leo's room, she was out of breath, but relieved that she hadn't run into anyone else she'd interviewed.

Denise smiled brightly when she entered the room. "Oh, Gemini. It's so good to see you today. We've missed connecting these last couple of days. Your double chocolate chip mint cookies were a hit. My boyfriend just raved about them."

"I was planning on baking again last night, but I had an unexpected visitor." She finally caught her breath and sat down beside Leo. "Did you hear about Carson Moore's death? Such a tragedy."

Denise shook her head. "It's all anyone can talk about. The police were up here again this morning, questioning everybody. They think there might be foul play. I can't understand why anyone would want to harm him. He didn't really have anything to do with the staff. He was more of a corporate guy."

Gemini thought back to the first time she'd met Carson Moore. He said he was "hands on" with all the patients.

"You didn't know him outside of work, then?"

"Not me, but my boyfriend. They used to golf together and really enjoyed each other's company. It devastated my boyfriend to learn of his passing. I kind of think Carson looked at Rodney as the son he never had. It was too bad when they had a falling out, but. You know how relationships can be. Hot one day cold the next."

Curious, Gemini thought. Gary said the same thing. Carson must've been a father figure to several men.

Denise wrote Leo's vitals and looked out the window. "It looks lovely out there today. I keep hoping they're going to build us an outdoor break area like they promised. Maybe once they add onto the hospital, that will be in the budget."

"Yes, I imagine that would be nice. Oh, and Denise? I was wondering if you knew his wife at all. Mrs. Moore?"

"I met her once. Mrs. Moore asked how well I knew her husband. Isn't that an odd thing to ask on your first meeting? I told her I didn't really, and she drifted off to talk to someone else. She moved away with their daughter last year."

"I'd like to meet her, just to understand Carson better."

Denise pulled the curtains the rest of the way open, so the sunlight hit Leo's face. "You never know what might stimulate him." She glanced at her patient. "I'll see you tomorrow, Gemini!"

Gemini waved goodbye, relieved to have some time alone with Leo. She sat beside his bed for an hour, whispering to him about her investigation. "I know you would find this fascinating, Leo. We would go pick out a new paint color and paint our bedroom. And as we did, I would tell you these stories and you would ask for more information that I didn't have. Then I would say, oh, what a good idea that is Leo. I'll ask about that next time." She kissed him gently on the forehead. "Tomorrow, my dear."

By the time she made it back to Feather Works, Shelley was sitting in the waiting area, her legs crossed. She was tapping her long, red manicured nails on her knee.

"I'm so sorry to hear about Mr. Moore. What a tragic thing." Gemini took off her jacket and hung it on the coat rack.

Shelley looked up at her with irritation. "You're late. I'm helping with the reception after the funeral and I have to meet with the event planner. Feather said we couldn't get started on my hair until you came here to wash it."

Feather gave Gemini the thumbs up sign.

"You are a little early, but I'm ready for you now." She motioned for Shelley to follow her to the washing station.

"Do you have any thoughts on Carson Moore's death? I don't mean to put it indelicately, but I was in the hospital when they found him and it didn't look like he died of natural causes." She began rubbing shampoo on Shelley's head.

"Oh, he was murdered. I'd bet money on it."

"Did he golf with your husband?"

"He golfed with several people. Are you asking if they killed him? They wouldn't dirty their hands with that. One of his many girlfriends murdered Carson Moore. You can ask around. One of them must've found out about all the others."

CHAPTER 28

"I don't know too much about these things. I'm going to be honest. I'm open to learning. In all of my experience in the law firm, there was never anyone who came in who had your abilities." Gemini took a sip of tea and sat down, holding the phone close to her head.

"It was so strange. Tug and I were getting ready for bed. Tug was finishing his fourth set of pushups and I was reading a book on starting a side business. I heard this sound, like a moan coming from the living room."

"Are you sure there wasn't a movie on television? It sounds like every horror movie Leo forced me to watch."

"That's what I thought too. Tug followed me and that's when it happened."

Silence.

"Feather? Are you still there? Are you hearing dead people again?"

"Yes, I'm here. It's still hard for me to process. We were standing in the hall and Tug said, 'Feath, I can see it! There's a man in a suit, standing by the bathroom! It wasn't just me, Gemini." Feather continued excitedly. "But Tug couldn't hear what he was saying. Zeb's study. In Zeb's study. He said that about four times and then he was gone."

"Cheese and biscuits. That's the strangest story I've ever heard." Gemini pushed the recliner back with her body, staring at the textured ceiling. "You're thinking this was Carson Moore?"

"It was Carson. I have to find out what he wanted me to see. Tug and I are going to break in to Doctor Wilson's home and find his study. It may be the key to his disappearance and Carson's death."

Gemini felt hurt she hadn't been invited. "I've been thinking of little else since Leo fell into the coma. I need to come with you. Maybe I'll find more clues while you're searching the study."

There was muffled discussion while Gemini took another sip of tea.

"Gemini? Tug is worried this isn't safe for you. Due to your…"

"My age? Not you too! My daughter- and son -in-law think I'm a doddering old fool. I thought you were different." Gemini hung up the phone and pulled herself upright. She would ask Howard how to go about breaking into an unoccupied home. It shouldn't be that hard.

She was washing dishes a few minutes later when her phone rang again. She wiped her hands on a towel and hesitated before answering. "Hello?"

"It's Feather again. I'm sorry. Tug and I have both had elderly grandparents who barely left their homes. We shouldn't have judged you like that. You've been right about everything all along and there's no way I'm doing this without you. You're kind of badass, Gemini Reed."

Gemini smiled and touched her chest while a warm feeling flowed through her body. "Me? I'm just a retired lady who's trying to make sure her husband doesn't end up like

Carson Moore, though he's not swallowing presently so, coffee wouldn't be an issue."

* * *

THE NEXT EVENING, they drove separately to the outskirts of Charming, where large homes sat precariously close to the edge of the seaside cliffs. They turned up an evergreen-lined lane and stopped in front of an elaborate wrought-iron gate.

Feather got out of her car and ran over to Gemini's car, opening the passenger side door. "I've got a tool to open the gate. The Open Sesame 140. Tug couldn't make it tonight. His mother is having a breakdown over something and she begged him to come. He sent me with all of his best products."

Gemini watch and waited while Feather attached a small box to the keypad for the gate. In a matter of seconds, the giant doors swung open. The two women drove inside and parked in a circular driveway in front of an all-glass, three story home. Both women got out of their cars and walked up to the front door.

"The Open Sesame 140 should work on this door too, since it opens using a keypad." Feather attached the machine to the door, and they waited. Nothing happened. She removed the box and examined it in her hand. "I hope it's not shorting out. Tug said this model is having some problems."

"May I?" Gemini asked. Feather handed her the box, and she examined it for a moment. "Back in my day, there was a very simple way to fix things." She found a battery compartment and pulled off the door. She took each battery out, wiped it on her shirt and put it back in. "Try it now," she insisted.

Feather re-attached the device and this time, a green light appeared over the door. "Code correct. You may enter," an electronic voice said. The two women stepped cautiously inside the cavernous home. "They pay this man far too much," Gemini commented, flipped her small pen light on. "How do we know where his den would be? We're going to have to leave a trail of breadcrumbs to get out, you know."

Feather shined her small light around them. "I've had several doctors as clients. They all talk about designing their homes. Always put the study next to the kitchen, they said, so the walk isn't too far."

Gemini's light reflected off shiny stainless steel appliances. "Kitchen at twelve o'clock."

They walked toward the kitchen and stopped when they got to a locked room beside it. Feather used her device one more time and opened the door. Inside, they found a book shelf with floor-to ceiling books on travel and a large desk.

Gemini immediately went to the drawers and attempted to pull them open. "Locked," she said disappointedly. "I don't think your box will help this time. These require a key."

Feather reached inside the pocket of her new leather coat. "Tug's got every tool imaginable." She bent down to the drawer. "Can you shine your light over here, please?" Gemini stood over the top of her, aiming her light at the drawer.

Feather placed a key inside the lock and began wiggling it around. "The Everydoor Key 220. It's a universal key that will fit in any lock," she explained. In a matter of seconds, the drawer was open.

"I wasted too many dollars on plastic containers when I should have been buying Tug's products!" Gemini marveled.

Feather continued until she'd opened every drawer. Each woman took a drawer and began pulling things out. "He liked his breath mints. Eight boxes so far."

"Do you know what I'm not finding?" Gemini moved slower, meticulously examining everything in the drawer. "Any indication that Doctor Wilson was planning a trip.

There's just a few hotel receipts from six months ago and a lawn mower repair bill."

"I've got it!" Feather held a folded paper up to her light. "This is it!"

Gemini dropped the receipts and stared with fascination. "How do you know? Is he giving you some kind of signal?"

"I can't explain it. I have a feeling. Maybe he's here, telling me and I don't hear him, but this is it."

"Code correct. You may enter." Loud footsteps moved across the floor. "Doctor Wilson? Just here for a security check. We got notification that your door was opened for the first time in two weeks and wanted to make sure you were okay."

The women looked at each other. "What do we do now?" Feather whispered.

Gemini thought for a moment. "Follow me."

"Hello? Gemini shined the light up and down until it focused on a middle-aged man in a security uniform. "Well, hello there. I'm Doris, Zeb's aunt. I'm checking on the place while he's on vacation. Brought my granddaughter with me to check on the cat since I'm not so spry anymore."

"Booger's fine, Maw Maw!" Feather added cheerfully.

"I didn't know Doctor Wilson had a cat. His dogs didn't seem like the cat-friendly type. Why don't you turn on the lights?" He moved over to the switch.

"Oh, no! I've got some problems with my eyes. They don't adjust well to light. Have to wear special glasses. That's why my granddaughter came with me."

The security guard shined his light on the two women. Gemini put her hands in front of her face and groaned. "Too much," she snapped.

"What's that you have in your hand there?" He moved his light to rest on Feather's hand.

"Umm"

"I'm making Zeb's favorite dinner when he returns: polenta, pork chops, and a fresh garden salad. Ending it with homemade brownies from his mother's recipe. He keeps it in a safe place. It's priceless to the Wilson family, you know."

"This doesn't sound right to me. I'm going to call the police and make sure we get everything straightened out."

"Uncle Zeb told me about your dad's brain surgery. He felt really bad."

The guard moved closer, shining his light directly into Feather's face. "I just mentioned that in passing once. He remembered?"

She put her hands up, trying to block the glare. "He said he talked to the board president about doing the surgery free of charge, but that guy was a big jerk and said no."

Gemini reached over and squeezed Feather's hand.

"I don't think we need to call the police. I'm confident you ladies are related to Doctor Wilson. He tried to help us with the surgery. Please thank him for me. You ladies have a nice evening."

When he was gone, they both let out a sigh of relief.

"Gemini, let's get out of here before something else happens. Meet me at the shop!"

The two women drove hurriedly into town. When they arrived at the salon, they looked at each other and laughed.

"Not exactly a normal night out for me!" Feather exclaimed.

"How did you know about his father's surgery? Are you hearing from Doctor Wilson now? Do you know he's dead?"

"It was Carson Moore. He told me where to find this note," she pulled the now-wrinkled letter from her pocket, "and gave me the story about the brain surgery. He told Doctor Wilson no when he wanted to donate his time for the surgery. One of many arguments they had."

"I can't wait anymore. Open the note!" Gemini insisted.

Carson, I don't want to threaten you, but that's where we are now, aren't we? You're in just as deep as I am, deeper, in fact. I've told you for months I wanted out. I won't be back. If you come looking for me, I'll go to the police and tell them everything. You dug your own grave, pal.

Zeb.

CHAPTER 29

Her mind was whirring. Besides this new piece of information, there were only a few days until they carted Leo off to Seattle. How was it going to work if she hadn't found out what happened to Dr. Wilson and Carson Moore, and she had to leave to be with him?

Sophia never thought about how this would make everyone else feel. Leo would shake his head and let Gemini do the talking, but later, as they lay in bed, he would cry as he told her how he had failed their only child.

"Gemini? You look so interesting! Sorry, that sounded rude, but I wasn't expecting to see you this way."

She hadn't realized that someone else had gotten on the elevator. Someone who knew her as Gemini Reed. "What floor are we on?" For a moment, Gemini wondered if she'd been so deep in thought she went to Leo's floor without thinking.

"The third. I'm picking up an extra shift this week." Denise squinted as she viewed the nametag proclaiming her friend as "Maureen."

"Oh boy, Gemini. What is going on?" The elevator doors opened and Denise yanked Gemini into an empty room and closed the door. "This isn't good. I don't know what to say to you right now."

"Well, you see," Gemini thought very hard. "Well, you see," she began again. "There is a retirement magazine put out by the Fassetville Times every Sunday. They asked me to write an in-depth article about Leo's journey with Atomycin and the drug trial. That's what I'm doing, I'm writing an article." She smiled with satisfaction.

Denise looked at her with skepticism. "It seems like you went to great lengths to do this. You could have just asked me, and I would have given you all the information you needed. And where on earth did you get this nametag?"

"Why do you need an extra shift? Are you and the boyfriend having money troubles?" Gemini spurted, trying to divert the attention from her problems.

"I told you Rodney has expensive tastes." Denise fidgeted uncomfortably. "We're saving up for the move, and that's hard to do when he buys so many clothes. He promised me he'd stop buying them."

"You deserve someone who values your company over a new suit, dear."

Denise sighed and held out her hand. "I need to collect those credentials from you, Gemini. I will not ask how you came to have them in your possession. Let's just say it could end badly for both of us. I'm also a little concerned about your mental health. I know it's been hard having your husband in this condition, but—"

"No! I'm just about done. The article is in the rough draft stage. I promise I won't use them again!" she pleaded. Howard would most likely get in trouble if anyone found out. "I'll have a badge burning with you front and center next week. I promise!" Gemini crossed her chest and gazed at Denise with her most mournful expression. "You're right. I needed a diversion from Leo's illness. It's been fun to be someone else. I haven't harmed anyone."

Denise put her hands on either side of her forehead and walked around in a circle. "Oh, Gemini. You are a unique person. If my own life weren't so complicated, I would push this." She grabbed the door handle. "I can't believe I'm letting this go, but I'm short on options. Next week is the end of this. I don't want to see Maureen in these halls again." She walked out without saying another word.

Gemini practically ran home. Howard Beachmont would need to know about this immediately.

He was outside, picking up his newspaper, when she arrived. "Afternoon, Mrs. Reed."

"You're getting a late start today. Howard," she commented while trying to catch her breath.

"I wasn't feeling so well. The beauty of retirement is deciding to stay in bed all day when I please. How are things going with your investigation? Are you finding everything you need?"

"I found a new piece of information." She pushed her tongue in her cheek, trying not to sound overly excited.

"Do you want to come inside?" he asked, holding the door open.

They walked into his living room and sat down. Today, the rich smell of cinnamon permeated the air.

"What are you making?" she asked, sniffing the air.

"Applesauce. It's good for what ails you. "Can I get you an iced tea infused with lavender from my garden?"

"Yes, that would be lovely." It sounded like a strange drink, but above all, Gemini Reed tried to be polite.

Howard returned carrying two glasses of tea brimming

with ice cubes. "Might be an acquired taste. Just warning you," he cautioned. "Tell me what's got you in such a twist?"

She took a small drink and found the floral taste wasn't bitter as she'd assumed, but lightly sweet and satisfying to her tastebuds.

"When I worked for my son-in-law at the law firm, I tailed lots of shady suspects. Not once did I worry I would be discovered. It was naïve, really."

"Was your cover blown?"

She took another sip and nodded. "Leo's nurse found me today. That was after an orderly figured out I didn't work in the mailroom. I'm afraid Maureen is dead."

"That's a pity." Howard put his fingertips together. "We always need more than one plan in case the first one fails. What is your backup?"

"Nothing yet. But I found this." She reached in her pocket and pulled out the note, handing it to him with a hint of pride. "It was in Doctor Wilson's study."

Howard pulled his reading glasses out of his pocket and read the note quickly. He turned it over multiple times, looking at the back and front and back again. "That's an interesting development. Could take you in several directions. I'd suggest looking into Carson Moore's personal life. If it were me."

She cocked her head to the side. "You've never explained to me why you are so well versed in investigative details. What happened when you were working at the hospital?"

Howard took in a deep breath and set the paper on his lap. "We were lured here two decades ago. My wife had a good job with the state of Louisiana, but they promised me twice my current salary. We couldn't say no."

"What kind of job? Are you a doctor?"

"I was the hospital president. It started out as a dream job

-I had excellent support staff and the hospital was making more money than it ever had."

"What changed?" Gemini tried to look around the room without moving her head. There was definitely no sign of a woman's influence.

"One day, I picked up a file that wasn't meant for my eyes. My secretary grabbed it out of my hands and said it wasn't anything important. When she went home that day, I searched her computer and discovered there were two sets of books–the reports I was seeing at the board meetings proclaiming everything was rosy, and the actual books which showed an enormous loss. The insurance companies were being overbilled, and it wasn't going to the hospital."

Gemini leaned forward, putting her elbow on her knee, resting her chin in her hand. "How did they react when you told them you knew?"

"They threatened to blackmail me. It went way deeper than I realized. They told me the reports I'd been signing after every meeting weren't the ones I'd seen. I'd been duped, and I was complicit in their scam. On top of that, my wife had been having an affair with a doctor here and they threatened to expose her if I said anything." Howard leaned back in his chair and put his hands behind his head. "It wouldn't have mattered. The police chief was in on it, too. They had me."

"Oh, Howard. That's all terrible. Did you leave your wife after that? I don't mean to be nosy." She took another sip, hoping he explained.

"My wife was a serial cheater. Another revelation. After I confronted her about this affair, she immediately broke it off and took up with someone else. They moved away as soon as the divorce was final."

Gemini thought for a moment. "What happened to the staff member?"

"He quit his job in radiology. You can't keep an opportunist down for long, though. They eventually elected him to the hospital board."

Gemini's eyes narrowed. "Is he still working at the hospital?"

"He was. Until his untimely death last week. Carson Moore got exactly what he deserved."

CHAPTER 30

Feather plopped down on the old, blue-velvet couch and tried to ignore the poof of dust that entered the air.

"Can I get you a drink? Maybe something with alcohol?" Wilma Quimby sat down uncomfortably close to Feather, patting her leg.

"I do better with a clear head, but thank you." Feather inched away.

Wilma pushed her short, round body closer to Feather. "I'm excited about this. I have so much to tell Pierson. You're so lucky to have this gift."

Feather scooted away again. "I'm glad you found me on the bulletin board at the grocery store. I wasn't sure anyone would see it."

"I scour the board every day. There are so many treasures right there beside the chewing gum and breath mints. I found all the artwork you see around you from artists who posted on that board."

Feather glanced around the room, where an eclectic mix of art covered the walls. An orange man balancing on his head hung beside a lovely landscape with green rolling hills. "I've never looked there, but I'm glad you did."

"I met my second husband by signing up for piano lessons," Wilma continued. "His advertisement was on that same board where I found you. It was meant to be." Wilma scooted still closer to Feather.

"I'll clear my head and we can begin." She paused. "It really works better if I have some space. I'll be able to hear Pierson much clearer."

"Because I'm gifted? My energy will impede yours? I thought so." Wilma stood up and moved to a nearby silver recliner. "I've been told I have spiritual energy surrounding me, too. They just haven't spoken to me yet-waiting for the right time, I suppose. You'll let Pierson know I'm ready to listen? He can be stubborn."

Feather nodded and closed her eyes. She breathed slowly in and out. "I can feel a presence here. Very strong."

"Yes, he was a bruiser. Everyone always said he had an unusually muscular body."

Why aren't you listening to me? This is important, Feather. You need to find my killer. You have all the tools. Use them!

"What's he saying? Does he miss me? We cuddled every morning before breakfast." Wilma reached forward and poked Feather on the leg.

"He's still thinking about just the right thing–"

I'll lead you to the evidence if you'll let me. Please, Feather! More people will die if we don't put a stop to this!

"PIERSON? I feel your presence! Come to me, baby!" Wilma stood up and raised her hands to the ceiling. "Inhabit me!"

"I'm hearing barking." Feather said softly. She opened her eyes abruptly. "Wait - was Pierson a dog? A big dog?"

"He's here! Woof! Woof!" Wilma dropped to the ground

and began walking on all four limbs. She moved over to Feather's feet and sniffed them before licking her leg.

"Stop that!" Feather pushed her away. "He's glad to be rid of you! Pierson hated that cheap dog food and the itchy spiked collar you made him wear!" She stood, embarrassed by her outburst. "I'm sorry. I shouldn't have said that. I should go."

Wilma jumped up and grabbed her arm. "No! Wait! He has to tell me what my third husband whispered in his ear every night! Pierson! Talk to Mommy!"

Feather was fairly certain she would not get paid today. She shook Wilma off and made a beeline for the front door. "Pierson isn't ready for a deep conversation. He suggests you buy a goldfish and see if you can keep it alive."

"A goldfish? Are they spiritual animals, too?"

She had to get out of there now, removing that annoying dog and Angie Bard from her mind.. Feather leapt from the porch and ran for her car. She got in and slammed the door, turning on her favorite group, Cat Banter.

She cranked the sound up so loud the doors shook and clutched the steering wheel, bopping her head with the beat. When the song was over, she looked up and realized Wilma was watching from the window.

Smoke and tire marks announced her exit as she sped off. By the time she got home, her head was clear. She'd been learning lately that she could decide when to let them in. "Tug? I'm back!" She threw the keys in the bowl and flopped down on her couch. She was grateful her boyfriend liked to keep things dust-free.

"How'd it go?" Tug appeared from the bedroom wearing his tight workout clothes. "I was just getting ready to leave. Do you want to join me at the gym?" He sat down beside her and gave her a quick peck on the cheek. "The gym was kind of like our first date. We could make it romantic in a sweaty, impersonal sort of way."

Feather grinned. "I would love to, another time. I'm beat."

"The reading didn't go well?" Tug's beautiful brow furrowed with concern. "What happened?"

"This woman is off her rocker, that's what happened." She looked at her black combat boots. "And one more thing."

Tug rubbed her thigh. "You can tell me anything."

"There's someone who won't leave me alone. I've been ignoring her as much as I can, but she's interfering with my readings now."

"Who is it?"

"My old boss, Angie. You remember that she came to me after she died and told me she'd given me all the tools I needed to run the shop?"

"And you've done an outstanding job, Feath. Business has tripled." Tug rubbed the back of her neck.

"Thank you, babe." She smiled. "Every time I open myself up to the dead, she's right there with her message. She says she was murdered."

Tug sat up straight. "How long has this been going on? What does she want you to do about it?"

"She wants me to find the person and bring them to justice. At first, I thought it was Gemini who needed her message, but now I'm sure she's talking to me. I'm scared, Tug."

CHAPTER 31

"Olive? What can you tell me about Carson Moore's personal life? Did you know his friends? What he did on the weekends?" Gemini took extra care to massage her scalp slowly. She wanted to keep her talking as long as she could. Although, with Olive, that was usually a simple task.

"That feels just divine. Thank you so much. Gemini. You are truly a gem. Ha! I made a joke, and I wasn't even trying! I can't wait for the two of us to do some sleuthing together. How did my Christmas knitting work out? Did it make for a good cover? Gemini and Olive are going to make a great team."

She didn't want to explain to Olive that she and Feather had already begun working together. "What do you know about Carson Moore's personal life?"

"He came here with his wife to work in radiology, If I remember correctly. They had a child-a daughter. After some time, the wife was just gone. There were whispers, you know how the hospital is, rumors of cheating with this person or that, but no one knew for sure what happened. I asked my grandson, and he was more irritated with me than usual. 'Don't involve yourself in Carson Moore's life, Grandma. You stay far away from him.'" Olive huffed. "Rodney thinks I'm an old fool."

Gemini thought for a moment. "That's strange. A couple of people have told me how he acted as a father figure to them. It's hard to think of him as a cheating spouse, a father, and a compassionate, fatherly man. They don't go together."

"I'm happy to ask questions. I have bridge next week. Nothing gets by those women. You should come with me sometime. We could make a day of it."

Gemini wasn't the bridge type. "Yes, I would certainly appreciate that. I'm just trying to figure out what happened to him. There is something odd going on."

"That was such a tragedy. Suicide is what they're calling it. Seems such an odd way to go. For a man always concerned about the way things looked, suicide by coffee makes little sense. There will be a funeral tomorrow afternoon. Public, of course. That way, everybody can come and say their goodbyes. Maybe you can catch up with his wife there? I'd bet she'd come to town to say one last goodbye."

"I didn't even think about that. I'll have to attend the funeral and introduce myself."

"Everyone will want to see how she looks, if she's genuinely upset about his death, or just putting on a show. It was a scandal when she left town, taking the child so abruptly. In small towns, this is the type of drama we live for." Olive smiled.

Gemini felt instant concern for Mrs. Moore. The last thing she needed was the scrutiny of Charming. "This is about Leo. His doctor is gone and now the hospital board president is dead. Where there's smoke, there's fire, Olive," she said defiantly. "Besides, on my frequent visits, Carson was always friendly." She gulped. She'd met him once, and she thought he was dismissive. "I'm sure his wife will be treated respectfully."

She rinsed Olive's head and blotted it with a towel. "What has your grandson said about Carson's death? It sounds like he didn't like him much."

"My grandson doesn't seem to know a thing; in fact, he pretends like it never happened. To be honest with you, I find that a little odd. He was such a tender thing growing up. His stepfather was very mean to him. Always calling him names and laughing when he cried. Every little thing set him off. We were all glad when that stepfather left. I often ask myself, Olive? What's worse? The poor, poor boy having a daddy that doesn't know how to care for him or having no daddy at all? I still don't know the answer."

Gemini glanced over at Feather, who motioned for Gemini to send over her next client. "I think Feather is ready for you."

When Feather was between appointments, Gemini asked to meet outside. She brought the plastic container of peanut butter oatmeal cookies with her she'd made the night before.

"Try one. They are my great-aunt Virgo's recipe." She offered the container to Feather, who took one cautiously.

"Gemini, you've been here now, a month, is it? And every time you bake, there's something on your mind. What is it today? Is it the letter? We haven't had any time to discuss what Zeb was talking about." She took a small bite of the cookie to satisfy Gemini and nodded enthusiastically. "Very good."

"It's my daughter, Sophia, and her husband, Brandon. They've been trying to micromanage Leo's case ever since he was diagnosed. And now, they want to move him up to Seattle soon. I told them I would fight them in court, but then I realized I didn't have the means to do that. I didn't want to use up all of my retirement funds fighting a battle that I would lose in the end, anyway. Brandon and his law firm have endless resources. I know that from my experience working with them."

Feather's face fell. "Oh, Gemini! I'm so sorry. That's just cruel!" She took another small bite of the cookie. "What are you going to do?"

"I can't really fight the two of them, but I also can't leave this battle. There is something wrong at that hospital and I'm not going away until I figure out what it is. Gemini Reed isn't a quitter and there are many people besides Leo who need my help." Her voice shook with emotion. "I need to get to the bottom of Doctor Wilson's disappearance and now-Carson Moore's strange death. I want to know if the two are connected."

"Are you going to stay? Even when your husband is transferred to Seattle? That's dedication, Gemini."

She nodded. "Just briefly. I'm sure Sophia will have restrictions placed on Leo, as far as I'm concerned. She enjoys making the rules. Leo was always behind me one-hundred percent, no matter what I was doing, so I know that's what he would want. He'll open his eyes one day in Seattle and I'll tell him everything that was happening here. If I told him I left right in the middle of an investigation, he would never speak to me again." She'd made it sound logical, but Sophia wouldn't see it that way.

"That's a totally different relationship than anyone I know," Feather said. "You are quite remarkable, Gemini Reed!"

Gemini smiled. "Thank you, dear. I think I'm pretty remarkable too. But so are you. And that's why I wanted you to come out here. I need to ask for a favor."

"What is it?"

"The funeral for Carson Moore is tomorrow afternoon. I need you to come with me so you can tell me if there are any entities there, and if they're giving you any messages. While you're doing that, I'm going to see if I can't find his wife or someone in his family who can give me more information about his history."

Feather's throat tightened. "I'm not much for funerals. My great aunt died when I was in the 5th grade." Feather looked up at the sky, where geese were flying by in a V shape. "We went out to the cemetery for the graveside service and it was very long. I had an uncle who pretended to be a minister. He wasn't really, he just liked to preach whenever he had an audience. And that day there were about 100 people there, so he was really in his element. He went on and on and on. I had to go to the bathroom and finally I couldn't take it."

"Terrible! What happened?"

"Desperate times call for desperate measures. I ran off to the furthest edge of the cemetery and went behind a grave. It was either that or wet my pants. I've felt terrible guilt ever since."

"You did what you had to," Gemini offered supportively. I'm sure everyone understood."

Feather chuckled. "Oh no, that's not the entire story. There were a couple of cousins who followed me. While I was, you know, in the act, they snuck up from behind and caught me. They laughed at me, in my vulnerable condition, and ran back to the family. They were so pleased with themselves, announcing what I'd done. I'd been kind of the family big shot before that day. All the adults were horrified, including my parents. 'That weird cousin Feather relieved herself on the tombstone of the town founder,'" she imitated their squeaky voices. "The oldest tombstone in the cemetery, as it turned out."

Gemini gasped. "Cheese and biscuits! That's rough! Your aversion to funerals makes sense now. What a horrible memory. Tell you what - let's make this a new start. We'll make sure that you go to the restroom before we leave, and if you have to go again while we're there, you just give me a signal, Let's just say you touch your nose three times and I'll know it's time to leave. I won't ask questions." Gemini stuck her free hand out to shake.

Feather hesitated only for a moment. "You have a deal," she said, offering her cookie-free hand. "I'm not big on cookies, but these are wonderful!"

Grand! I'll pick you up at one o'clock tomorrow afternoon?"

"Just keep in mind, I can't summon people. They have to come to me. If no one floating around feels conversational, I can't force them. That's just the way it is."

"I understand." Gemini opened the door to the salon. "I just appreciate your coming with me."

"And also," Feather continued as they walked inside, "because it is dead people central, maybe everyone wants to send some kind of message to their loved ones. They might look at me as the postwoman who will deliver their mail and things could get complicated."

Gemini nodded. "No expectations. I promise."

CHAPTER 32

Gemini wore the black dress Leo called "Shabam in Mourning." The bodice was low cut and tight, hugging her figure. Her sleeves were made of a see-through material, the only loose component. It was a little too tight for her taste and she felt exposed, but it was all she had on short notice.

She'd bought it two years ago, when Leo's mother passed away. It was a middle finger to the woman who would often say, "Gemini is a name hippies give a child hoping she will wave down men on street corners. Utterly disgraceful." She was 104, and everyone figured, or at least hoped, she would be dead long before then. Leo was such a nice man, but his mother was a bitter, angry woman who complained about everything. Even Sophia, who was the darling of the family, wasn't immune to her wrath.

Feather wore her new leather jacket over a rainbow-colored blouse with black pants and combat boots. She wasn't about to dress as a funeral goer when she didn't know this man. It seemed disingenuous. She dyed the ends of her hair brown. That was as appropriately subdued as Feather Jones was going to get.

When they arrived, they both recognized faces from the hospital–doctors, nurses and board members. Feather styled their hair, and Gemini had grown familiar with many of them during her trips to the hospital, both as herself and her alter-ego. She hoped the people who knew Maureen wouldn't make the connection to Gemini. Luckily, she wore a small hat with a stylish black net veil that partially covered her face. She noticed Denise with a well-dressed man, who she assumed was Denise's boyfriend. Denise kept touching him as though she needed reassurance.

Feather grabbed Gemini's arm as they approached the group. "There are so many voices out here, Gemini. I don't know if I'm going to be able to tell which one is Carson Moore."

"Can you ask them nicely? Is politeness in the afterworld a thing? Are they nice? Are they rude?"

"They are the same people they were in life. Some are nice, some are rude." Feather continued moving, nodding her head up and down or back and forth, depending on the message she was receiving. They found a seat in the very last row of folding chairs.

"I can't say anything right now because it wouldn't be appropriate at a funeral. Do you get that?" Feather whispered to herself.

Gemini put her finger to her lips, reminding Feather the mourners wouldn't understand her conversation.

They sat in silence, listening as different hospital board members praised Carson Moore's dedication to the hospital.

When she could stand it no longer, Gemini leaned over and whispered in Feather's ear. "Who is it? Who do they want to talk to?"

"Someone named Mavis. She's hid a secret from her

husband. Something to do with her fascination with fetish movies."

"Where is he?" Gemini asked.

Feather pointed discreetly to the section of the mourners facing them. A bald, elderly gentleman wearing a suit far too small for his large girth stared blankly at the casket.

"He doesn't look like a person who would take that news well."

A hospital board member, the fourth since the women had arrived, got up and began giving his recollection of Carson Moore. "I remember the first day he approached me about being on the hospital softball team. I was not a softball player, but I offered to watch from the stands or keep the stats. He insisted we were all amateurs, and working together was what was important. Well, he was right. I haven't quit playing softball since, and I was on the league-winning team two years in a row. Go Slushy Slammers!"

There was a smattering of laughter from the crowd.

"Now I'll hand the microphone to Carson's widow." He gestured to an attractive woman in her forties wearing large, dark glasses and a black floppy hat. She moved to the microphone with hesitation. She wiped her eyes and paused, examining every person in attendance.

The crowd became a little uncomfortable as she stood there, not saying anything. The previous speaker went back up and whispered in her ear and she grabbed his arm and shook her head 'no.'

When she composed herself, she put the microphone to her lips. "I'm sorry. I didn't leave this town on the best terms. I've been asked to say a few words about Carson. As many of you know, we were married for fifteen years. Most of them were lovely. It was only within the last nine months that we had disagreements we couldn't get past. That doesn't mean that we didn't love each other, or that we didn't both love our child." She sniffed and took in a deep breath, letting it out slowly. "I never imagined this was how it would end for Carson. He wasn't that kind of person. He was a good father, a good man and–" she broke down, doubling over as she sobbed. The folding chairs squeaked as several funeral goers moved around uneasily.

"He promised he'd change his ways. 'Just a few more months and I'll meet you girls in the Midwest. I'm almost done here, darling,' that's what he told me more than once. I believed him. What choice did I have? He was my first love." She broke down into deep, throaty sobs. The hospital employee who spoke previously came up to the mic and gently escorted her away.

Gemini leaned over to Feather and whispered in her ear. "That was a strange eulogy, don't you think?"

"Very," Feather agreed.

"And now, I would like to have the board vice president come up and say a word or two. Harry?" He gestured to a short man in the front row. Gemini had never seen him before, despite all of her time spent in the hospital. He looked like he was a Mafia boss. Very stout and sure of himself. She could see him in a white hat and a pinstriped suit with a cigar hanging out of his mouth.

"As many of you know, we all golf together every Thursday. This last week was very hard for all of us. We missed our golfing buddy. Carson was a fixture at the hospital and things won't be the same without him. I doubt we can find a replacement on the board that is as dedicated as he was."

Gemini saw out of the corner of her eye that Carson's widow was walking away. She touched Feather's arm and pointed. "I'm going to see if I can talk to her," she whispered. She dug in her purse and pulled out her car keys, handing them to Feather. "In case you need to know."

Feather shook her head in disapproval, taking the keys.

Gemini ran as quickly as her restrictive dress and unusually high heels allowed.

By the time she'd conquered the uneven ground and made it to the waiting car, she was out of breath. "Mrs. Moore? I'm so sorry for your loss. I just knew your husband briefly, but he seemed like a lovely man." Gemini touched Mrs. Moore's arm lightly, just as she was getting into the backseat of a sable-colored limousine.

The woman wiped her nose. "Thank you," she said breathlessly. "Are you part of the hospital staff? You don't look familiar to me."

"In a way." Gemini put her hand on her chest, trying to slow the rapid pace of her heart. "This may be inappropriate right now, but I don't believe your husband killed himself. He was doing just fine. I know you can never tell what a person is feeling inside, but it's hard for me to imagine him ending his life, especially in that manner."

Carson's widow stared at Gemini. "Do you work for the police or something? They've been less than helpful, and I would be pleasantly surprised if you said yes."

"No, I don't. I don't want to say more right now. Can I take you out for coffee before you leave? We could discuss this in more detail. I mean, if you're feeling up to it. I know you've had an enormous shock and you need to deal with your grief."

"I'd like that very much. I'd like to get out of here and do that right now, as a matter of fact. I'm glad I left my daughter with her grandparents, but being alone today is hard. All of this funeral business is too much for me. I could use the friendship of a kind woman."

Her words caught Gemini off-guard. "There's a place not far away, within walking distance, actually."

"Forty Cups! I used to go there after I dropped my daughter at school." She looked out the opposite window and then turned her head back to Gemini. "I'm supposed to go to a gathering at one of the other board member's homes, but honestly, I'd rather have all of my teeth pulled at once."

Gemini smiled and stuck out her hand. "Gemini Reed. Happy to offer friendship without dental tools involved."

"My name is Janine, by the way. Do you want to ride with me?"

"Sure!" Gemini walked around the other side of the car, relieved to get off her feet. As soon as she sat down, she texted Feather and told her she would meet up with her later. The coffee shop was close enough. It was only a matter of minutes before they were sitting in front of it. The women got out of the car and went inside the diner-themed establishment. They both instinctively walked to the back of the room and sat in a cherry-red, vinyl-covered booth.

After they'd ordered, Gemini ran through the list of questions in her head. "May I ask where you are living now, Janine?"

Janine removed her enormous hat and set it next to her. Her wavy, brunette hair framed her beautiful face dramatically, in a way that reminded Gemini of glamorous old Hollywood stars.

"Denver. I moved in with relatives when things went south with Carson. This is a nice place, but the hospital is too full of gossip. I couldn't go anywhere without people staring and whispering . Ironically, everyone here has a secret or two they wouldn't want known publicly."

"What do you mean by that? Have people told you their secrets?" Gemini asked innocently.

Janine nodded and smiled. "You must not have lived here long, if you haven't figured that out yet."

"I moved here recently. My husband is ill in the hospital, so I spend my days helping at a hair salon and meeting new people."

"That's so kind. Are you a stylist?"

"A stylist wannabe. I wanted to go to beauty school, but Leo needed me to help start the hardware store, so I put that on hold. Years passed, I had a baby and found a job at a law firm. Our lives sometimes take us down different paths than we envision."

Janine clasped her hands together in front of her. "I agree with you. I never thought I'd be a widow, or even a single parent."

"It's a terrible shock, I'd imagine."

"Black coffee?" The server in a pink uniform stood in front of their table.

"I had that." Gemini raised a finger in the air and nodded.

"Eggy Sando with chive cream cheese and latte?"

"Mine, please." Janine responded.

The server set Janine's order down and walked away.

Janine took big bites of her sandwich like she hadn't eaten in days. When she wiped her face on a napkin, she glanced up at Gemini. "Oh, sorry. These used to be my favorite. I got lost in memories there for a minute."

She wiped one more time and crumpled her napkin into a ball. "You were asking about Carson. It was always the same with him. He'd tell me he was working on something hush-hush that would pay for our daughter to attend any college she wanted. His 'wow-factor side gig' he'd call them. Every time he found another side gig, he spent more time away from us, doing things in secret. I told him I didn't like it and that I wanted him to quit. That's where the conversation always ended. It was the same thing with our daughter. 'I'm going to make so much money for you, little girl.' Never asking about dance lessons or her best friend. She didn't want to come today, and I wasn't about to force her. She's seven and she already has such a negative opinion of her father."

Gemini thought about Sophia at seven. They had so much hope for her future. If someone would have offered to fund an expensive education for her, Gemini would have spent time in consideration before turning it down. "What kind of thrill-seeking had he done in the past?"

"One time, he convinced another doctor to accompany him on a snorkeling trip to the Cayman Islands. This other doctor was deathly afraid of water, but agreed to go. Carson had no trouble convincing people to do whatever harebrained scheme he cooked up. I got a phone call in the middle of the night. It was Carson, in tears, because his friend had disappeared. He pushed him off the boat as a joke and he never came up."

It didn't sound like any joke Gemini had heard. "That's terrible! What happened to the other doctor?"

"He taught Carson a lesson of his own. He set it up ahead of time with another boat to pick him up. Zeb and Carson never fully trusted each other after that. The Circle T resort banned them both for life."

Gemini mulled this over. "I certainly understand why it's hard for you today. Your emotions have to be all over the place."

"It's the same story that everyone tells when they get involved in things they shouldn't. Money. Greed. He wanted those things more than he wanted us. I decided I didn't. I wanted a normal family life. Not to mention the fact that he was having an affair. That word should be affairs, plural. He didn't let a little thing like marriage slow down his social life." Janine rolled her eyes.

The hairs on Gemini's arms rose. "With someone from the hospital?"

Janine put the last bite of her sandwich in her mouth and closed her eyes. "Mm. I will have to get one more of these before I leave town. The only good thing about this place."

She opened her eyes and licked her fingers. "I'm sorry. You're probably loving this little seaside hamlet. Right next to the ocean."

"You're entitled to your opinion, too. I'm so sorry about the affair with Mrs. Beachmont."

"Not that one. It was the lady who owned the hair salon. Angie something. She had a thing for doctors. She and Doctor Wilson had their moments, too. I expect that was another thing that tore the two men apart. They were both sharing a bed with the same woman."

The server filled their mugs and stared hard at Janine. "You look familiar. Do I recognize you from somewhere?"

Janine shook her head. "No, I don't think so."

The server walked away and Janine leaned forward. "She used to tell me stories about everyone at the hospital. I'm not in the mood today."

Gemini leaned forward, too. "Did you know that Doctor Wilson is missing?"

"No, I didn't. It doesn't surprise me. He and Carson had lots of late night meetings. I think whatever was going on involved both of them. Maybe even that Angie person. Deals made after midnight are always sinister."

"Do you think this has something to do with Atomycin?"

Janine's mouth dropped open. "How do you know about that?"

"My husband is a part of the study. That's why I'm so concerned." She took a deep breath and let it out slowly. "A friend gave me something that might interest you." She didn't know Janine well enough to explain that she'd let herself into Doctor Wilson's home. "It is a note, written threateningly, saying Doctor Wilson would make his findings public if he wasn't allowed to get out."

Janine leaned back and crossed her arms. "Well, well, well. The boys had a little spat, did they? Of the two, I think Zeb had more of a conscience, no matter what I said at the funeral today. I could see him deciding he wanted out if they were altering the study. The boys joked about changing the results of their first study in order to increase their payout. What I can't understand is why Carson would get rid of him. They were friends at some point. Do you have any other ideas of people who might be involved?"

"I wish I did, Janine. Everyone has their own story about his death at the hospital, but I've yet to find proof any of them are true. No one thinks he killed himself."

Janine put a manicured finger in the air. "There was one person. A maintenance man who thought the world of Carson. He came over and mowed our lawn several times. He was always asking for more work. Poor guy, Carson, paid him a few dollars for each back-breaking chore, but he always received it with a smile. I doubt he'd involve himself in anything shady. Carson was like a father figure to him."

Janine looked at her watch. "They'll be coming for me any time now. And I've already told you more than I should. What have you told the police about all of this?"

"The police aren't interested in the rantings of an old woman." Gemini remembered her experience with the detective. "They think I'm crazy, I guess."

"Sometimes it's better if people underestimate you. Gives you some breathing room. Carson never thought I'd leave him because I'd always put up with his shenanigans, no matter how embarrassing. He'd convinced me I wasn't able to live on my own. My daughter and I left in the middle of the night, when he and Zeb were having a late meeting. He never saw it coming."

The bell on the door of the cafe jingled. The last board member who had been speaking at the funeral walked in and looked around. Janine waved at him until he saw the two women in the back. He walked with purpose to where they sat and put his hands on his hips. "There you are! You left the funeral without a word and I was concerned!" His eyes traveled to Gemini, and he looked at her questioningly. "Do I know you?"

"I'm an acquaintance of Janine's. New, actually. We're just having some coffee and discussing life."

He glanced at them both and frowned. "It's not a good time for that. You need to come with me and see to the guests."

Janine's mouth tightened. "I don't want to. I don't think my husband would have expected me to entertain all of his golfing buddies and ex-girlfriends. That's too much, even for him."

"We have a very large reception with all the hospital staff. I'm sure your presence would bring them comfort. You did promise, Janine."

"You mean it will provide optics, Harry. It has very little to do with comfort." She sighed. "I suppose you're right, though. I agreed to this ridiculous show of unity." She pulled out her purse.

"Oh no, Janine. I'm going to take care of this. I appreciate you sitting with me and visiting for a few minutes. I wish you all the best with your daughter and everything in the future. Maybe you'll find some new direction."

Janine smiled and took her hand. "Thank you so much. Gemini. I needed a good friend today. I hope you find what you're looking for."

CHAPTER 33

Feather arrived minutes after Janine's departure. She drove over the curb, almost crushing Gemini's fancy black high-heeled feet.

"I have to tell you something!" both women said in unison as Gemini sat in the passenger seat. They laughed together.

"You go first," Gemini offered. "Mine will take some time to explain."

Feather pulled the car into a diagonal parking space and turned off the car. "It's probably better I don't drive and talk."

"Good idea, hon. My Sophia once wrecked her fancy car while she was lecturing her nanny about feeding Taurus yellow cheese. Now she pulls over to yell."

Feather put the car in park and unhooked her seatbelt, turning to look at Gemini. "I had premonitions about today. I was up most of the night and even tried some of Tug's Doctor Whipley Sleep Powder. Nothing helped."

"You did? You never mentioned a thing earlier. Poor dear!"

"I suppose I should have told you everything, but I

worried you wouldn't agree to go to the funeral if I mentioned it."

"All right, now you need to spill."

"Well, last night I was getting ready for bed. Tug finished his evening meditation and was in the middle of his twelve-minute headstand. I went to get myself a glass of water, like I always do before bed. While I was in the kitchen, turning the water on, that's when it happened." Feather gripped the steering wheel. "I saw an apparition. You know, normally they aren't visible. They just speak to me and I sense that there is a presence, but this is the second time I've witnessed something like this in a week. I don't like it."

"What did they look like? Handsome, short, tall, funny looking?"

"It was a man. It wasn't anyone who died recently. His clothing looked like something from 1960s. He said that was his best decade."

"Oh," Gemini said disappointedly. "Well, who was it then? And what did they say? Don't keep me in suspense, girl!"

"He told me I needed to be careful at the funeral. I felt like he was telling me the murderer would be attending."

"What? Did he tell you who that might be? Was it someone else at the hospital?" Gemini tapped her foot nervously.

"Tug came into the kitchen to check on me. He's such a sweetie. But when he went back to bed, the man had disappeared."

This entire investigation was like this apparition: there and then gone. "That doesn't give us much to go on. Did you look around? Was there anybody at the funeral who spoke to you?"

"Yes, voices in my head. During the funeral and they said that the murderer was there too. I tried not to be conspicuous when looking around. I watched for people who might be nervous or act out of place, but the only strong feeling was that everyone there had a secret of some kind."

Gemini smiled, remembering her conversation with Janine. "Yes, I'd imagine they do. My information is about Carson Moore. This may be hard for you to hear, Feather. Both Carson and Doctor Wilson were having an affair with your boss, Angie."

Feather's mouth dropped open. "I knew she was having an affair with Doctor Wilson, but I didn't know about Carson Moore."

"Why didn't you tell me about that sooner? I've been trying to understand Doctor Wilson's secret life. You might have mentioned something." Gemini didn't hide her frustration.

"I'm sorry, Gemini. I'm still trying to process this skill I'm developing. It can all be too much like you witnessed the other day. I never meant to hide it from you. I just didn't have the mental space to remember. It was all so painful when Angie died."

Gemini patted her leg. "I know, dear. You're going through quite a lot. I'm in a quandary, trying to put these pieces together before Sophia forces Leo and I to leave Charming. You mentioned talking to someone else?"

Feather squirmed uncomfortably in her seat.

Gemini reached across her and opened the door. "Run in, dear! I'll wait. Remember, we decided there would be no embarrassing accidents today? Re-writing history, so-to-speak?"

"Huh? Oh, I don't have to go."

"I just thought, the way you were wiggling–"

"No, it's not that. The apparition who visited me last night had more to say."

"More facts for our investigation? Winning lottery numbers?"

"Something helpful. It concerns your problems with your daughter."

CHAPTER 34

Gemini went home and took off her funeral dress. She put on some comfortable lemon-yellow slacks and a yellow-and-white flowered top. Removing the dress added some measure of relief to her day. Thinking about losing a spouse was difficult for her, while Leo was in such a delicate state. She walked over to Howard's house and knocked on the door.

"I'm here to ask for another favor. I seem to do that a lot."

Howard scratched his nose and stared without emotion. "Come on in, Gemini." She smelled another intoxicating scent coming from his kitchen.

"What is that delicious aroma today, Howard?"

"It's Paraguayan chili. I got the recipe when I was touring South America. It's got coriander in it, that's what makes it different. I had it over the course of two weeks while we were there. You would think my digestive system would have complained, but when you're in a strange land, having something that becomes familiar is a comfort."

"I would love that recipe. Leo judged a chili competition once. It was his favorite. It IS his favorite." As soon as the words came out, her emotions took over. A tear rolled down her cheek. "That is not at all what I wanted to do here." She reached into her pocket and pulled out a tissue, wiping her nose and face. "It's been a hard day. I rarely burst into tears like a hormonal teen."

"I'm not much for emotion. But I possess a healthy respect for those who are. Is there some way I can help?" Howard guided her to her usual spot on his Naugahyde couch and handed her another tissue.

She sniffed, replacing the tissue in her pocket. "I went to Carson Moore's funeral today. I wanted to speak with his widow. She told me about her husband being involved in illegal activities, though she didn't know exactly what they were. She said he was obsessed with wealth and power, and that Carson had many affairs. I felt–I felt–"

"Like it could be you in the funeral garb? Makes sense."

She sat back against the couch, relieved she could be honest. "Leo is the polar opposite of Carson Moore. But seeing his widow reflecting on her husband's life was too real," she sniffed. "I've been so involved in this mess, in part because I don't want to think about what's going on with Leo. Brandon was right about that."

She realized she'd come to another person who also had negative feelings toward Carson Moore. "Oh, Howard. I'm so sorry. I forgot that your wife also… you know."

Howard made a shoving gesture with his hand. "Don't worry about it. I'm glad they are both out of my life. I can still have sympathy for his widow. Horrible man." He gazed out the window as if he was miles away. "They can't be cooking the books the way they did when I was there. Too easy to uncover. And with only two people involved, it has to be simple."

Gemini sat tall. "Did I say there were only two people involved?"

"That's what you've implied. I've never heard you speak of anyone other than Carson Moore and Doctor Wilson."

A realization hit Gemini. "You're absolutely right. If Carson Moore killed Doctor Wilson over, let's say a gambling debt, or a woman, then who killed Carson Moore? I've been looking at this all wrong."

"What did you want from me?"

"I'm looking for another identity. This time, I'll go to another floor. Maybe I'll start in housekeeping. There is a woman who almost lost her job because of Carson. There has to be a third side to this triangle. Angie said-" she caught herself. Howard wouldn't believe Feather spoke with the dead. "There may have been another murder last year, but I don't have proof. They involve someone else in their business. Janine Moore mentioned someone in maintenance who spent a lot of time at their house."

"No need for a new identity. I'll do some poking around. Still have my contacts, remember?"

"I really want to ask you why you're still involving yourself in hospital affairs, Howard. But I exhausted the circuits for today. Should I stop over tomorrow? I have a most delightful phone call to make in the morning, but that's all." She smiled, thinking about Feather's revelation.

He shrugged. "You could."

"Howard, I want to tell you, you are the most resourceful person I've ever known."

Howard smiled, making him appear very handsome, Gemini noticed.

"I'll take that as a compliment. As I told you before, I found myself in the middle of a very sticky situation once. If and when the time is right, I'll continue my story."

Gemini wiped her face. "I'm feeling better already. Things are moving forward!"

Howard looked at her with amusement. "So it's about the

chase, is it? Your juices get going when you've got someone to track down?"

Gemini hadn't considered it in that light. "I guess I do. I like a good mystery and I like to solve it. And it doesn't hurt that this will be helpful to my husband."

"Well then, I will get on it. I'll look forward to your visit tomorrow. Not too early, remember? I enjoy rising later in the morning and then making myself a large breakfast. I expect eleven or so would work." He stood and walked toward the door. Gemini followed.

Howard paused and turned around. "And Gemini? There is nothing wrong with having the sleuth mentality. It makes you an adventurer of sorts. Since you're not getting your trip around the world, you're getting your mental stimulation here. I rather admire that."

Gemini walked a little taller as she headed up the steps to her home. She decided this wasn't the time to plan her morning phone call. She had no emotion left, and this required everything she could muster. Instead, she made herself a pot of tea and got out a sleeve of crackers and some peanut butter. She found the mystery book Leo bought her two Christmases ago and sat, eating crackers and drinking tea until her eyes couldn't stay open any longer.

The next morning, she heard a soft knock at the back door as she was putting marionberry jelly on her toast. She was in her pajamas and the fuzzy lavender robe Leo insisted she buy for herself. Normally, she didn't like anyone to see her in that condition. It was just another excuse for crass comments about being elderly and staying in her pajamas all day, and she wasn't in the mood. This time, her curiosity got the better of her.

When she opened the door, she discovered a brown wicker basket covered in a checkered cloth. "I hope this isn't a baby!" She called to no one in particular. "You've come to the wrong place, if that's what you're delivering!" The only person out on the block was the paperboy, four houses down. He didn't understand what she said, but waved at her. She waved back and shook her head before stooping to pick up the basket. She immediately recognized the unique savory smell of Howard's chili. When she got it inside, she took the cloth off and found a container of chili, a slice of fresh cornbread, and a note:

Mrs. Reed,

I've had some bad days myself. Resourceful is at the top of your resume as well. I admire your drive and determination.

Howard

CHAPTER 35

"Brandon, it's Mom." She always felt that was an awkward way to refer to herself. She wasn't Brandon's mother. But from Sophia's fourth date, he decided he was a part of their family and so called her parents mom and dad. She wondered to herself if Sophia called Brandon's parents, mom and dad as well, which left her inexplicably jealous. It wasn't her business. She would have much preferred it if Brandon just called her Mrs. Reed.

"Yes, Mom. So nice to hear from you. We miss here you at the law firm. The new girl we hired just isn't quite up to par. She takes a long lunch break so that she can fix her hair after her jog. Makes me appreciate the fact you didn't care much about your appearance."

Brandon always tried to compliment her, but it ended up being an insult. Perhaps Sophia was attracted to the "fixer-upper" aspect of his personality.

Gemini smiled. "Thank you, Brandon. I'm glad to know that I'm missed. I would imagine your new person isn't much for stakeouts, either."

"Those aren't really in the job description, Mom. You

took that upon yourself. She's just doing what's required, no more, no less."

"You certainly didn't complain when I got you the information you needed to win your cases, did you?"

Brandon sighed. "You've got me there. It certainly got me in hot water with Sophia, though, and I didn't need any more issues to work out with her. So, what can I do for you today? I've got a five-thirty golf game and I've got to pick up my new clubs on the way."

For a split second, she wondered what illegal activities Brandon planned for the golf course. "I wanted to talk to you about moving Leo. He's doing just fine here. I know his nurse very well and she's a lovely person. It really wouldn't make any sense to move him at this point. He's stable right now."

"Sophia's been through this with you already, Mom. She explained to you he needs better care, and the only way to achieve that is to move him somewhere bigger and more sophisticated. Isn't it for the best? Don't you want him to get the treatment he deserves and recover?"

She hated the condescending way he spoke to her when they weren't at work. Like she was a doddering old fool. "Of course I do, Brandon! How can you think I don't? This is my husband, and I want him to have the very best. But if Leo wanted to seek treatment in Seattle, he would have done that himself. You always respected him and he you. What would he say to you now?"

Brandon was silent for a moment. "I understand what you're saying. I do," he uttered. "But Sophia and I already made the arrangements. I've got a colleague up there who pulled some strings. He's going to check in every week and make sure Dad has the best of everything."

"So this is all about advancing your career, then? He did you a favor and now you're stuck because you may need his cooperation with a case down the road? I didn't want to do this, but you're forcing my hand. I've got something on you, Brandon."

"What are you talking about? Mom, are you drinking?" Brandon laughed at the absurdity of her comment. "Blackmail is not a good look for you."

Gemini cringed. "I'm talking about your grandfather, Morris Floris. He had a conversation with a friend of mine."

Brandon huffed. "This isn't funny, Mom. My grandfather died long ago. Are you playing games with me, or are you really confused? Sophia may need to research facilities for you, too."

"You don't want Sophia to know about your secret past. If you did, you would have told her already."

There was silence on the other end of the line.

"Brandon? Did you hear me?"

"This playing detective has got to stop, Mom. You're not a professional, you're a retired woman with too much time on her hands."

She let that comment go, knowing what she had to tell him would more than satisfy her urge to make him hurt. "Your grandfather knows all about the used car lot. The fake insurance policies you put together for them to sell to poor, unsuspecting car buyers. He says there is proof and it won't take long for me to find it."

"How would you know what my grandfather says? You never met him! This is absolute crazy talk. I'm getting worried about you."

"Are you really going to argue with me, Brandon? You want to outright deny what I'm saying? That won't end well for you."

"I ended my relationship with those brothers years ago. Besides-would you do this to the father of your grandchild? Do you want your daughter out on the street with a small child?"

"Sophia is perfectly capable of taking care of herself and her son," Gemini scoffed. "She's an intelligent woman with many resources."

Brandon sighed. "I don't understand how you got ahold of this information. Maybe you went through confidential files while you were here, or god forbid, you've been talking to people you shouldn't. It's disturbing you would do this to your own son-in-law. A shake down. That's what this is."

"Are you done?" she asked patiently.

"What is it you want, Gemini?"

"To leave Leo right here. Let him finish the drug trial and if he still hasn't shown improvement, then you can move him."

Brandon chortled. "That isn't happening. We've already made the arrangements. You think because you've uncovered something that happened more than six years ago that you've won this battle." He was using his lawyer voice, the one he used when he wanted to make the other side's clients feel small. "It's over and there isn't anything you can do about it. The statute of limitations has run out. There's really no ammunition in your gun, Mother. Just a silly flag that won't harm a fly."

Gemini was glad that Feather had taken the time to ask Morris for all the details. Morris was embarrassed his grandson would sully the family name as he had. "The statute of limitations has run out on money laundering, that's true. It's too bad you also perpetuated that fraud through the mail. I did the paperwork for the Jaymeson case, remember? Your jail time would be six years for criminal fraud and contract violations. On top of that, one might say, the cherry on the sundae, there is a ten-year sentence for a federal crime. You've still got some of the fraudulent policies in a locked box, buried under the new fence post we put up two years ago. Shame on you, Brandon. Involving your wife's parents in your crimes."

She could hear Brandon thumping the phone on his chest. When he put it back up to his ear, his tone was much more conciliatory. "I can't believe this. You aren't a vindictive person. Just a quiet little retiree. This isn't right."

"So we've got a deal then? Leo stays here for the time being?"

"How will I explain this to Sophia? She'll hit the roof!"

Gemini suppressed a giggle. Oh, to be a fly on the wall when that conversation took place. "I'll leave that up to your lawyerly mind. You can be very persuasive when you want. I'll let you both know when there are any changes in Leo's condition." She hung up the phone quickly, before he tried to change her mind.

CHAPTER 36

Feather walked timidly into the house. The floorboards creaked as she moved, causing her to tense up in expectation of a scary scene. In the carnivals she'd attended, that was always how it worked. Feather Jones wasn't normally frightened by strange sounds, but today, with the murder at the hospital, she was very much on edge.

The house sat upon a hill that overlooked the ocean, as most of the imposing homes of Charming did. A long porch lined the front of the house and a swing hung on one hook, a sign of better days. It was one of the oldest homes in the community.

"Hello?" she called. Normally, she didn't like to enter without the owner by her side, but this client had given her permission. "I'm here for my appointment at 2:00 PM. You said to meet you in the living room of the Peregrine Mansion. I'm ready for your reading."

There was no sound at all except for the window that rattled every time there was movement. She walked through on her own while she waited for the owner. Sometimes it helped to get a feel for things before there was other energy around. There was definitely someone else in the room with her. She thought it was the previous owners at first, but when she asked, she got no response.

"I know you're here. Please come and talk to me. I am not your enemy. I'm just here to fact find."

The hairs rose on the back of her neck. That was usually her cue that someone was there and wanted to speak. "My name is Feather. I live in the modern day and I'm just wondering what's making you so sad and keeping you around? Are you here to guide someone to the other side?"

She continued walking through the kitchen and up the back stairs to the bedrooms. The air was electric. Something was guiding her forward. As she walked down the long, ruby red carpeted hallway, she was drawn to the bathroom. Inside, she saw a claw-foot bathtub with ornate swirls on the feet. The design at the base of the pedestal sink matched the tub feet, though the porcelain appeared cracked in several places. Beside the sink sat a half-removed toilet. The energy in the room had changed from electric to dark and clouded, and she was feeling like she was suffocating. "Is this where it ended? This was your last experience on earth? Help me out here. I'm just trying to get a lay of the land and you can give me whatever information needs to be relayed."

"Where are you? I saw your car out front. I'm the owner!" A voice announced from the living room.

In an instant, the energy left the room. "I was hoping we would have some time alone before she arrived. You can continue to communicate with me. I may not be able to respond, but I'll be listening."

"Here!" Feather called as she walked down the stairs. An older lady with thick glasses and blue hair that Feather had fortunately not been responsible for stood in the foyer. She smiled as she saw another living human in her home.

"Thank you for coming today. You know, people in this town look at ghosts as a necessary evil. Part of the history, but nothing they'd acknowledge in public. It's been going on too long though, and I've decided I can't ignore the signs anymore. You wouldn't believe how many houses in Charming are haunted. And this one," she pointed up randomly, "is no exception."

"I'm Feather, by the way," Feather stuck her hand out eagerly. "When we spoke on the phone, I was at work and I couldn't be more specific. I'm sorry about that."

"Lottie Morgan. Nice to meet you, Feather. You come highly recommended. My friend Ida said you told her where to find the money buried in her backyard. Word is getting around and it won't be long before folks book you from morning till night." Lottie glanced around the room at the furniture covered in white sheets. "I'm sorry for the mess. We'd planned on fixing things up nice, making it a real showpiece. Then all of this nonsense began. No one wants to be here until they're sure they aren't square in the middle of a horror movie."

Feather chuckled. "It's usually not quite like the movies. Why don't you begin by telling me what's going on here? What is scaring everyone away? What is it that has you concerned?"

Lottie touched her fingertips together. "Well, it all started three years ago. My sister passed away and left me this house. Despite all of her flaws, she loved her home. Bought it from the Peregrine family for a song and she treated it like a museum. She even purchased their furniture, original to the place from 1907." Lottie pulled back a sheet on one couch to reveal the deep purple velvet covering of an ornately carved settee. "As you can see, only the finest quality materials," she said proudly.

Feather moved to the couch, touching it to see what she

could pick up in the way of people who had passed through. Nothing.

"She died unexpectedly and you could've knocked me over with a feather when I heard the house was mine. I got the keys and then came the next shock. Apparently, she'd given up on the place several years ago and let it go. My poor sister fell into a deep depression and quit caring for what was once her pride and joy. I wanted to cry when I saw the extent of the mess."

Maybe depression was keeping her from confessing to Feather?

"When I came in to start the remodeling work, strange things began to happen. I'd leave paints and tools by the railing and they'd be gone the next day. One time, I came in and discovered a broken mirror on the floor. Now, mind you, those things can fall at any given time, but it was in a different room from where it had been hanging on the wall for the last thirty years."

"Is it possible that someone else was in here? Maybe a squatter, or a neighbor who was just curious about what remained after your sister died? Sometimes there can be straightforward explanations for things that we don't understand."

Lottie crossed her arms. "The neighbors never liked my sister. I didn't blame them. She was a bit of a crank. I asked if she wouldn't please try to be a little nicer to folks, but that wasn't her way. She never invited anyone in or spoke to folks if it didn't please her. She even yelled at the newspaper boy if he came too close to her porch. When she died, I think everyone was relieved."

Lottie looked at Feather apologetically. "Shouldn't talk about family like that, but it's the truth. As far as squatters go, anything is possible, I suppose. But there would have been some sort of jimmying of the door or other evidence of someone breaking a window. There's been none of that; it's all locked up tight when I'm not here."

Feather took in a deep breath. The hairs on the back of her neck rose once more. "They're here with us now. Is it alright if I speak to them?"

"Yes, yes. Please do!"

"I'm here with Lottie and we want to listen. What's making you sad?"

A dusty candle holder sitting on top of the china hutch slammed to the floor.

"Oh, my goodness!" Lottie grabbed her chest. "What does that mean? Are they angry with us?"

"Possibly. Is this your home?" Feather called. "If it is, please give me a sign."

The window rattled again. "OK, so I know this is your home now. Please tell me what you need. Do you want to speak to your sister?"

She turned to Lottie and whispered, "What was your sister's name?"

"Drucilla."

Feather did a double take. "Drucilla?"

"Horrible name, isn't it? My parents knew what they were doing when they named her Drucilla. Horrible name for a horrible girl."

Drucilla? Is that you? What's going on?"

Feather closed her eyes and stood grounded for a minute. "She's telling me there is something you need to know. Something that she's been trying to tell you ever since she passed. Actually, before she passed. You continually ignored her."

Lottie shook her head vigorously. "I never did like to visit with her. She was so negative that I shut her out. The last night of her life, before she choked to death on that banana, she said we had to talk about something serious. I didn't want to. Everything was serious with her and she was such a downer."

"Can she tell you now? She'd really like to speak. And then she will leave you in peace."

Lottie nodded.

"She wants you to know that it wasn't your fault. You didn't push your brother into the street. You remembered it wrong all these years."

Lottie's eyes swelled with tears. "Duncan?" she whispered. "I was mad at him for tearing the head off my doll. I pushed him down and he staggered as he got up, moving into the path of a car driving down the street way too fast."

Feather put her hand in the air. "No, Lottie. That's not what happened. Drucilla says she was the one who pulled the head off your doll. When you confronted her, she pushed you into Duncan. That's why he fell, because she caused a chain reaction." Feather opened her eyes. "You felt guilt when she didn't, and that's why you took this burden on these years. She never corrected you before, and now she wants it out in the open. That was what she needed to say. I think she is at peace now."

Lottie pulled a tissue from her purse and wiped her nose. "Thank you for that, Feather. I can see why it would have bothered my sister. Every time she wanted to speak with me about it, I shut her down. It's just too painful after all these years. I should have listened. If I'd let her tell me years ago, we wouldn't be in this pickle." Lottie looked up at the ceiling. "Drucilla, I'm so sorry. We should have taken care of this when we were young. I thought you wanted to remind me of what I'd done. I misjudged you."

"It's out in the open now. And I think you can renovate your home and everything can just go back to–" Feather closed her eyes once more and the hairs on her arms rose again.

Lottie finished wiping her eyes and returned her tissue to her purse. "What? What's going on now? Is there something else she's irritated about? That girl always found something to complain about. My mother called it a bug up her bum. As you can tell, we struggled a lot as a family."

Feather gazed at her solemnly. "Drucilla has something else to say, but the message isn't for you, it's for me."

"What's this about? Is she going to call you names for being in her home? I'm sorry if she's being rude. That's just how she is." Lottie began pacing back and forth.

"There is someone who's been trying to talk to me, and I've ignored them. It's a woman. Someone I used to work with. She wants me to know she was murdered. Drucilla has a message to deliver, since I won't listen to Angie."

"Oh, dear. That's serious. Who killed her? Will she tell you? Drucilla, you have to help this poor woman!"

Feather's face twisted. "There's more than one death. She says Angie wants me to know she wasn't the only one murdered. Carson Moore was murdered too."

Lottie stopped. "The hospital guy? I thought he committed suicide?"

"The deaths will continue unless we bring it out into the light. I've been ignoring the facts, and it's time everyone learns the truth. Stop them. Stop them."

Feather's face was stoic as she repeated the sentence over and over. When she opened her eyes, her legs were wobbly, so she reached out for the couch and collapsed on top of the sheet.

"Are you alright, dear? Do you need some water?" Lottie hovered over her, touching her forehead to see if she had a fever.

"Letters. She said—the letters are crucial," Feather stammered.

"I've got a pen in my purse—just a minute." Lottie went to

the kitchen and came back with stationery with the heading, "Let us charm the pants off of you! Charming, Oregon.

"I'm ready. Tell me what letters Drucilla wants you to remember."

"She didn't finish. I don't know if it was specific to the alphabet or letters that are written." Feather was getting her wits about her again. She sat up and looked around. "I'm sorry, Angie. I should've been paying attention."

"Should you call someone? I'm sure the authorities won't understand, but is there someone else who might be able to help you figure this out?" Lottie asked. "You've performed a great service for me today. I'd like to do something for you." She opened her purse again and pulled out three fifty-dollar bills. "For your troubles. I won't forget what you've done."

"Oh, no, I couldn't–"

"I won't take them back." Lottie said firmly, placing the money in Feather's hand. "Now go find someone who will help you track down this murderer. You and Drucilla did the world a huge favor today."

Feather stood, placing the money in her front jeans pocket. Tug would be pleased she'd made a tidy profit. "I've got a friend who's looking into things at the hospital. Once she gets ahold of this information, she'll be like a dog with a bone."

CHAPTER 37

*G*emini watched out of her window, waiting until precisely 11:10 a.m. to walk over to her neighbor's home. Even though he'd been up early to deliver her basket, she didn't want to assume he was ready for company until the specific hour he mentioned.

"His name is Gary Johnson." Howard Beachmont rubbed his chin as they sat in his living room, the rich smell of cinnamon-heavy banana bread permeating the air. "He's been my friend ever since we moved here." He took a drink of lavender-infused lemonade and smacked his lips. "It's a good crop of lavender this year."

"What?" Gemini's face fell. "Cheese and biscuits. Gary J.? He was the first person we met when we arrived at the hospital. He was so kind." She couldn't believe the words coming out of Howard's mouth. "It feels like a betrayal, Howard."

"You're looking at it all wrong, Mrs. Reed. Gary's always wanted to impress the people in charge. When I was there, he brought me donuts and coffee every day. Finally, I told him I didn't eat that crap and I sure didn't drink hospital coffee.

The next morning, he showed up in my office with a protein smoothie. He wanted so badly to make me happy."

"When you left, did he maintain a friendship with you?"

Howard shook his head. "Like I said, Gary has a great admiration for power. His proximity to powerful men makes him someone important. Once I lost my title, he wasn't interested. I asked him to help me move my things out of the office. He never showed."

"Do you think he understood all of Carson Moore's dirty dealings, so he killed him? Was killing him better than watching another hero fall from grace? No offense, Howard."

Howard took a long drink of his tea. "None taken. In answer to your question, I'm not sure. He isn't a violent man, but we all do strange things when we're pushed to our limits."

"This sounds like the precursor to another story of your sordid past." Gemini winked and then instantly felt ashamed she would make such a childish joke in front of a man of Howard's caliber. "I just meant that you have a rich history," she added.

"I know what you meant," he replied. "If you and your Leo end up staying after his release, I'll invite you both over for a barbecue. I marinate my ribs for twenty-two hours in a secret sauce." He brought his fingers to his lips and made a kissing sound. "Perfection. After a good meal, you'll be ready to hear about my escapades."

"Leo and I would enjoy that very much." Gemini set her glass on the table and stood.

"Mrs. Reed... Gemini, what is your plan of action going forward? If you're going to confront Gary Johnson, you shouldn't go alone. If you're approaching this as a fact-finding mission, I won't be overly concerned."

Gemini stopped walking and turned around. "I'm not sure yet. If this were my own home, I would go to our store and get some paint. When Sophia gave her best friend a black eye, we painted the kitchen Daisy Doll Yellow. Leo's mother asked to move in with us. That's the year we painted our bedroom Barely Blush. It turned out off-white, but that's okay, because by the time we'd finished painting, we always had an answer to our biggest problems."

"Nothing to paint in the rental?" Howard stood, placing his glass on an ornately carved wooden table, and followed her as she walked outside.

Gemini gestured to her house. "I've hated this mud-brown color ever since we moved in. Not only that, it's peeling under every window. If it were mine, I'd begin scraping off the old paint and applying new right now, at least the part that faces the street. By the time I finished that project, I would have a perfect plan in my head. I suppose I could go home and bake, but that usually only works for small ideas."

"And what color do you think would be appropriate? Instead of the 'mud brown', as you call it?"

She looked across the lawn and thought for a moment. "A pleasant light, breezy blue. We had a color in our store called Oceanberry Blue. We painted a wall that color once and we liked it. It would cheer up the house enough to make it look like somewhere I'd live."

Howard nodded. "I've got some wooden slats from the fence I took down last fall. Haven't done anything with them. You're welcome to take them home and paint until the lightbulb goes off in your head."

"That's kind of you, Howard. But I'm sure I'll be fine. I've been baking cookies for my co-workers and the process of stirring and mixing will have to suffice. I've got a new chocolate chip cookie recipe I found on the internet."

Gemini bent down to smell his deep, purple irises. "These

were always my favorites. Thank you for the chili, by the way."

"Huh? Don't have any idea what you're talking about." Howard turned abruptly and went inside.

Gemini looked at her watch. It was almost noon, and she needed to go up and see Leo. Today, the thought of being inside the hospital walls made her sick to her stomach. What if she ran into Gary before she was ready to confront him?

She turned around and walked back to Howard's home, opening the gate and walking into the backyard. She found several six-foot pieces of old, grey wood laying on the ground by fresh new fence posts. Instead of asking, she took two of them and transferred them to her garage. She placed the tarp they'd used during their move (to cover her grandmother's rocking chair) over the cement floor.

They'd brought their painting supplies from home and stacked them neatly on the garage shelves. Even though Leo was ill and Gemini was sure she wouldn't feel up to it, paints, brushes, tape and buckets were a wonderful part of their memories of life together and neither of them could bear to leave them behind.

The can sitting on the most accessible shelf, Very Violet, was a temporary bathroom paint job. Leo had to find a way to tell his mother she needed a full-time caretaker and Gemini needed to find the words to ask for a raise. They both painted furiously, until each were covered in deep, purple splatters. Husband and wife sat on the kitchen floor, exhausted.

"Do you know how to tell her?" Gemini asked.

"Yes. Do you know how to tell him?" Leo asked.

They looked at each other and nodded solemnly. "Now," Leo continued, "what do we do about this awful bathroom color?"

When she opened the top of the paint can, she inhaled the

scent, and her soul filled with joy. It was the scent of renewal. Starting over. Every time they painted something, it was a beginning. She dipped her paintbrush and began stroking the paint on the old wood, changing the color from one of despair to a bright, hopeful color.

Her mind wandered as she painted the same two boards over and over until the half-used can was empty. Gemini shuffled cans on the shelf until she found the Burnt Sunset, dark orange dribbles running down the side. She took an old brush and flicked bits of orange onto the dark purple, making a lovely contrast of colors.

The strokes of paint on the wood did their magic, lifting her spirits and her mind. By the time she'd finished both boards, she realized she'd splattered paint all over her nicest pink pants. It didn't matter.

Now that her mind was clear and her mission clarified, she felt energized. When she'd changed and began her walk to the hospital, she pulled out her phone. "Feather? I'm going to leave a message because I'm going to the hospital. Of course I'll see my Leo, but then I need to see someone else. I think I've figured out who killed Doctor Wilson and Carson Moore. I just wanted you to know, in case something goes horribly wrong."

CHAPTER 38

Feather turned off her phone ringer. She'd been putting this off for too long. Anginette made it very clear that she needed her help and she wasn't going away until she got it. While utilizing her friend's help would be crucial, she needed as much information as possible first.

When Angie died, Feather didn't want to touch anything in her apartment. It felt like an invasion of privacy to Feather to paw through her things. They weren't close, at least not in Feather's mind, and at that point she didn't have any sign that foul play had occurred.

Curiosity got the better of her, however. She returned on that same day and started sifting through her boss's drawers. There would be no one else to clean out the apartment, she reasoned, she might as well start now.

She pulled out the clothes first, carefully packing them into Angie's suitcases. By the looks of her luggage, she was a frequent, upscale traveler. Everything matched and had multiple tags attached to the handles.

Feather continued removing clothing until she got to the

bottom of the drawer, where she discovered a thick folder marked "accomplishments."

Angie organized the folder chronologically, with little yellow sticky tabs placed on each year of note. The first tab read, "The beginning." Angie started her salon ten years earlier, working out of a former laundromat on the edge of Charming. She had two stalls and one employee. "Only eight clients the entire first month," Angie wrote in the margin of the document. Attached at the bottom was a photo of a young and vital woman, beaming as she pointed to the sign above the door that read, "Cutz Hair Salon."

The next tab said, "Marketing." In this section, Angie included flyers advertising a two-for-one deal if you brought a friend in with you to get a haircut. "My business quadrupled in four months!" she wrote. There were several pictures of Angie at social events, her look increasingly sophisticated.

Feather glanced over at the closet, where expensive dresses hung. She'd never seen Angie wear any of them.

The final tab included photos of Angie in her current salon, the ribbon cutting attended by the mayor as well as high-profile people from the hospital. Feather recognized several doctors, former clients of Angie's that she inherited when her boss died.

The top drawer contained half-price pizza coupons and crafting project ideas.

In the second, a moldy, half-eaten carrot sat atop a book called Making Your Employees Feel Like Family. She threw those in the trash and was going to shut the drawer when something else caught her eye.

There were at least twenty photos rubber-banded together, as if they had an important purpose. "No one takes actual pictures anymore," she said to herself. She picked them up and her mouth dropped open.

Angie, in various stages of undress, photographed herself

with prominent men from the community. She appeared to be intoxicated in most of the pictures. Feather walked over to the box where she'd placed the folder from the dresser. She opened it up to the last tab. She recognized several of the men in that photo from the pictures Angie had taken in more intimate moments.

The most shocking photo was one with Angie and a doctor, the hospital pediatrician, hugging under a bridge. She was completely unclothed, except for a long strand of pearls and high heels. Angie was holding a scribbled sign that read, "Portland!" Her eyes were bright red, as though she were under the influence of something. Each photo was stamped with the date and time.

Feather recognized the hospital pediatrician because he was a client of hers. She took the photo and put it in her pocket. Searching for some kind of positive memento to take, she discovered a large, purple candle in the bottom drawer called Blackberry Memories. She picked that up and took it with her as well. That was enough for one day.

It took her an entire month before she could return. By that time, the eviction notice hung on the door and she realized she only had a few days to remove Angie's possessions. Tug came and helped her move large boxes to storage. Weeks later, he confessed he'd found more photos of Angie with different men.

One-by-one, Feather took the photos and held them over the flame until they caught on fire. She placed them in a dish beside the candle and watched them burn. Tug held her hand as she cried for the woman who'd been such a support to a new stylist.

Feather turned off her phone ringer. She'd been putting this off for too long. Angie made it very clear that she needed her help and she wasn't going away until she got it. She asked

Tug to join her in the living room as she lit the Blackberry Memories candle once more.

"Tug? Are you ready?" she called.

"One sec." He appeared in the living room, pulling a shirt over his head. "After you had your cleansing, I found another. I didn't want to ruin your vibe, so I didn't say anything. It's been in my sock drawer ever since."

He handed her a photo, and she placed it on the table without viewing it. "Thanks, Tug. I need to concentrate right now. Will you sit down and hold my hands?"

He knelt down beside her on the floor. "I don't know how much help I'll be. I don't hear voices in my head, unless it's flashbacks of my mom yelling at my brother to get up for school. He was pretty adamant he would not go most days." Tug chuckled.

"I need your positive energy, babe." Feather took both of his hands and kissed them before holding them tightly and closing her eyes. "Tug, you close your eyes too," she instructed. "Angie, I'm here. I'm ready to listen to whatever you need to say."

They sat, smelling the intense, sweet and spicy scent of the candle for a few minutes in silence.

"What? You need to speak louder," Feather insisted. "Angie, now is the time for you to tell me everything. I'm listening."

Tug opened one eye. "What's she saying?" he whispered.

"Shhh!" Feather squeezed his hands. "Living beings need to can it so I can hear those who aren't!" She tilted her head to the side. "You're coming through now. I got it. The letters. Did your murderer write you a threatening note? I didn't see anything when I cleaned out your place. Just a bunch of pictures."

The two sat for another five minutes, Tug patiently

waiting for further instruction. Finally, Feather opened her eyes and sat back, releasing his hands.

"Well? Who killed her?"

"She kept repeating the same thing over and over. In the letters. In the letters. I couldn't get any more information." Feather looked at the carpet, discouraged. " There was nothing in the letter we found at Doctor Wilson's house about her. I don't understand, but I'm still new at this, so I might be doing it wrong."

Tug pulled her in close. "It's alright. We'll try it again in a day or so. Maybe my energy was too cloudy. I did eat two burritos last night. That had to put some kind of a fog in the room."

Feather laughed. "How is it you can make every situation uplifting?"

"It's a gift, I guess." He stood and offered her a hand to stand beside her. "Couldn't live up to the family name, but I sure know how to work a room."

"You've far exceeded the family name, from my experience with you, Tug Muehler."

He kissed her neck. "You say that to all of your boyfriends, don't you?" he whispered, rubbing his lips softly across her skin.

"As much as I'd like this to continue, I'm not ready to give up on Angie," Feather said breathlessly. "I'm going to stay here by myself for a few more minutes, just to see if she returns. Then I suppose I should call Gemini and fill her in. She'll want to know all the details."

"That little old lady has turned out to be a real plus for you, hasn't she?"

"She's not frail and I don't think of her as old," Feather retorted. "She's smarter than half the people I know my age. Gemini is my friend. My good friend."

"I'm sorry, Feath. Didn't mean anything. I'm sure she's a

wonderful person. You're a great judge of character and if you like her, she's okay in my book. You should invite her to dinner soon. I'd love to meet her!" Tug pulled on his jacket. "I'm running for a smoothie. You want anything?"

Feather shook her head and smiled. If she had her boyfriend's metabolism, she wouldn't waste it on protein shakes. "I'm good, thanks."

As he pulled the door closed, Feather leaned over to blow out the candle. One day, she'd light it again. On the anniversary of Angie's passing, she could set up a memorial at the salon. That would be a real "coming together" moment for everyone and maybe, for a day, there wouldn't be any drama.

She looked down at the picture Tug found. Angie was on some tropical getaway. She and Doctor Wilson were standing in front of a fancy hotel. The sign in front said, Circle T All-inclusive Resort.

She put her hand up to her mouth. "It was this simple? The entire time? Oh, Gemini, you're going to love this one," she said out loud, reaching for her phone.

CHAPTER 39

Gemini stood in front of the main doors to Charming General Hospital. It wasn't like her to hesitate. Whatever she did, she went full steam. If she made a mistake, she'd deal with it later: that was one of the many glorious parts of aging.

Today, however, she had some reservation. She was about to confront a murderer. This was the first time she had this particular experience. She'd been on many stakeouts that looked like they would end badly, but her guardian angel had been watching over her every time. Leo called her Myrna. "A happy-go-lucky, quirky woman who always seems to find the light," he'd say. She hadn't told him half of the sticky situations she'd survived, thanks to the wiles of Myrna.

When Gene Bartles was released from prison after serving time for selling illegal diet pills out of his laundromat, he'd tracked Gemini down as she was going home from work one night.

She'd been thinking about what to make for dinner. Leo wanted something using garden vegetables. She thought they would enjoy a nice ratatouille. He'd been feeling strange lately and thought a healthier diet might help. As she exited her car, she sensed someone standing behind her.

"You're Cinnamon Plum?"

She shut her door and stood, facing her car. She went through all the alias used in her undercover work. Luckily, she made a file for them and hid them from Brandon.

"I could be. Who are you?" Her voice remained cool. Panicking would only escalate the situation quicker.

"You know who I am. You ruined my life. My wife left me and took everything, all because of you."

"If I recall, Mr. Bartles, your wife was already planning a divorce when your illegal activities came to light. The only thing I did was assure she and your children had enough money to live on. Would you have wanted them to starve?"

He moved in a quick motion to her backside. She felt cold metal jammed into her ribs.

"That's not true. We were madly in love. Now I'm going to ruin your life the way you ruined mine. You can get in my car on your own, or I'll pick you up and carry you. Your choice."

She'd insisted the entire office take a self-defense course for this very reason. At the end, they were all awarded certificates. Brandon joked his mother-in-law needed options to keep him in line.

"You don't want to do that, Mr. Bartles. That will send you straight back to prison. Is that how you want your children to remember you? In prison garb?"

"Nobody will know it's me. I've got it all planned out. Nobody will know it's me. I'm tired of chit chat. Are you coming willingly? I had plenty of time to lift weights in prison - I can throw a little thing like you over my shoulder in two seconds. Won't even break a sweat."

"There is a camera across the street to your left and one

to your right. After our newspapers were stolen, they kindly agreed to point the cameras at our driveway."

"I'll come back and take care of them," he sneered. "Not worried about a couple of cameras."

Gemini counted to ten. She focused all of her energy into one fiery ball. She spun around so quickly, Gene Bartles lost his balance. Steve's Safety First School graduate, Gemini Reed, jabbed her car keys in his eyes and he fell backward, wincing as he put his hands to his face. Her neighbor came running from across the street.

"Gemini! There's a car on the way! Are you alright?" He looked at her with concern and then sat down on top of Gene Bartles, grabbing his arms and pinning them behind his back.

Gemini bent over. "Ooops. I forgot the part about my neighbor being the police chief. He's always on the lookout."

"She poked me in the eye!" he wailed.

Gemini always thought of that day when she was feeling unsure of herself. That day, she'd done everything right. Luckily, Leo was asleep and hadn't heard a thing.

She took a deep breath and opened the doors to Charming General Hospital. Gemini walked up to the reception desk, where Beverly B. was talking on the phone. She waved at Gemini. "Oh, really? I'll see what I can do. Don't worry about it. We'll figure it out." She hung up the phone and looked at Gemini apologetically. "Sorry. That was my sister-in-law. My niece wants to have a sleepover where all of her friends get their hair done. My sister-in-law doesn't think she can afford it. Eight little girls is a lot of hair, you know?"

"I might know someone who could help. I'll get back to you later today after I check with her." Gemini tapped the counter nervously. "Before I visit with my husband, I need to see Gary J., the maintenance man. Have you seen him today?"

OCEANBERRY BLUES

She picked up the phone. "I can page him for you. Do you want him to meet you in your husband's room?"

"No! That's too private," Gemini said quickly. "What I meant was, we like to keep things calm in Leo's room. If he could meet me right here, I would appreciate it." She pulled her necklace from inside her blouse and rubbed it anxiously.

Beverly nodded. She called the extension for maintenance and instructed them to send Gary to the reception area. "You can sit down and wait for him, if you like? We actually received a few recent issues of some beauty magazines! Can you imagine? This is the first time in all the years I've worked here that I've seen new magazines!"

Gemini picked up a magazine and glanced at the cover. Ten Ways to Make Him Say I'm Sorry. "Oh, and Beverly, it appears someone vandalized my car in the parking lot. Could you call the police for me? It's far too warm to wait outside, so I'd like them to come in and get me first."

"Gosh, Gemini, I'm sorry to hear that. I'll call them right now." Beverly picked up the phone again.

Gemini was too nervous to sit, but she didn't want to raise suspicion so she perched herself on the lime green couch closest to Beverly. She tried thumbing through the magazines, but the "Ten Minute Diet" and "Twenty Things to do with Liver," couldn't keep her attention. She reached into her purse and clicked the recording device to the "on" position.

There was a tap on her shoulder.

"Mrs. Reed? Did you need my help?"

Gemini swallowed hard and stood. "I do." She folded her arms across her chest. "I'm confused about something, and I'd like your help to figure it out." She fiddled with the necklace hanging on her chest, rubbing the red gemstone against fingers.

Gary adjusted his stance, planting his feet wide and

putting one hand under his chin. "You know I'll do what I can, ma'am. Are there problems with your husband's room?"

"No, nothing like that. It's about Doctor Wilson."

"Oh? Have you heard somethin' about him? Last I knew, he was still on vacation. Those rich folks run off whenever they feel like it. The wife says that's normal for them."

"Yes, you mentioned he was on vacation. Where did you say? Somewhere with lots of water?"

Gary nodded. "That man loves his water sports. He told me so many stories about his adventures. Has a real nice big boat too."

"That's where I'm needing help, Gary. I know for a fact that Dr. Wilson hates the water. Terrified of it, in fact. Carson Moore's wife told me an interesting story about the two men taking a vacation together. Carson tried to trick Doctor Wilson into getting in the water. That's what ended their friendship."

Gary shrugged. "Must've gotten that wrong then. I could swear he told me he liked to swim."

"My theory is that you killed him. Maybe you didn't want a third person in your side business any more. Or you were having financial problems? I haven't figured that out yet. But after you got rid of him, you decided it was Carson Moore's turn. He must've caught on to your plan and you had to get rid of him too," Gemini said boldly. She glanced around at the lobby, mercifully full of people.

"You don't know what you're talking about." Gary's voice lowered an octave. "Carson was my best friend. I'd never do anything to hurt him."

"That day I saw you in the elevator, you were a mess. It's not easy to kill someone you care about, I'd imagine."

Gary looked around too. "I don't know where you got your crazy ideas, but I would never harm a friend."

"But you would harm Doctor Wilson? He was wanted out.

I found the letter. Was it about the drug trial? Was there something wrong with the Atomycin my husband received?"

Gary's face turned beet red. "Mrs. Reed, I'm afraid I'm going to have to call security and have you escorted off the property."

"Why? Because I figured out what happened? The police are on their way. What will they find when they search your place? Is that where you buried him?"

Gary gripped her arm. "It wasn't like that. Carson asked me–" he caught himself and released her. "I'm not going down for this. I could make some calls right now and have your husband's machines 'accidentally' turned off. Is that what you want? How about you call the cops and tell them you weren't serious?"

Gemini pulled her arm back and straightened her sleeve. "Why don't you explain to me exactly what happened? I used to work for a law firm and I can help you find good representation. If it was an accident, they'll be understanding. Doctor Wilson was arrogant, wasn't he?"

Gary motioned toward the lime green couch and they both sat down. Gemini made sure she kept her purse in her hand. She had lots of potential weapons inside–including her car keys and some pepper spray she'd kept on hand ever since the incident with Mr. Bartles.

"Carson, my best friend, had lots of problems with Doctor Wilson. The two of them argued about business all the time. They had a misunderstanding, and Doctor Wilson threatened to tell the rest of the hospital board about it. That's when Carson asked me to do a favor for him. He never actually told me to get rid of anybody, he just wanted to make sure his business dealings weren't in jeopardy." Gary tapped his foot nervously.

Gemini nodded, just as Olive had taught her. She sat silently, giving him room to continue. As she did, she pushed her purse up against her chest., ensuring the recording pen was close enough to capture everything.

"I offered to mow Doctor Wilson's lawn after work. He said his mower had just been repaired and should be working fine, but I told him I couldn't get it to start. When he came out to see what the problem was, I hit him over the head with a hammer. I put him in the lawnmower bag and dragged him to my trunk. Carson said–I mean, I decided to throw him into the ocean. Probably shark meat by now."

"And what about your friend, Mr. Moore? Did he threaten to expose you?" Gemini leaned back.

"No, he wouldn't do that. He was my buddy." Tears formed in Gary's eyes. "I've never had a friend as good as Carson. He gave me tickets to baseball games and steaks at Christmas. I don't have anyone else who cares if I live or die now that Carson is gone."

Gemini actually felt bad for him. She leaned forward and put her hand on his leg. "You deserve to be loved, Gary. Are things bad with your wife?"

"Ma'am? Did you call us?" A police officer appeared beside them. Gemini rose to her feet quickly.

"Yes, officer. This man just confessed to the murder of Doctor Wilson."

The police officer had a puzzled look on his face. "What? I thought they called us for a break-in?"

Gary stood and put his hands in his pockets. "She's crazy. We've been trying to get rid of her for months, but she keeps hanging around here. Last week, she said someone was poisoning the cafeteria food."

Gemini opened her purse and pulled out the pen-shaped recording device Feather gave her. "It's all here. Every word." She hoped that was true.

Gary took this opportunity to make his getaway. All of his

time spent doing Carson Moore's yardwork had not been wasted. He was agile for a middle-aged man.

"Go! I'm a very fit sixty-eight, but running isn't my thing!" Gemini yelled at the police officer. He stayed firmly planted in place.

"I'm still not sure a crime was committed, ma'am. I'm going to need more information from you. I can track him down later."

Gemini rolled her eyes. "Cheese and crackers! You're letting a murderer escape!" She watched as Gary ran outside. Immediately a well-built man caught him and slammed him to the ground.

CHAPTER 40

*G*emini and the police officer hurried outside.

A young bodybuilder was sitting astride Gary. He was holding Gary's hands together behind his back with one, beefy arm. "Where is she? What did you do to Gemini Reed?"

"She's fine! I didn't touch her! Get off me!"

"Are you Tug?" Gemini asked.

The man glanced up, and with his free arm, shook her hand. "Yes, I am. You must be Gemini. Your alarm went off from the Sanity Saver 2000, just as Feather was listening to your message. I came as fast as I could."

Gemini pulled the octagon-shaped device from her shirt. "I wasn't sure the police would arrive in time. I was hoping you would get the alert. This thing is a wonder!"

"Do you want to tell me what's going on here?" the police officer asked. "You might want to get off that man before I'm forced to charge you with assault."

Gemini reached into her purse, where she'd dropped the recording device, and pulled it out. "Tug, show me how to play a recording from this pen thingy."

Tug took the pen and pushed a tiny button on the side. "This is the cheap version. You'll have to hold it up to your ear, officer."

Gary continued to struggle as Tug held him firmly. "You might as well give up, buddy. All you're doing is wearing yourself out."

After hearing the entire conversation, the police officer handed the pen back to Gemini and asked Tug to move so he could handcuff Gary. A sizable crowd was gathering in front of the hospital, some angry that a longtime employee had been arrested. A man Gemini recognized from Carson's funeral as acting board president came outside and spoke with the police officer and they both moved to Gemini's side.

"Mrs. Reed? Could you tell this man your story?"

"As a member of the Charming Hospital Board, I would you to tell me exactly what happened with Doctor Wilson."

He acted as though he'd never seen her before. This man who treated Janine like a business associate and dismissed her as unimportant the day of Carson Moore's funeral. "No, I don't think I will, sir. I'm going to see my husband and tell him all about my day. Then I'm going home." She walked around him and inside the hospital.

When she rounded the corner into Leo's room, Denise was sitting beside Leo, holding his hand. She looked up with surprise. "Late for you today, Gemini. I thought maybe things got busy at the beauty shop. They're going to try taking him off the ventilator again!"

Though it should have been a comfort to see his nurse in such a caring pose, something was off. She'd never seen Denise acting this way with her husband. When Gemini focused her eyes on Denise's hand, she pulled it back and put it in her lap.

"My shift ended an hour ago. I thought I should check on Leo. I wasn't able to spend much time with him, unfortunately, because it was a busy day. Donna Ryan, the woman who was originally in this room passed away. Her children were upset and refused to leave."

"Is that why you're here now? You're worried that Leo is next?" Gemini moved to his other side. "The Atomycin was a mistake, wasn't it? I should have listened to Sophia and Brandon when they told us to skip the drug trial." She brought his hand to her lips and kissed it. "You could've spent your final months reading your silly weather journals and watching sunsets instead of in a hospital bed in another town." She whispered.

Denise stood. "It shouldn't have turned out this way."

Gemini was caught off-guard for the second time. "Of course not. He was sick when he made this decision and I should have listened to my family when they told me this was a mistake."

She glanced at Denise and was surprised to see tears in her eyes. Gemini moved to her side to comfort her. "Leo's going to be just fine. We need to stay positive in front of him. Just because you lost one patient, doesn't mean you'll lose another."

Denise smiled and wiped her eyes. "I should be the one comforting you. I don't act unprofessionally in front of patients and I'm sorry." She left the room abruptly.

Gemini sat back down, taking her husband's hand once again. "What a strange day this has been, Leo. I caught a murderer, and I thought that might be the end of it. Though he didn't confess to both deaths like I expected. I promised you we'd find out what happened to your doctor and I did. I suppose it's time to move you to Seattle and see what their fancy doctors and drugs can do for you." She bent over and kissed his forehead. "I know you'd fight me on that. When you're well, I expect a big blowup, one that would make your mother proud."

Instead of trying to solve the disappearance of Doctor Wilson as was her usual routine on her way home, she was thinking about what she might make for dinner. She still had a package of pasta she'd brought from Fassetville. The sun was setting by the time she walked in her door, a brilliant fiery red and blazing orange, two of her favorite paint colors she always suggested for play rooms. Immediately, her phone buzzed.

"Gemini? Are you okay? Tug told me what happened today. I have so much to tell you!"

"Slow down, Feather. It was quite the drama. The hospital rumor mill will go into overdrive this time. I'd love to hear about your experiences, but I'm exhausted." Gemini set her purse on the counter. "Can we talk tomorrow?"

"Sure." There was disappointment in her voice. "Do you want to come to the salon early? Tug said he wanted to bring donuts and coffee for the woman who solved the disappearance of Doctor Wilson."

"Okay, I'll be there by eight." She chuckled. Tug was everything Feather said he was. Enthusiastic, charming and handsome. "Oh, and Feather? I've made an important decision I'd like to share with you."

CHAPTER 41

The sun shone brightly as she opened the door to Feather Works salon. She walked to the break room, where Tug and Feather sat. They both looked up with big smiles on their faces as she entered.

Feather stood up and threw her arms around her friend. "You are so brave, Gemini. The bravest woman I've ever had the pleasure of knowing. I'm proud to be your friend."

Gemini patted her arm and blushed. "I'm not sure I'm worthy of that title, but thank you."

Tug, who shoved that last of a chocolate-covered donut in his mouth, held up his tablet. "The front page of the paper today." The headline read, Hospital Employee Admits to Murder. "I'm surprised they didn't interview you."

This morning when she'd gotten out of bed, there were five missed calls and three messages. She'd just assumed Sophia was in crisis, and Gemini needed a night of rest before dealing with that.

"Come and sit! Tug, who has the metabolism of a ten-year-old boy, brought donuts and coffee. I don't know if you've heard, but Forty Cups makes donuts every Friday and they sell out in fifteen minutes. To actually find yourself with a dozen donuts means you'll have luck the entire week!"

Gemini sat down and chose a small donut with pink sprinkles and took a small bite. "Mmm. These are good!"

"Tell me everything! What did he say when he confessed to killing those men?" Feather asked excitedly.

"Well, he killed Doctor Wilson for Carson Moore. He had a real devotion to that man, for some reason."

"That's odd. Why would he commit murder for the man and then turn around and kill him?" Feather asked.

"Guilt? Maybe Carson was threatening to blackmail him?" Tug offered, taking the last two donuts from the box.

"That doesn't really fit. Gary willingly did all of Carson's dirty work. There'd be no reason for Carson to blackmail him. Other than threatening to tell Gary's wife, I can't see that Carson Moore would have any leverage there." Gemini took another bite of her donut. "It's the police's problem now. I'm sure they're investigating and will figure it out."

Tug shook his head. "Nope. It says in this article that they are still considering Carson Moore's death a suicide."

"Hmm. That's very strange." Gemini thought for a moment. "No, I'm done. This is no longer my problem. I've decided that—"

"Yesterday was a day for revelations," Feather began excitedly. "I figured out something too. With Tug's help," she looked at her boyfriend lovingly, "I spoke with Angie again. She kept insisting that the key to her murder had to do with letters. It made no sense to me. I didn't find any letters when I cleaned out her apartment."

"Show her the picture, babe," Tug encouraged. "She's so smart."

Feather pulled the photo of Doctor Wilson and Angie out of her pocket and slid it across the table to Gemini. "Look at the sign in the background. Where the picture was taken."

Gemini picked it up. "The Circle T Resort." She put the photo down, stunned. "Cheese and biscuits! She was there with both Doctor Wilson and Carson Moore?

"One of them killed her. I'm certain of it," Feather said proudly.

"Janine Moore said their friendship ended after that trip. I wonder if besides the dirty tricks they pulled on each other, if they didn't know the other was dating Angie? Why would she agree to go on a trip with one when she knew the other would be there?"

Tug looked from one woman to the other. "Neither of you is going to get any sleep tonight if you don't go down to the police station and ask some questions."

Feather stood. "He's right. Gemini, will you go with me? My first appointment isn't for another hour. I'm so close to figuring this out."

"Of course. I'd like to put some heat on Gary." Gemini stood and put her purse over her shoulder. "Thank you for breakfast, Tug. You're both lucky you found each other. Every powerful woman needs an equally powerful man in her corner."

Tug jumped out of his chair and hugged Gemini in one motion, almost knocking her over. "You're the best, just like Feather said."

The police station was four blocks from the hair salon, so the women decided to walk, enjoying the sunny day. Gemini chose to wait to tell Feather her news until they had finished their interrogation.

As they entered the small interrogation room, Gemini could feel a cool draft around her. She wondered if one of Feather's friends from the hereafter was trying to tell her something. "This could use some paint," she said as they sat at a dented metal table in front of peeling, pea-colored walls. "Maybe a bright, Gallant Green," Gemini remarked as they waited for the prisoner to be brought in.

"Someday, you're going to give me a whole new paint scheme for my salon. You have an eye for color."

"About that—"

The door opened and Gary walked in, shackled at the waist. He was wearing a grey one-piece jumpsuit and looked as though he'd not had any sleep. When he sat down in front of them, he leaned forward. Gemini prepared for his anger at her to spurt from him like a fountain.

"Mrs. Reed, I'm glad you came today. I need you to give my wife a message."

Gemini and Feather looked at each other with astonishment. "What do you want her to know?" Gemini asked.

"That I'm sorry. She realized I would do anything for Carson, and she was fine with that. She didn't sign on for murder though. She refused to take my call last night. Since then, I've been worried sick about her."

Gemini took a deep breath. "I would be happy to convey your message. However, we need some information from you first." She nodded to Feather. "Go ahead."

"We need to hear who killed Angie Bard. We've already figured out that she took a vacation with both Carson Moore and Doctor Wilson. Which one of them was angry enough to end her life?"

Gary looked down. "Oh boy. I want my wife to trust me again. I love her—"

"This is the only way, Gary," Gemini insisted.

"Alright. Here's what happened. Carson didn't know that Angie was coming on the trip with them. She flew down separately and when he saw them together, he flipped his top. That's when he decided to kill Doctor Wilson. He knew the doc didn't like water, so he was going to stage an accident and let him drown."

"Except that Doctor Wilson was one step ahead of him."

"How'd you know that?" Gary's eyes narrowed. "The two of them were involved in some shady stuff and the longer it went on, the more Doctor Wilson told me he didn't trust Carson. That's why he brought Angie down, knowing it'd set him off. The doc paid to have Carson's hotel room bugged, and he figured Carson was going to either kill him or make it so he couldn't return to his job. He decided to set Carson up first."

"And when the plan didn't work, what happened?" Feather asked.

"Carson found the bugs in his room after he realized the doc hadn't drowned. He called me from the resort and said, 'This time, buddy, you're gonna do it. No backing out. If you're my loyal friend, now's the time to prove it.'"

"What did he mean by, 'this time'? Had he asked you to kill before?" Feather mentally went over previous deaths in Charming, wondering if they were actually murders.

Gary crossed his arms. "Carson was madly in love with Angie. That's why he left his wife—"

"She left him!" Gemini growled.

"Whatever. But that's what ended the marriage. Then he found out she was seeing other guys. Lots of them. He told me to get rid of her. I didn't blame him, she'd lied to him all along."

"I'm sure she had her reasons," Feather retorted, thinking back to the file she'd found, where Angie listed all the men she'd been with to boost her salon. "She was living on crackers and water. She didn't have any other way to get her business off the ground. He probably decided they were in love without ever asking her."

"I don't know anything about that," Gary continued. "He wanted me to wait for her to get in her car after work and then run her off the road on the way home. I started following her, but then I chickened out. I ain't killed nobody before and I didn't want to hurt her."

"If you didn't kill her, then who did?"

"He was so mad when I told him I didn't go through with it. He went over to her place and made her choose. It was him or Doctor Wilson. She said she didn't want neither of them. That's when he threw her down on the bed and shoved some pill in her mouth. She died right away and he set it up to look like suicide."

The women sat in shocked silence.

"I'm sure he arranged for the accidental cremation before the autopsy, so no one would question her death," Feather said solemnly.

"You got what you came for, now you'll go see my wife?" Gary asked hopefully.

"If it scared you to kill Angie, why was it so easy to kill Doctor Wilson?" Feather asked. "That doesn't make any sense."

Gary fidgeted, causing his handcuffs to rattle on the table. "He wronged Carson. Not only did he steal Angie and make him look like a fool on their trip, he wanted out of their business deal. He would've squealed to the cops about that. I was angry at him for what he'd done to my buddy, so I had no problem killing him. I stick by my friends-I'm the most loyal guy you'll ever meet."

"What was this business deal they were involved in?" Gemini asked. "Was it something at the hospital?"

"They made a deal with the drug rep for Canipril. They're doing a similar drug trial in Seattle and wanted their results to read better than the Atomycin study. Doctor Wilson administered three times the correct dosage to a couple of patients and made it seem like they'd died from the experimental drug. He'd done it before through the same drug rep. Made a gigantic pile of cash."

Gemini's blood ran cold. "Wait. What you're saying is that people were given the wrong amount of this drug? On purpose?" Her mind began connecting all the dots.

The guard came in. "Time's up, ladies," he said, motioning for Gary to stand.

"We've got more to ask him!" Feather protested. "Can't he stay just five more minutes?"

Gemini stood. "I know everything I need to know, Feather. Gary's of no more use to us."

"You'll call my wife, right? Make sure she knows I'm loyal and decent. That's why I'm here! I stood by my buddy!"

CHAPTER 42

"Are you sure you don't want me to go with you?" Feather asked, as they stood in front of her salon. "I could move my appointments around. After everything we've learned today, and the rest that you've figured out, you will need support."

Gemini hugged her. "You're a good friend, Feather Jones. I don't want you to cancel your appointments. Tug was an excellent backup for me yesterday, though. Would he mind coming with me again today?"

"I'm sure he wouldn't. He doesn't have class until noon. Wait, a sec and I'll run in and get him."

Gemini hadn't processed the information about Doctor Wilson, the man they'd pinned their hopes on. She thought about the excitement in Leo's voice for the first time in months as they spoke on speaker phone.

"I'm so happy you've agreed to join us, Mr. Reed. The results of this drug have been tremendous. Just tremendous. A forty-year-old woman told me she felt like she was twenty again. Imagine what this will do for you, Leo?"

Leo squeezed Gemini's hand. "Can't wait to work with

you, Doctor Wilson. I've been researching Atomycin too. They seem to have the edge over their competitor. You're offering me what we've been dreaming of. My wife and I can't wait to meet you."

"Have the front desk call me when you check in. The Reeds are going to be some of my favorite faces!"

Zebulon Wilson turned out to be a calculating opportunist. She was almost glad Leo wasn't awake to hear this. He'd been so proud of the research he'd done and his decision to come to Charming for treatment.

She'd had her doubts about Carson Moore since the first day, so that came as no surprise. What to do next, though, was still up in the air.

"I'm here at your service, Mrs. Reed!" Tug opened the door and practically bounded out beside her. His grey Doctor Whipley–Good for What Ails Ya! T-shirt was taut across his chest. He was wearing shorts that complimented his bulging thigh muscles. He looked every bit the bodyguard she needed.

"You can call me Gemini," she said, as he struggled to keep up with her brisk stride.

Tug told her all about his unusual upbringing, feeling uncomfortable in a wealthy family and then becoming their biggest embarrassment. "That's what got me interested in fitness. The way I looked was something I could control."

"I can see how much you love and respect Feather. It takes a decent man to treat a woman that way. You should be proud of who you are, with or without their support."

"Thanks, Gemini." When he smiled, his two perfect dimples framed a face like some she'd seen in magazines.

As they entered the hospital, Beverly B. hopped out of her chair and came running to embrace Gemini. She was so boisterous it knocked Gemini off balance and Tug had to steady her.

"What's this about?" Gemini asked after catching her breath.

"You are such a hero. I spoke to that man every day and had no idea he was a killer. None. How did you figure that out?" Beverly smiled at her admiringly.

"It would take too long, but one day soon, I'll bring some cookies and we'll chat on your break. I'll tell you the entire story."

"I understand. You want to see Leo. Have a good visit! And thank you again!" Beverly waved and returned to her seat.

"You're a local celebrity now," Tug commented as he pushed the elevator button.

"Hit number four, please. In my younger days, I sometimes dreamt of that. Our dreams change, though. Even day to day."

The doors opened, and they walked out, side by side. "Do you want me to go in, or wait out here?"

There was no sense in being a hero today. "Come in with me, please, Tug."

Denise met them in the hallway in front of Leo's room. "Did you bring more cookies today, Gemini? We loved the last batch!"

"None today, Denise. I was wondering if you'd mind stepping into Leo's room. There's something I'd like to ask you."

Denise looked curiously at Tug and followed them into Leo's room. "What's going on?"

"Yesterday when I came in, you were apologizing for Leo's condition. I thought you were just being kind. But then it hit me."

"I was being kind! Leo is one of my favorite patients!" Denise protested.

"Be that as it may, you left me clues early on that I ignored. The first time I met you, you talked about your plans to retire to an island. I was surprised that someone so young could afford such a thing, but I had no idea of the levels you'd stoop to achieve your goal."

"What are you talking about?"

"You said if your boyfriend would only quit buying his expensive suits, you could afford to retire now. When Carson Moore died, one of the nursing assistants remarked that he'd been arguing with someone in a fancy suit the day before. Your boyfriend, who is a drug rep, spent time with Carson on the golf course and would have had access to his office. I believe they got into an argument over the drug trial for Atomycin and he killed Carson Moore."

Denise's face was ashen. "Gemini, that's insane! After I caught you dressing up, I should have realized then and there you weren't in your right mind. I can find someone to help you!"

She moved toward the door, but Tug blocked it. "I'm going to call security if you don't let me out!" she warned.

"Oh, you'll want to hear the rest of this. It's fantastic," Tug replied, displaying his lovely dimples.

"You pushed me to go visit Donna Ryan, so I did. She told me she caught you administering two extra doses of Atomycin in her I.V. You told her it was a mistake. She threatened to sue the hospital, and you asked what you could do for her if she didn't say a word. That's when she was moved to the nice suite with the view of the ocean. Completely free of charge."

"I made a mistake, Gemini. We're all human."

"You planned to kill her. You had another lethal dose ready to go. The day of Leo's coma, Esther C. from the main desk told me you had a phone call soon after, presumably with Rodney telling him the deed was done. Another nurse came in and gave the dose to Leo because it had his room number on it. Let me know when you want me to stop, because I've got more."

"Okay, okay." Denise put her hands up. "All of that is true. Rodney made a deal with the drug company to throw the study. It's enough for us to retire. He approached Doctor Wilson and Carson Moore last year about manipulating the results of another study. They all made good money. I don't know what happened between those two, but this time, Doctor Wilson wanted out and Carson got greedy, He wen t to Rodney and said he wanted Doctor Wilson's two-thirds." She paused, clutching her throat. "We're going to retire to an island. We needed that money more than he did. Rodney was left with no choice; he has an experimental spray used to fight infections that can be lethal in strong doses. He went into Carson's office and sprayed it in his coffee mug."

Gemini gave Tug a sideways glance, hoping he would take the cue and restrain Denise. Instead, he gave her an encouraging thumbs up.

Denise moved to Leo's side. "I can end Leo's life right now. I'll pull the plug and prevent anyone from coming in to save him."

"From your favorite patient to someone you could so easily discard? That's very cold, Denise."

"If you harm Leo or Gemini, I'll take you down so fast you won't know what hit you!" Tug threatened.

"So what do you think you're going to do now, Gemini? It seems we're at a standoff. I'm not losing my reputation over this. Rodney and I are days away from leaving to start our dream lives."

Gemini moved closer to Denise. "That's what I thought too. There is no such thing. Dreams are just something pleasant to distract ourselves with. Real life is never so perfect. You should know that from all the patients like Leo you've seen." In one quick move, Gemini grabbed her arm and pulled it backwards while forcing her down on Leo's leg with the other. "Tug! I could use some help!"

Tug moved swiftly to Denise's body and held her in place. "Go call the police. It's all recorded."

"I gave my pen to the police yesterday!"

"I'm wearing one around my neck right now." He motioned for her to pull the gold chain from around his neck out of his shirt. On the end of it was a small device. "The Listen UP 150. I wear them all the time just in case I run into a potential buyer."

When the police arrived, Denise tried rescinding her story, but Tug played back the entire conversation for them. All the while, Leo rested peacefully.

The same police officer who'd helped yesterday was surprised when he recognized her. "We could use someone like you on the Charming police force," he joked. "I would like you to come to the station and write out a statement, Mrs. Reed."

"I will," she replied. "After I spend some time with my husband."

Eventually, the room cleared. Tug was the last to leave, promising he'd fill Feather in on the day's developments. "Call us if you need anything, Gemini. You know we'll be there in a heartbeat."

The sound of police radios and staff subsided, and the only noise that remained was Leo's machine gently beeping out his pulse. The noise had become comfortably familiar. Gemini crawled into bed beside her husband, tucking her arm around him. "I know you've heard this all before, but I need to tell you this crazy story again from the very beginning. It will feel better to get it all out at once."

CHAPTER 43

"Olive called this morning. She said she doesn't want to come back here until I warn everyone they're not to gossip about her grandson, Rodney and his girlfriend, Denise." Feather burst out laughing. "The town gossip wants everyone to stop gossiping."

"She's hurting. It's going to be hard to process that her grandson is a murderer." Gemini bit her tongue, resisting the temptation to say something more.

Feather motioned for Gemini to follow her back to the empty room. "I was re-thinking our conversation two days ago, before you and Tug took down another criminal. You said you had something to tell me and I never let you finish."

Gemini pulled out a chair and sat down. "What I needed to tell you has changed." She put her elbows on the table "After everyone left yesterday, I had a deep conversation with Leo. Even though he can't respond, it did my heart good to just get the story out. I came to some conclusions."

"This sounds dramatic!" Feather pulled out a chair and sat beside her.

"Before all of this, I thought maybe Brandon was right,

that Leo should be moved to Seattle. Of course, we can't do that now, when I know that the company running that trial is corrupt. My next idea was to stay here and go to beauty school."

"I thought you might, Gemini! What a great idea! I'll keep a stall waiting for you, right next to–"

Gemini put her hand in the air. "Our dreams change with the ebb and flow of life. I've enjoyed my time washing clients' hair. But I think there is a better use of my talents. If you will be agreeable."

"Whatever you want, Gemini! I need to be honest—I was going to try to talk you out of moving to Seattle, anyway."

Both women chuckled.

"There is a genuine need for people to talk about their lives. It's a restrictive experience, living in a small town where whatever filters through their mind and out their mouths may end up as dinner conversation across town."

Feather cocked her head to the side. "Where are you going with this?"

"I'd like to take over your empty room. First, it must be painted. I'm thinking a soothing Luscious Lavender with Buttercup Yellow accents. Then, I'd bring in baked goods and plug in the coffee pot. People could come in and visit with me or anyone who has time to chat.We'd put a sign over the door that says, 'Coffee and Comfort' or something to that effect. It would be a way for people to feel safe talking about their troubles. We could also place brochures in the room so everyone would know about your great talents as a paranormal investigator."

Feather processed the information. "I think that is a wonderful idea! But I learned that we make a great team. I'll only make a brochure if we can put your name on it too. As my partner." She tapped her fingers on the table. "I can get

OCEANBERRY BLUES

Tug to help you. Some days I wish we had a treadmill at home to burn off his extra energy."

Gemini stood. "Thank you, Feather. I look forward to our partnership."

"You can't stay? I don't have an appointment for another half hour."

"No, I have quite a lot to do. Oh, by the way, Beverly from the hospital front desk wants to set up a children's party with you. All the little girls will be getting their hair fixed. Just call the front desk and tell her I recommended you for the job."

"Will do."

"'I'll be in touch." She reached over and hugged Feather. 'I'll be in touch."

For the third time, she walked to the hospital uncertain what lay ahead. She sat on a bench next to the giant Charming General Hospital sign and texted, "I'm here." She tilted her head back and closed her eyes, enjoying the warm summer sun.

"Mrs. Reed? Are you sure you wouldn't be more comfortable talking in my office?"

She opened her eyes and sat up straight. "No, Doctor Natchez, I've had plenty of foul air in that hospital lately. I want to sit here while we speak."

"All right then." He sat down beside her. "We're on the same page about your husband's care."

"He's not going to get better, is he?" she asked dully.

"I can't say for sure. Over the years, many miracles have happened in this hospital. Your husband's story hasn't ended yet. We're thinking about testing him off the respirator again today. By the way, our lawyers are working on a settlement offer that you should find to your liking."

"What would be to my liking is for my husband to return to the person he was," she snapped. "Before he was over medicated."

Doctor Natchez crossed his arms. "I just looked at his most recent test results this morning. While the dosage was inappropriate for him, it appears his cancer is in remission. We'll run more tests to be sure."

She wasn't prepared for this information. "What? Leo's cancer is–gone?"

"I can't explain it. The drug trial is over for us, for obvious reasons. But other hospitals will study Atomycin and maybe Leo's tragic situation will help someone else down the road."

Despite all that had occurred, Gemini felt warm inside. "That's what he would have wanted. Leo's goal in life has been to help others in any way he can. It makes sense in our crazy upside down world that he would have to end up in a coma for that to happen."

"We need to talk about what comes next, Mrs. Reed. If you want him transferred to an extended care facility in Fassetville, we can make those arrangements for you."

Gemini thought about the Fassetville Cozy Care Center. She'd been in there when Leo's mother was at the end of her life. It was a dark and drab place, suitable for people like her but not at all where a bright light like Leo should live.

"I've heard from people in the beauty salon that there is a cheerful place here. Charming Waves Assisted Living. That's where I think Leo should be. Until he recovers."

"I'll make the arrangements." Doctor Natchez stood. "As I mentioned on the phone, our intention was never to put you or your husband through this. Words don't convey how bad we feel. If you're staying in town, we'd like to invite you to be part of a hospital advisory committee. To ensure patients' care is the utmost."

Gemini smiled and shaded her eyes as she looked up at him. "Keep your friends close and your enemies closer, eh Doctor?"

"Something like that." He glanced at his watch. "I've got a

meeting soon. You've got my personal number. You'll call if you need anything?"

"You can count on it."

She got up and dialed the number for the property management company again. Still no answer. The short lease they'd signed would be up soon and she wanted to see about extending it, just while Leo was in the care facility.

There was one more call to make. She'd been pondering it now for two days, as she worked over everything in her head.

"Mother? What's going on? I haven't heard from you in forever. You could've been dead in your recliner, or–"

"Sophia, stop." Gemini said sharply. "There are many things to tell you and they won't all come out in this conversation. You're going to sit and listen. You won't respond until I'm finished, got it?" There was silence on the other end of the line. "Sophia? Are you still there?"

"You said silence, right?"

Gemini sighed. "Your father is going to an extended care facility to finish his recovery. He's going to stay right here in Charming with me. As much as I'd like to see my grandson more often, I don't want to be his caretaker. I want to be his grandma who spoils him with things he shouldn't eat and smothers him in kisses. You'll need to make other arrangements."

She waited for Sophia's sharp response and when it didn't come said, "I'm done, for now."

Sophia cleared her throat and began. "First, I know how awful the extended care facility is here. After Brandon convinced me the Seattle trial wasn't going to work, I thought he should probably find something like that."

"That's a relief, Sophia. I was worried that you–"

"I gave you the courtesy of silence, Mother. It's your turn," her daughter snapped. "The second thing I wanted to say is that we're interviewing new nannies. Brandon said you weren't really interested in living here. You must've had a real heart-to-heart with him. I like being in control, and Daddy's illness has left me feeling powerless. Maybe I went overboard, but I only want what's best for both of you. Now it's your turn."

"We came to a mutual agreement," Gemini replied. "I'm glad he's understanding me better. I will need to speak with him about some legal matters, but not today. Sophia, despite our differences, I want you to know that I love you deeply. I appreciate you for the powerful woman you are."

"Thank you, Mother." Sophia's voice cracked. "I admire you, you know? Always putting Daddy and me before yourself. I hope while you're in Charming you find some time to do things you enjoy, like knitting and playing bridge."

Gemini smiled. "Well then, I'd better get to it. Knitting waits for no woman. Maybe you could come down for a picnic on the beach soon?"

"We'd love that." She paused then, like there was something she wanted to say but couldn't get out. "Bye Mother."

Gemini walked home, feeling satisfied by all she'd accomplished. When she rounded the corner, it shocked her to see several men setting up scaffolding around her rental. Her neighbor was standing outside his home, watching.

"Howard, what's going on? I've been trying to get ahold of the management company to extend my lease. Are they kicking me out without giving me any notice? It'll be another matter for my attorney if so."

"No need for that kind of excitement, Mrs. Reed. Rumor has it, the management company heard one of their rentals was an ugly mud brown. They decided it wouldn't do, so they are painting it a crazy sounding color–Oceanberry Blue." There was a hint of a smile on his face.

"Howard, you own this house? Why didn't you tell me before?"

He shrugged. "Never seemed like the right time. Seeing as how you'll be here for the foreseeable future, the place you live should be pleasing to the eye, don't you agree?"

Her phone buzzed and she thought about ignoring it, but when she saw the number, she answered immediately. "Is something wrong with Leo?"

"No, Mrs. Reed," Esther C. couldn't hide her delight. Just the opposite. Your husband is conscious."

Buy Book Two in the Charming Mystery Series

If you liked this story, please consider leaving a review. It helps others find my books! Reviews are vital for an author's survival in a tough business.

Leave your review now

Sneak Peek

Tangerine Troubles

Gemini Reed took a sip of her lemon ginger tea and moved uncomfortably in her seat. "Howard, as you know, I owe you a huge debt of gratitude for all you've done for me. Letting me rent this house–"

"Never had a millionaire renter before. Kind of ludicrous," Howard Beachmont grumbled, bringing his own steaming cup to his lips.

"The settlement isn't final yet. It will be nice to know I don't have to worry about my needs or Leo's," her voice trailed off. The overdose he was given of Atomycin cured his cancer but also put them both in this state of limbo. She cleared her throat and pulled herself up straight. "I don't want to worry about the upkeep of owning a home, at least not until Leo is here and strong enough to help out."

Howard noticed a dead bloom on his scarlet mum plant

and set his cup on the glass table before bending down to pick it. "You were saying? I have a garden club meeting in an hour. They want me to be in charge of the annual Charming Iris Festival this year. No matter how disagreeable I become, they seem to think I'm the best man for the job."

"I was saying that I just don't think I should get involved with your personal family business. If it were a different topic, I wouldn't hesitate to help you." She put her hand to her chest, touching the sticky late-summer skin that must have been blotchy and red.

"My helping you obtain false hospital credentials wasn't personal? I know more about you, my next-door neighbor than I do my ex-wife."

Gemini crossed her legs, staring at the bronze-colored vines winding their way across the fence that separated their two properties. Last week Howard came over to and trimmed the ones that dangled to the ground on her side. "You're right. I owe you this and it's selfish to think otherwise. I'll do it."

"Thank you, Mrs. Reed-Gemini. It should be known that I wouldn't trust anyone else with this information. That should give you a sense of pride."

Gemini chuckled. "I'm the only one you trust with your family's dirty laundry? Is that a compliment?"

Howard frowned. "I've been out of his life for more years than I was in. Strange thing to say about one's own offspring. Even your Sophia, for all of her difficulties, has never pushed you out."

If you liked this story, please consider leaving a review. It helps others find my books! Reviews are vital for an author's survival in a tough business.

Leave your review now

Made in the USA
Columbia, SC
06 March 2023